Praise for Douglas Robbins

Baseball Dreams and Bikers

"*Baseball Dreams and Bikers* skillfully weaves a tapestry of relatable characters and universal themes, inviting readers to explore the intricate layers of human existence through vivid prose and profound storytelling." —Kevin Wells, Educator, Milton Hershey School

"Very enjoyable and thought-provoking stories that resonate deeply, evoking empathy for characters in their quest to fill the void within. Each story stands satisfactorily alone yet interweaves similar themes, leaving a lasting impression as some characters become timeless in memory" —Veronica Richards, Librarian

Love in a Dying Town

Kate Hutson
5 out of 5 stars: A heartwarming story of hope
Reviewed in the United States on June 3, 2023

"I SO enjoyed *Love in a Dying Town*! Jim is a flawed, but likable protagonist and the author brings the struggles of single fatherhood to life. Jim and Lily's heartwarming father-daughter relationship was my favorite part of this book. The characters and the setting were so vivid, and I was majorly invested in the Bowen family, rooting for them the whole time. *Love in a Dying Town* was a moving book and I couldn't recommend it more!"

Chris
5 out of 5 stars *Love in a Dying Town* reads like a Springsteen Song
Reviewed in the United States on May 20, 2021

"I just finished *Love in a Dying Town* and sincerely enjoyed it. It's a book about where I'm from and made me feel a lot of the same war-torn feelings. Robbins takes a slice of America that has seen better days and makes you feel the pain and anguish, hope and possible redemption of a fading way of life. It reminds me of a Springsteen lyric from 'My Hometown':

> *They're closing down the textile mill across the railroad tracks,*
> *Foreman says "These jobs are going, boys and they ain't coming back"*
> *To your hometown.*

The book reads like a Steinbeck/Springsteen novel/song. Very true feelings of sadness, bright happiness, nostalgia and above all, Love. Love for your child, love for your partner, love for yourself, and love for where you are and how that made you who you are. In this book, Doug Robbins has created a story that will make you feel life viscerally."

Narican: The Cloaked Deception

"Readers who embark on this journey will be rewarded with a rich and immersive narrative that challenges their perceptions and leaves them pondering the intricate dance between light and darkness within us all." —Maccabee Griffin, *Beyond the Pen* podcast

The Reluctant Human

Ashley P
5 out of 5 stars: For the highs and lows of life! Great book!
Reviewed in the United States on October 18, 2024

"*The Reluctant Human* by Douglas Robbins is a compelling read that dives deep into the human condition. Scott Bauman is a relatable character who navigates the complexities of life with a mix of humor and introspection. Robbins' sharp wit and engaging storytelling kept me hooked from start to finish. The book explores themes of depression, personal growth, and the search for meaning in a way that feels both profound and accessible. If you're looking for a thought-provoking and entertaining read, I highly recommend this book!"

Max Johnny

Alan Sidransky
5 out of 5 stars: Feeling *Max Johhny*
Reviewed in the United States on January 30, 2013

"I've read numerous works by Douglas Robbins and this is by far his best. He sets out the character arc well by introducing us to the character and maintaining his secret for a good portion of the story. We're not sure why Max is so devastated. When the event occurs it comes quickly like a good left uppercut. I didn't expect it, certainly not in the form in which it was delivered. There's a lot here for men too, in particular. I might add it's good to see a man writing fiction for men as most fiction is well, let's face it, written for women. Robbins' characters are real and they let us know what men are thinking and how they feel emotion. The end is quite satisfying as well. Well done."
—A.J. Sidransky author of *The Interpreter*

Black Cloud Rises

Also by Douglas Robbins

The Reluctant Human

Max Johnny

Leaves Piled High

Narican: The Cloaked Deception

Love in a Dying Town

Baseball Dreams and Bikers

DOUGLAS ROBBINS

This book is a work of fiction. The names, characters, places, and incidents are products of the writer's imagination or have been used fictitiously and are not to be construed as real. Any resemblance to persons—living or dead—actual events, locales, or organizations is entirely coincidental.

Black Cloud Rises
Published by Rebel Press

Design by David Provolo
Edited by Winsome Lewis

ISBN (paperback): 978-1-7333978-2-7
ISBN (hardcover): 978-1-7333978-3-4

LCCN: 2025923256

www.douglasrobbinsauthor.com

Not all wounds heal—some run deeper than medicine can reach. But others, touched by light and truth, can find their way to mending.

"Humankind has not woven the web of life. We are but one thread within it. Whatever we do to the web, we do to ourselves. All things are bound together. All things connect."

—Chief Seattle, Duwamish and Suquamish tribes

ONE

Pine Ridge Reservation, South Dakota
Present Day

Four-year-old Little Wonder pokes his head outside the screen door of his mother's single-wide trailer, dark curls bouncing in the morning light.

"Come on, Unca Bwack Cwoud, the parade's startin'."

Uncle Black Cloud stands in the dirt yard, beer can dripping in the fall air, locked in the sacred ritual of horseshoes with Bull Nose Pete and Tall Tim—two other so-called "elders" on the rez and life-long friends. Pete earned his nickname as a boy: his wide nostrils flared with every charged emotion, and he demonstrates it now with every bad throw. And Tall Tim's six-foot-two frame never quite lives up to the "tall" in his name. Both men are a few years older than him, if you consider mid-fifties to be elder.

"Oh, I would not want to miss that," Black Cloud deadpans, stressing the vowels in his native rolling tongue. It is a dry fall morning with temperatures in the low forties, cool after a rainstorm blew out to the plains two days prior. He takes aim and throws his last horseshoe. Fifty-two years of life have taught him that some things can't be forced—accuracy, forgiveness, history.

He leans left then right and just misses the iron spike for the win.

"Ah, horseshoes and hand grenades," is all he says. The two other men understand that their visit is now over and grab their cans of Camo Black Ice.

After all, today is the Day of Mourning, or what the rest of America calls Thanksgiving. It is a reminder etched in blood across all native lands. Who would want to miss the Macy's Thanksgiving Day Parade? Yet Black Cloud's family has always marked this day, starting with his father, a Vietnam Veteran, who dreamed of his children belonging to a larger American story.

Always be thankful," he'd say, "for what we've been given."

Black Cloud calls after his friends, "Happy Thanks-for-Taking." Meaning, *thanks for taking our land*. He doesn't add, but they hear it anyway.

His two friends respond in kind, with Tall Tim raising his can in salute.

"Yup, Happy Thanks-for-Taking. Hello to your mum and sis." The two older men half stumble down the dirt driveway past the knee-high brown scrub brush, some old tires, and a long-forgotten garden. The rusting skeleton of a chain link fence leans with the weight of time.

Black Cloud equally carries the weight of history on his shoulders and in the name his grandmother had given him. His family always said he carried the past like black clouds rolling over the hills. The name stuck partly because of his disposition, but mostly because he never let things go quietly and deeply felt injustices. He has much darkness about the way Native Americans, America's first people, have been treated.

But lately, that weight has started to feel less like a burden, and more like a purpose. Time and mortality calling to him like a distant message etched upon the stars.

As a teenager, Black Cloud dreamed of being like Leonard Peltier—not the prison part, obviously, but the fire in his belly. Peltier was a leader in the American Indian Movement, or AIM, a group that stood up loudly. In the early 70s, they took over the Wounded Knee Memorial, demanding change for how they were treated, drawing national attention. The standoff with the FBI ended badly—two agents killed, and Peltier sentenced to life, a case still debated today.

But for Black Cloud, it wasn't about the headlines. It was about someone finally saying, *Enough*. That moment planted a seed in him—not rage exactly, more like a stubborn kind of refusal. A refusal to pretend everything was fine just because someone said it was. During this time, his mother often dragged him to rallies.

Stepping toward the white vinyl and blue trimmed trailer, he stops in front of Little Wonder who looks up at his uncle as if he were some giant from the old stories. The boy tilts his head so far back he starts to wobble when Black Cloud places his hand behind him, saving him from toppling over and bumping his head on the doorknob. His name is Little Wonder because ever since he was a baby, he's been staring up at things with great, big, black eyes.

Inside, two other children bounce on the brown living room couch, their energy barely contained waiting for the parade to start.

On the TV screen, Chip Wegney, pop singer and master-of-ceremonies, preens in front of Macy's flagship store, his long, tan mohair jacket swaying with each movement. Up on the wooden platform, where the New York City skyscrapers pierce the gray sky like glass totems, he performs his latest hit. His voice echoes down 34th Street as he spins through his signature dance moves that everyone's been copying, ending with a flourish up on the toes of his stylish black leather boots.

Just a few feet away in the kitchen, Black Cloud's sister White Feather tends to the duck roasting in the oven—a gift from their cousin Joseph who still hunts the wetlands down by the creek. No turkey this year, but on the rez you learn to be grateful for what the land provides. White Feather is ten years younger with fair skin and a lightness to her brown hair.

She cooks with her friend Morning Sparrow, a plump black-haired girl no older than twenty-three with a big smile and a bigger face. She lives up to her name as nervous words spill from her mouth like water falling from a spigot without a shutoff valve. It has been said she wakes up speaking and rarely stops until she closes her eyes at night.

They chatter nervously about their husbands overseas between basting and seasoning, their hands keeping busy and holding the fear at bay. Both of their husbands are enlisted men. Morning Sparrow's husband John is a medic, while White Feather's husband Robert drives supply trucks through the desert heat.

"John says the medical training is intense," Morning Sparrow says, her hands never still. "But he can't wait to open a practice when he gets back..." Her voice trails off, heavy with hope and doubt.

"Same with Robert and his trucking dreams," White Feather nods, lifting the lid to let steam escape from the mashed potatoes.

"He says every mile he drives over there is practice for his own company here. Without the landmines, of course."

Their shared hopes rise with the duck's aroma bursting into the room from the open oven door. Silent prayers for futures that feel both impossible and inevitable are offered.

Both women know the statistics—how many reservation dreams die waiting for the right moment, the right money, the right break. But today, in this kitchen, they let themselves dream of a better tomorrow and their husbands standing safely alongside them.

Black Cloud settles onto the couch with the three children. Little Wonder is warm against his side, watching the twenty-five-inch screen flickering with another world. This is how Thanksgiving begins on the Pine Ridge Reservation—ancestors honored at sunrise, then horseshoes, beer, family, and that damn parade.

The spectacle unfolds on 34th Street outside of Macy's in New York City. Characters from Broadway shows lip-sync and dance with product endorsements shamelessly offered up. A movie trailer plays while up-and-coming actors and actresses follow on a float and wave to the mass of onlookers bulging on the sidewalks. A marching band beats the drums of someone else's rhythm. Large animal balloons dance clumsily along.

As the parade unfolds, gasps of joy erupt from the children. Their expressions are pure and uncomplicated. Black Cloud watches their faces glow in the TV's light, feeling disconnected from that glamorous world, on a poor reservation rampant with poverty, alcoholism, and unemployment. They might as well be a million miles away.

He understands darkness. His people know it well, but he also understands that laughter, that bubbling joy within is like the dance of songbirds in the morning light. Human connection is free, insuppressible. It can't be bought, sold, or taken.

Still, the parade's wealth mocks him. This is everything that's wrong, he thinks. Glamorous and superficial while ignoring the unemployed and dying.

Thanks for taking our land, assholes. We should've scalped you when we had the chance.

But then Little Wonder squeals at a float shaped like a dragon, and Black Cloud remembers: joy finds its way through any crack in the darkness, even through his own. The children bounce to the music on the couch's edge, their faces bright as new pennies, and for a moment he lets himself bounce along with them and claps to the music.

Black Cloud's birth name is Abraham, not after the biblical figure, but for Abraham Lincoln. His father, having walked between two worlds, chose this name with deliberate care—a bridge between histories. His father, a history buff, knew Lincoln was a bold man, a man with vision, and he believed a man with a vision could change the world. He wanted his son to be equally great no matter the circumstances.

To the government and the white world, he would be Abraham, but to his people, he was Mahpiyasapa, "Black Cloud." His name was given to him during his teenage years when his grandmother saw him standing against a storm-heavy sky, his silhouette merging with the gathering darkness and ensuing rains. He stood within the tempest while everyone else took shelter indoors.

His father, who spent hours poring over dog-eared history books while other men drowned their sorrows, would tell young Abraham stories of Lincoln's rise from a log cabin to the highest office.

"See this man?" his father would say, tapping a scratched photograph in the history book. "Born with nothing but determination in his pockets. A man with a vision," he'd continue, tapping his son's chest with a weathered finger, "can part the clouds of impossibility. Remember that always, Mahpiyasapa."

Then, his father went off to fight in Vietnam and returned to these ancient hills carrying history books like medicine bundles where truth and answers could be found. He believed understanding the past was the best way to heal it and influence the future. But the hills—these sacred Black Hills of South Dakota—their homeland had their own wisdom, as his wife Zitkala would say, her medicine woman's eyes hearing the truth of it on the wind.

"These hills," Zitkala would whisper to Black Cloud while they gathered sage in the early dawn light, "they hold more than earth and stone. They hold souls, my son. Some souls come here to heal, others get trapped and never find their way out." She would pause, her hands moving with practiced wisdom. "Your father's spirit circles these hills now, looking for peace."

Hope died slowly in his father. The history books gathered dust while rejection letters for job after job piled up like fallen leaves.

"What good is knowing their history," he'd spit out between swallows of whiskey, "when they won't let us be part of their future?" The bottle became his new medicine bundle, and the words a *good Indian is a dead Indian* began to poison his tongue—words he'd once fought against turned upon himself.

He died in his forties. His spirit finally joined the others trapped in the hills, leaving behind a son who carried two names and the memory of earlier days when hope filled their home. Earlier in his life, before the darkness took him, he had planted seeds of possibility in his young son's heart and the idea that hope can change everything.

He'd say to Black Cloud, "Never forget, son, your name carries two worlds: strength and wisdom. Use them both."

After this, his mother took him to more rallies on how to stand

and be seen. She became more active in community affairs. He watched men and women working together carrying their heads high and proud to protect their land and families, and demand better treatment, against great odds. He learned that hope can spread like wildfire given the right circumstances.

At the commercial break, Black Cloud tries to get up, but the kids paw at him in protest. "No, don't go," Lilyanna, Little Wonder's eight-year-old sister, says.

"I have to check on Grandma," he responds.

"Nooooo," Little Wonder and his sister shout in unison. Morning Sparrow's three-year-old daughter, Maisy, joins in the protest, then sucks her thumb and watches the older kids.

"No Unca Bwack Cwoud," says Little Wonder. "Don't go. We'll miss you too much." He shakes his head back and forth then reaches up, his small fingers finding Black Cloud's weathered ones. Black Cloud looks down at their joined hands and is still surprised by the smallness of his nephew's hand. He remembers his daughter Samantha Blue when she was this age. All smiles as his family of three would walk a trail together searching for butterflies—holding hands with his wife, Gloria.

Lilyana pats the empty cushion with the authority only an eight-year-old can muster.

"Yeah, Uncle Cloudy," Lilyanna says, laughing.

"Fine, next commercial," Black Cloud surrenders, settling back into his seat. A mischievous glint crosses his face. "But now what?' He pauses for dramatic effect rubbing his chin. "Oh, I know…"

Before they can squirm away, he's attacking them by blowing playful raspberries, his lips buzzing against their necks and arms like a swarm of tickling bees. Their laughter bubbles up, pure and clean, filling the trailer with its music.

The parade marches on, a glittering procession of untouchable dreams. Broadway dancers spin stories they'll never witness, while glossy products flash promises of better lives their wallets can't afford. Black Cloud feels it then, that familiar itch under his skin. He rises from the couch, too restless to keep playing spectator to this world beyond their reach.

As he rises from the couch, he's again pelted with "Don't go" protests from the kids.

"I have to check on Grandma," Black Cloud says, trying to soften his voice. "*Unci*. Can you say *Unci*? Mother."

"*Unci*," Morning Sparrow's daughter whispers around her thumb. Then her free hand clamps over her nose, a gesture they all understand. The children never want to visit her trailer, where incense fights with mothballs in the heavy air, and strange voices chant words that slip past understanding. Something old lives in those rooms, something that makes even the bravest child want to run.

White Feather wipes her hands on her apron, eyes meeting her brother's. "We'll come by in a bit, bring some food."

"We can't, Mom!" Lilyanna's voice rises again. "We have to watch the parade!"

"Oh hush." White Feather's tone carries no discussion. "You better come visit me when I'm old." She turns to Black Cloud, who's already reaching for the door. "Cloud, ask her if she needs anything." He nods, one foot stepping outside. "And Cloud…" he pauses, stepping back in, "ask if her ladies need anything…"

"Okay, okay." The screen door slaps behind him as he steps into the air that smells of coming winter. The dying of things has begun. His mother's trailer waits next door, patient as the hills themselves.

In the next trailer over on the same shared property, three women sit near his mother's bed, chanting and swaying their bodies with ancient rhythms. Two wear traditional gowns alive with symbols and fringe, while the third sports blue jeans and a blue bedazzled shirt that reads "Beyonce" beneath a weathered cowboy hat. They sit in a triangle around her bed—one on each side, one at her feet—in a room that is small and sparsely decorated.

The healers continue their work as Black Cloud enters, drawing sacred smoke across their bodies in practiced motions. His mother lies beneath handwoven blankets of earth tones, her head propped on feather pillows, her once-wild black hair now carefully brushed.

She says, "My son has come to visit on this sad but happy day. There is hope where there is life."

"I know, Mum." He settles beside her on a wooden chair, fighting the mingled scents of cotton balls, chemicals, and smoke. "The ancestors know that too. But what good is hope when I can't buy you proper medicine?" He pauses, trying for lightness. "Maybe we need a ghost dance to bring back the ancestors, huh?"

She lifts one hand in dismissal. "No dance needed. When I sleep, they return." Her eyes find his face. "You will do something special, Black Cloud…you are also in my dreams."

A chanter's arm rubs against him as he takes his mother's weathered hand into his. "In fifty-plus years I haven't done anything special yet…"

"You were a special baby and spoke to the ancestors…you just do not remember."

"I can't talk to no ancestors, Mama. Unless I'm drinking and talking to Tall Tim and Bull Nose Pete." He attempts at a smile. "But they ain't no ancestors, just old."

"This is no time for jokes, Abraham." Her voice carries sudden strength, and her eyes bore into him. "Jokes do not set us free. They only hide our pain. My time in the physical world fades like a rainstorm's final drops. But you will do something special. This I know." Tired, she closes her eyes and releases his hand. "We will not be forgotten like antiques in a barn." She folds one hand on top of another and rests them on her stomach.

The chanting grows louder, filling the small space. Smoke burns his eyes. The windows are sealed against the November chill. Black Cloud's lungs fight for clean air as the chanters' voices rise. Then, as one, their eyes open and their palms turn outward toward him, offering something he can't name. Their words shift to what might be ancient Sioux, or what might be something else entirely—sounds that belonged to his grandmother's grandmother, and to the land itself.

He knows her time is limited. He's known since she took to this bed and now seldom leaves. Soon she'll "walk on"—not die, never die—but continue her journey to join his father and the ancestors, to be with Wakan Tanka, the Great Spirit.

He leans in closer so she can hear him over the chanters. Before speaking, he wonders if the smoke alone might kill her.

"White Feather will bring food later with the kids." He presses his lips to her hand, then her cheek, and places her hand back onto her chest. Stepping back, he nods to the chanters whose eyes are closed, and palms are raised.

Thinking she's fallen asleep, he turns the doorknob quietly when he hears her voice, soft but clear, "Listen as you go."

He turns back, yet her eyes remain closed.

Outside, the golden sun caresses the rolling hills and the thin stretch of land between their mobile homes. The hills rise black and brown against the sky, and he feels their weight in his bones as if he is the soil and rock itself. Fifty-some years of life and what does he have to show for it? He shakes his head in disappointment. There have been no great accomplishments, only opportunities lost, just out of reach.

As the screen door slaps behind him, White Feather's voice carries from within the trailer, along with the fragrances of basted duck and green bean casserole.

"How's Mom?"

"She's fine. Talking her crazy stuff as usual." He watches the children, still lost in their parade. "Eh, we're all half-crazy out here." He drops onto the couch and reaches for Little Wonder. "But they're one-hundred percent cuckoo." He nods toward the TV screen and tickles his nephew until the boy tumbles off the couch giggling.

No time for jokes, his mother's voice echoes. *Listen as you go.*

He stops the tickling and runs his hand through his thick black hair. His face grows solemn and his eyes droop. Something heavy settles into his chest as he watches the parade march across their small screen—that glittering world a million miles from their reservation. Little Wonder climbs back onto the couch, but Black Cloud barely notices. His thoughts run sideways into another, leading nowhere and everywhere all at once.

He looks out the window of his mind onto the reservation, into town, and across the Indian Nation and sees the same turmoil and heartbreak everywhere. The parade comes back on. If only he could do something big, he'd show them how they weren't antiques. He grabs another beer from the cooler near the couch and cracks it open, swilling half of it down in one gulp.

Lilyana smiles while brushing her long black hair with a hairbrush, captivated by the dancers, their outfits and glamor. She is eight after all and believes in princesses and kingdoms. She stands and twirls herself like a ballerina in perfect form. Black Cloud watches her proudly at first, then feels a deep ineffable shame within—maybe they are antiques. People from another time and place who roamed the earth as tribesmen and tribeswomen. Where did they belong in these modern times? Where did his customs? His culture? These beautiful children? Him?

It all appeared so out of reach, out of touch. The glamor of New York City could've been on another planet: a place these kids will most likely never know. Offerings and opportunities they would never experience unless they abandoned their home on the reservation, their ancestors and heritage.

Conflicted, he pats her on the head and says, "You dance beautifully." She smiles and curtsies. The two other kids clap. All of the kids now stand and dance to the music, even four-year-old Little Wonder who holds hands with Morning Sparrow's girl Maisy. All of them shaking their butts.

"Dinner!" his sister shouts, but something lingers in his mind and keeps him trapped in place.

He wonders how he could bring that joy to his people—not dancing for the pains of the past, but for the joys of the present. How can he bring their beauty and their culture to the world?

"'Food,' I said," his sister shouts again from ten feet away. The parade fades to commercial and the kids race over to the round table for food, not wanting to miss a minute.

Black Cloud is usually the first one in line for food. His sister places her hands on her hips, "Cloud, you coming?"

Nothing. He sits mesmerized by the flashing images and the

marching band's rat-tat-tatting exploding drums like gunfire from a Gatlin gun—the first machine gun that left so many dead across the Indian Nation. He can feel the banging of Indian drums in his blood, in his heart, pulsing through him.

"Earth to Cloud. You coming?" Still nothing. "ABRAHAM!" she shouts.

The sound of his given name snaps him back to the present. He finds them all staring, plates in hand. With a shake of his head, he scoops up Little Wonder, pretending to munch on the boy's neck.

"No Unca Bwack Cwoud!" Little Wonder squeals. "You're supposed to eat the tuwkey."

"Duck," White Feather corrects, but her eyes stay on her brother. "Are you okay? You're really into that parade today."

"Huh? Oh yeah," he mutters, accepting a plate. The drums from the TV mix with older rhythms in his blood: buffalo hooves, ceremonial beats, history itself moving across the land.

The kitchen feels too small, too hot. Sweat breaks out across his forehead as he stands with his plate in hand. White Feather serves him, her eyes never leaving his face. He barely notices the food, his mind caught between the marching bands on TV and older rhythms within.

She serves him and watches him as he sits. "Cloud, I thought you hated the parade..."

"I do. Did." He falls silent, watching without eating, a duck leg gripped tightly in his hand.

Morning Swallow leans over and whispers to White Feather, "Your brother is so weird."

"Tell me about it." The women share a laugh.

His niece suddenly twirls in perfect imitation of the ballet dancers on screen again, her long black hair flowing. Pride swells in his chest, then sinks just as quickly. These children, these beautiful children, watching a world that barely knows they exist.

The parade host's voice carries over their laughter, "And now, coming down 34th Street..." Black Cloud watches the children dance to someone else's music, and something clicks into place.

Black Cloud had always hated that parade for the obvious reasons—a celebration of stolen land and the murder of so many people, lies, broken treaties. But he never understood the deeper reason that fueled his hatred until this day. What felt like hate had in fact been jealousy, like wanting a parent's love and attention while being ignored and pushed aside. He wanted to see his people get their due respect and to show the world what they were capable of. He had many friends in other tribes who felt the same way. Yet it all felt impossibly out of reach. How can you make a country see you? How can you make a country acknowledge its past?

White Feather calls again for him to eat, but he's caught in the space between worlds—the TV's bright lights, the drum beats in his blood, his mother's words echoing *listen as you go*.

The money wasted on the parade could go to medicine and industry. Looking at the food in his hand, he gives thanks to the spirit of the duck and to the land for feeding his family as it had for centuries. He tears at the flesh, not wanting to be an antique in some damn barn or sealed off the way he's been. That succulent meat never tasted so good, and he'd never felt so ravenous for it. He chews slowly on his duck leg, the taste rich and earthy. Gratitude, he thinks, is also a form of rebellion.

"Delicious, sis. Thank you," he says wiping his mouth with a hand. She raises an eyebrow and glances at her friend as they laugh some more.

Modern dancers with colorful costumes and graceful movements come onto the television. He says to White Feather, "Wish they could see you dance our traditional dances, sis. You'd be the best one out there."

"That was long ago…I've got more jiggle than wiggle now," she says as they bring out the desserts. The parade ends soon after and the kids fall asleep. He kisses them on their foreheads and stands to leave.

"I'll bring Mom some food after I clean up," she says to him at the door.

He nods, floating outside of time as if seeing history and events from some broader perspective. "Uh, can I help with anything?" he offers blankly.

"Nah, you're good."

He leaves without another word and steps outside into the cold. The prairie stretches in all directions—rolling and silent. He feels the ancestors and their history in the wind. His name, Mahpiyasapa—Black Cloud—presses against his spine like a stone carried a long way.

Full of duck and dark thoughts, he walks the dirt path to his own trailer. The chanting from his mother's home carries on the afternoon air. They're saying his father's name: Man with Two Ears, the one who listened more than spoke.

Confused about the events of the day, and having never put his finger on it before, he lets his thoughts tumble. Antique, his mother had said. The word lingering in his thoughts.

Inside his trailer, he grabs a Budweiser and takes a long pull. The word turns over in his mind like tumbleweeds blowing across the prairie. He lays down on his bed. Not antique. Not forgotten. Just waiting. Waiting to be seen.

His eyes close, heavy with converging thoughts and a sense of disconnection from the larger American family.

"We will not be forgotten," his mother had said. Maybe that's what he'd been hearing and struggling with all along.

TWO

A Stirring Within

As he sleeps, the land whispers. When he awakens, he isn't sure of the time, but it's dark, and he's sweating. A yellow moon hangs low like a lantern over the ancient hills. His mind startles into consciousness knowing his mum's right: no ghost dances or sun dances will change anything.

He sits upright in bed knowing they cannot keep asking their ancestors to save them. "We must ask of ourselves," he says aloud, surprised by the sound of his voice in the middle of the quiet, dark night. He glances over at the empty side of their bed where his wife should be sleeping. Gloria's side remains untouched. Two years gone, and it still feels wrong to stretch out into that space. He presses his hand to her pillow. Cold. He misses her most at night, in those long dark hours when the ghosts have room to stretch. Sometimes in the dark hours of the night, he swears he can feel the warmth of her presence, like sunlight on a cold day.

Some mornings, he half expects to find her at the kitchen stove, humming out of tune and burning toast. Gloria, with her wild laugh and bony elbows. Gloria, who once stood up to five marshals harassing kids who were hanging around at the local store. Gloria, who once danced barefoot through the rain with their daughter clinging to her hip. When she was sick in bed, Gloria would say, "We're allowed to grieve, Abraham, but not forever. That's not living." Her hand would slip out of his when she needed rest.

His wife of twenty-three years died from breast cancer, and he often feels her presence, her love.

After losing Gloria, their daughter Samantha had become his anchor, his reason to rise each morning. They called her "Samantha Blue" because the sky had never looked bluer than on the day she was born. For twenty-two years, she'd been the bridge between her father's reservation roots and her mother's dreaming heart.

She'd been the light after the storm, their girl with the unshakeable curiosity. He used to joke that she didn't walk—she wandered. Just like her mother. After Gloria passed, Samantha became his compass. The reason he brewed coffee in the mornings. The reason he kept the house from falling in on itself.

They sat side-by-side for months after the funeral and grieved. On the steps. In the backyard. In the quiet. Not needing words. Just watching the sky shift colors of reds, blues, and greens, like a bruise healing.

The day transitioned into night, and they watched shooting stars that somehow resembled the light she brought into everyone's life. A prayer, a miracle, as if Gloria were listening and responding back to them.

On rainy days they'd drink hot chocolate together at the small kitchen table where they had shared so many family meals, where young Samanatha Blue had drawn pictures and did homework assignments.

Between tears, they'd trade memories of Gloria's laugh, her terrible jokes, and the way she'd dance while cooking Sunday breakfast. How she'd tell stories about the day Samantha was born, always ending with, "Your daddy cried harder than you did," and a kiss on her daughter's head.

Father and daughter held each other up through the worst days, hospital visits and watching her body wracked with the disease, sharing the weight of absence until Samantha's own grief began pulling her toward different horizons. He understood—she was young, and young hearts need space to heal and explore. She had her mother's wandering spirit, her light, and that need to chase something bigger than pain. But understanding didn't make the silence of her absence any easier to bear. Some mornings he'd find himself making three cups of hot chocolate out of habit, the empty chairs at the kitchen table like wounds that wouldn't heal or dissolve. He'd eventually pour it down the sink after letting it sit all day. Or he'd pour it into the soil outside in case she wanted some.

A year after Gloria passed, their only child left for California. He remembers the morning Samantha Blue told him and the way the kitchen light reflected in her purple sunglasses—her pixie-cut brown hair tucked under an LA Dodgers cap. It was their last breakfast at the small table that had held so many conversations.

"It's just so heavy here, Dad." Her fingers spread photographs of magazine cutouts she'd been saving across the worn tablecloth—California cliffs dropping into an endless blue sea. "But it's sunny there every day and the Pacific Ocean is so blue and goes on forever." Light danced in her eyes as she traced the coastline.

"Matches your middle name: Blue." He smiled weakly.

"You're right, it does." She smiled at the pictures then tilted her head, smiling at the thought. "After mom died," she continued, gathering the photos closer, "and watching her long illness, her suffering, I'm just lost and need to go…somewhere. Somewhere new. Anywhere. You know?"

He nodded, understanding that same restless yearning to explore and find oneself. Knowing we're all born explorers. We only stop when we get stuck.

Understanding the desire to outrun the past and start again. But you can't start again in the same place you've always been. A new place allowed for new thoughts and new experiences.

Yet in the process, some lose themselves further while some may find what they didn't even know they were looking for. Some souls drift into shadow while others step into light.

"I just want to a be a girl and meet people and live and laugh, maybe fall in love. I'm twenty-two and just want to see…"

"I get it, hon." His words were gentle but firm. "There's a whole big world out there. You're beautiful, vibrant, and so smart. You certainly take after your mother." Their laughter filled the small kitchen, a sound grown too rare. "Just don't forget your pop."

"I won't. I promise." She leaned across the table, pressed her lips to his cheek. "I just want to wake up with the sunshine every day and the salty smell of the ocean and run along the beach. I just need to go." After a pause, she looked away, "You should leave here too." He had considered that, yearned for it. Get on the road like he and Gloria had always wanted and see the country. But he couldn't leave his home.

Touching his cheek where her lips had been, he lays back down, curling into the blanket, missing his family. Loneliness creeps in with the night air as sleep carries him gently back into dreams. His wife stands with the ancestors in silhouette atop the Black Hills, whole again, her body radiant as dawn. Her long brown hair streams with colors—blues, reds, yellows, greens. She reaches for him, fingers almost touching, before the dream dissolves into morning mist.

When he awakens with the sound of songbirds and soft light filling the room behind his closed eyelids, he hears, *You must go, Abraham.* Startled by her voice, his eyes pop open. Her sweet, soothing voice is right there, as if Gloria were lying next to him. For a moment he hoped to see her there, his wife, to feel her, but only cool sheets lay tussled about.

This idea follows him into the bathroom as if it is alive and demanding his attention. He stands and crosses into the bathroom. The mirror does him no favors. His eyes are puffy, and face sags.

You must go, Abraham!

"Go where?!" he shouts and shakes his head while looking in the bathroom mirror. "Um, I'm trying to go to the bathroom here." He looks around the room.

No jokes, Abraham.

"It's no joke. I am in the bathroom." He splashes cold water on his face and can hear the soft hum of the fridge, and the creak of the wood floor contracting in the cool.

He continues his morning, the voice quiet for the moment as he dresses into blue jeans and a long black sleeve shirt. Morning light spills across the kitchen as he makes coffee, her voice finding him once again.

You must go, my love.

"To the parade?" he asks the empty room as he spins around searching. "To watch? I'm not some kid needing to go to some stupid parade and stand in the rain. Or travel two thousand miles to be a tourist." Surrounded by faux wood paneling in front of a white speckled countertop, he argues with the silence.

But the urge persists. The sense that he must go continues, like taking out the garbage or fixing a leaking pipe. The idea simply won't leave him alone. He eats cornflakes and drips milk on the round Formica table. He stares at the milk running along the tabletop as his cornflakes go soft, his breakfast forgotten as the past melds with the present.

He steps outside for some air in his socks, forgetting how the cool air bites at this hour. Feeling stifled and confused, he finds a gold finch perched like a small sun on the fence post staring at him while other birds gossip in the brush. Rubbing his foot over the hard baked landscape, the earth feels wide this morning, the past whispering its truths.

And then, the chanting starts.

Low and throaty, it drifts from his mother's trailer next door. The healers have returned. His mother must be having another one of her visions. The voices in his head align with her chanting—rhythm matching rhythm, the past flowing into the present like an electrical surge.

Voices from the dream demand his attention again as if standing alongside him. He shouts at them, questioning why he must go.

"You want me to hijack the Macy's parade? Make a scene? Build a float? It's suicide. I'll get killed." But the voices won't relent.

The chanting from next door grows louder. The wails continue, and he hears his name, not Black Cloud but Abraham, liberator. He looks over to his mother's house and she is shockingly up and banging on her window.

"You must go!" she shouts like a crazy person. She isn't looking at him, but past him with crazy wild hair. "You must go!" He turns away, and when he looks back, she's gone.

Shaking his head, he walks over and sits down on a wooden bench under a ponderosa pine. Grabbing the cell phone from his back pocket, he calls his daughter, wanting to tell her about his waking dream, seeing mom, and that weird thing Grandma just did. But more than anything, he just wants to hear her voice and laugh with her.

The phone rings, and he is forced to leave a message. "Call your dad. Let me know how you're doing." But she isn't so good at calling him back.

He stands, placing the phone into his pocket. Alone, he considers drinking too much whiskey and feeling sorry for himself. The dream and message confuse him. Instead, he thinks of Gloria and the strength she carried in her small body.

He chuckles to himself and says, "Miss you, woman." Then sighs, appreciating the day filled with blue skies and soft clouds. Empty pastures, bare cottonwoods, and the red dirt road that leads out to the highway.

THREE

Thirty Years Earlier

The Bureau of Indian Affairs office in Boise stood like any other government building: fluorescent lights, beige walls, and cubicles. But for Black Cloud and Stan Whiteman—summer interns vying for the same fall position—it held the promise of futures yet unwritten.

Black Cloud had come to the Bureau believing he could change things from the inside. His father, despite his eventual bitter end, had always preached about working within the system, about being the change they needed. About dreaming big and lifting others.

"Someone's got to be first," he'd tell young Abraham. "Someone's got to walk through their doors and make them see us as more than numbers in their reports."

So Black Cloud had done everything right. He graduated top of his class, wore suits that didn't quite fit his shoulders, spoke carefully in meetings, and dreamed of the day Native faces would be common in these halls, rather than just subjects in filing cabinets.

But it was during those long summer days of filing papers, red tape, and learning how bureaucracy *doesn't* work that Black Cloud discovered something unexpected: not just the grinding wheels of government, but a spark of hope in an unlikely place.

Gloria, a case worker, electrified that mundane space. She stood five feet five inches in heels, but her presence filled the office. Her straight black hair caught the overhead lights, and her smile could make even government paperwork seem less dreary. At two years his senior, she carried herself with a quiet confidence that drew both Black Cloud's and Whiteman's attention. She was the first in her family to get a college degree and also wanted to make a difference. Fierce, when need be, but her usual disposition was light and kind. She laughed easily.

Working together in the same office with several others, the three of them had a bright future in their young eyes. Both he and Whiteman became friendly and interested in her. Whiteman gave her flowers and chocolates and sat at her desk and laughed at her jokes.

She liked his curly blond hair and baby blue eyes. So Black Cloud backed off, thinking she was with him.

For weeks, Black Cloud buried himself in work, taking extra assignments, staying late to study policy; anything to keep his mind off her. He told himself it was better this way. After all, Whiteman could offer her things he couldn't: stability, status, a car that wasn't the city bus. Every time he heard her laugh at one of Whiteman's jokes, he pressed his pen harder into the paperwork, leaving impressions that went pages deep.

Until one day by the filing cabinet, she turned to him and said, "Are you ever going to ask me out? I see you looking."

He glanced up from his nearby desk. "Huh? I thought you were Whiteman's girl."

"I'm nobody's girl until I say I am." Her plaid skirt swayed as she walked away. Her hair was done up with a fashionable yellow bow set off to the side. He was hooked.

The three friends fell into an easy rhythm that summer: drinks after work, bowling on weekends, dancing on Friday nights at the local VFW. But beneath the surface, tensions simmered and desires grew.

During Black Cloud's last week—while he was out of the office—Whiteman made his final play for her.

He looked over his shoulder and said, "Black Cloud can't take care of you the way I can. I mean he doesn't even own a car and takes the bus here. He's a great guy, but you can do better than him." He sat on her desk with pleading blue eyes.

"That's not very nice, Stanley. I'm not sure I would want to be with someone who speaks about his friend like that. Now if you will excuse me, I have work to do," she said as her eyes refocused on paperwork.

Both Black Cloud and Stan Whiteman prepared for the next level position after the summer internship. Both took the test and interviewed. One would begin a career with the Bureau and one would simply go home. Better luck next year.

After the job went to Whiteman, Black Cloud felt sorry for himself and unsure about his future while he packed his desk belongings into a small box. Gloria walked over and asked him to call her, passing him a note. Whiteman saw the note from her and saw Black Cloud slip it into his breast pocket, smile and nod. Then he saw their eyes meet. He saw the way Gloria looked at Black Cloud—not with pity, but recognition. And something broke inside him.

His bitterness grew over the years at losing Gloria: the resentment, the revenge he kept hidden, waiting for a chance to get back at him. He'd never married and never forgot, yet often thought about what could have been if Black Cloud hadn't interfered in their "love," as he thinks of it.

Black Cloud said on their first date, over plates of chicken fried steak at the diner down the street, "The Bureau of Indian Affairs and yet there ain't no Indians working there. That never made no sense to me. Bureau of White People, more like it." The words carried all his frustration about trying to change things from within.

"I'm Native American, twenty-five percent Coeur d'Alene. Thank you very much."

"Oh right, so you are. Well, let's call it the Bureau of Gloria then," he said, smiling at her.

She smiled back from across the restaurant table, then slid her hand into his.

"I'm *your* girl."

They married six months later, Cloud proposing on the steps of that same Bureau building where they'd met, but this time with a bouquet of sunflowers in his hand and an inexpensive ring in the other.

"It might not have worked out the way I planned," he'd said, down on one knee, "but I found something better than a government job. I found you." Gloria wore that same yellow bow in her hair the day she said yes, and again at their wedding.

Later, the truth came out in whispers around the office—how Whiteman had cheated on the test, paying off an intern from another department for the answers. The higher-ups buried it, of course. Investigating would have meant questioning the whole system, and no one wanted that kind of trouble. So, they let it go. Whiteman got the job, yet bitterness grew with what had been taken from him. He told himself he'd done it for love, that he would have done anything for her—even cheat and lie. Three decades later, he still carried that same poison in his veins.

FOUR

A Crazy Dream

Cards are played at the recreation center that night. Black Cloud sits with his usual crew: Bull Nose Pete, Tall Tim, and Samuel Red Deer (though he doesn't ever go by Red Deer and doesn't intend to start now). The oldest of their group at fifty-seven, Samuel is a quiet man, except for when he's calling out someone's foolishness.

They gather around a folding table in a large room meant for greater things: music lessons and children's dance classes that never materialized. The instruments were never bought. The funding, like so many promises, never came. Now it's just hardwood floors, empty walls, the soft slap of cards on their meeting table, and the occasional belch.

As the cards are dealt by Black Cloud, he speaks casually.

"So, I had this crazy dream," he says, eyes fixed on the cards sliding from his hands, "that we should have our own float in the Macy's Thanksgiving Day Parade."

Tall Tim snorts, reaching for the empty potato chip bowl. "Why? We can watch it from here and play horseshoes."

"Besides, we weren't invited," Bull Nose Pete adds, arranging his cards.

Tall Tim wonders, "Wouldn't we need to buy tickets to participate?" The bowl of potato chips has run out, and he picks at the crumbs from the bottom.

"I ain't going to no stupid parade," Samuel declares. "You need money for that, and *we* have no money…"

"Yup," Tall Tim adds. "That's one thing we've got plenty of, no money."

"Go fish," Black Cloud says, then takes a swig of beer.

Bull Nose Pete squints at his cards.

"Any eights?"

They all shake their heads in unison.

"Go fish."

Tall Tim continues, "I was just thinking about not having enough potato chips and you want to have a float in some parade. I've got holes in my socks, Cloud." The man raises his shoeless foot to demonstrate.

Shaking his head at his friend, Black Cloud's voice drops lower, serious now. "We'll pay for it with the land that's been stolen, the genocide of native people, and broken treaties. It'll be our last stand."

"What the hell does that mean?" Samuel chides. "For a float in that dumb parade? I'll pass."

Black Cloud raises his eyes. "We need to be in it, a part of it. Show them who we really are. And I don't mean dancing and waving like good little Indians. Or stoic, somber, and wise." He crosses his arms and puts on a serious face. "But real people." His fingers tap the cards slowly. "It's time America heard the real story. Make them listen for once. There's more to it than just a float," Black Cloud says, not fully understanding it himself, his eyes back on his cards. "It's so much more than a float."

Bull Nose Pete mocks, “You’ve got your head in the clouds again, Cloud. It was just a dream. Let it go.” His nostrils flare as he laughs along with the two other men.

Black Cloud responds, “Yeah, yeah. I’ve never heard that one before.”

“You’ve got that look, Cloud. The one that always leads to trouble,” Tall Tim says.

“That kind of trouble leads to jail,” Samuel adds, shaking his head. “Count me out.” Then adds, “Any twos?”

They check their cards and shake their heads.

“Go fish.”

“At least we’ll be remembered,” Black Cloud persists, “and not antiques forgotten in some barn.”

Samuel spits out words like daggers.

“Sounds stupid. We’d be outcasts and jailed. We’d eat crow.”

Bull Nose Pete chimes in, “We already eat crow. On second thought, prison don’t sound so bad compared to this place.” He’s still sober enough for those words to ring true. He takes another swig of his beer.

“This place is a prison,” Tall Time proclaims. “No jobs, no money, no good women.”

The men grunt in agreement.

Black Cloud counters, “The women might say the same thing about no good men.”

“Hmmm,” Tall Tim spits chewing tobacco into an old coffee can that dings as it hits.

Silence descends until Black Cloud breaks it.

“We ain’t going to jail if they don’t catch us.”

“Catch us for what?” Samuel’s mocking laugh holds no humor. “Entering a float in a parade? Are we just going to show up with a float and say, 'Here we are?' Just deal you fool. Too much sunlight on your brain."

The dealt cards slide across the table, catching under the receiver's fingertips.

"You're right about one thing, Cloud," Tall Tim studies his hand.

"What's that?" He asks looking up.

"It's crazy all right."

The other three men nod in unison.

"Now that's something we can all agree upon," Samuel says.

"It might have been a vision," Black Cloud stokes the idea, not ready to let it go.

"Oh god," Samuel's eyes widen with mock revelation. "Nope, it was just a dumb dream. I had a dream of Marilyn Monroe the other night. Or was it a vision?"

Laughter fills the empty room.

"Okay, okay," Black Cloud joins the chuckling, the dream folding like a bad hand, realizing they're probably right. "Let's just play cards."

FIVE

The Persistent Seed

While drinking coffee the next morning, Black Cloud watches steam rise from their cups like smoke from a ceremony as he tells them about his dream. His sister and Morning Sparrow sit across the small kitchen table listening, their faces soft in the early light. He needs to release it from its cage and set it free, even if they laugh like the others did.

"It's just a silly idea, isn't it?" His words feel strange, like a betrayal exiting his lips in the quiet of the morning, before the kids are awake. He shrugs, "A float carrying statistics about our lives here. Past and present information for all to see. Warrior traditions of mounting horses, shooting bows and arrows. Maybe some dancing and song. But also who we are in the present. How we're living."

White Feather and Morning Sparrow exchange a look that makes him sit straighter. Morning Sparrow leans forward, her usual chatter replaced by something more serious.

"What happened when you went over to your mother's? Did you touch her?"

"Yeah, of course." He wraps his hands around his coffee cup. "Why?" He gave a slow nod, unsure where this was going. Then remembering, "One of the chanters' arms was touching mine."

Morning Sparrow's eyes widen. "That's no ordinary dream. That's a transmission," she whispered, as if the room had ears. "The spirits don't brush against the living for small talk."

"Oh, come on." He looked at his sister for backup.

White Feather shrugged, blowing on her coffee.

"I'm serious!" Morning Sparrow leaned in. "You were part of a purification rite. You touched the circle. That dream wasn't yours alone."

Black Cloud looked down into his coffee as if it might tell him something. "It felt…bigger than me. Like something was pushing it into me."

Morning Sparrow nodded. "Exactly."

He rubbed his temples. "It's just—what do I do with it? Build a float? We've got no money. No plan. Just a stupid sketch on a napkin and a headache."

"The ancestors don't waste dreams," Morning Sparrow said softly. "Maybe it starts with a float. But it's big, whatever it is."

He thought of his mother's smoke-filled room, her hand wrapped in his, her words, *You will do something special.* He hadn't believed her then. Maybe he should have.

The morning light catches the rising steam like the refraction of light from their cups, and for a moment, Black Cloud sees it again: the sacred smoke that had filled his mother's trailer, carrying whispers he's only beginning to understand.

That night, sleep eluded him. When it finally came, it brought more than rest.

In his dream, he stood in the middle of Manhattan, the Macy's parade unfolding around him like a surreal painting. Balloons floated overhead, dancers spun past in a blur, and there in the center of it all—his people. Not as stereotypes or side attractions, but proud, defiant, whole. A wave of emotion passed through him like thunder. Then came the voice again—Gloria's—whispering, *Make them see.*

He awoke at 3:12 a.m., drenched in sweat, breath ragged. The house was silent but for the faint creak of wind against the trailer. He didn't hesitate. He grabbed a notebook and scribbled furiously under the weak light of the kitchen.

Diagrams. Ideas. Names of parks and hiding spots. Timelines and symbols. It all poured out of him.

He pauses with a pencil in hand realizing that this is so much bigger than a float in some parade; it's a grand stage with the eyes of the world upon it. It is a reclamation in plain sight. His pencil scratches across paper in the pre-dawn darkness, catching whispers before they fade.

An hour later, spent from the download of information, he dozes off in his blue recliner, papers clutched to his chest. When he wakes hours later to sunlight streaming through dusty windows, the memories feel distant, like something he witnessed rather than thought, like far off stories told long ago.

Later that morning, Tall Tim knocks on his trailer door. Black Cloud opens it; his hair and clothes are a mess like some mad scientist after working all night in a lab. Sprigs and tufts of hair shoot in all directions, shirt wrinkled and untucked. Drool is encrusted upon his face.

"What happened to *you*?" Tall Tim looks up at him from the metal step of the trailer, squinting. Cloud shakes his head.

Without stepping inside, Tall Tim asks in flat native tones that rise as the question exits his lips, "So anyway, how could they not catch us?" He stares up at Black Cloud and the eyes of these two best friends meet.

Black Cloud glances around the empty yard and hurries him inside.

"Come in. Come in."

They settle at the small round table, and though his hands already shake with excitement, Black Cloud pours them both coffee and spreads out his night's work.

He taps the notebook filled with fevered diagrams about their float with signs on it and participants coming in from all directions.

"The plan is so much more than I first understood. It isn't just about a float in the parade at all—it's about being witnessed. Imagine it—our people, center stage. Telling the truth in front of the whole damn country."

"So…no float?"

"Yes, still a float."

Tall Tim shifts his jaw from left to right, then left again while looking at the notes. "My five-year-old granddaughter draws better. But ah, we don't want to be witnessed, Cloud. If we're witnessed, that means we get caught. Right?"

"No, no, that's not what I mean. Witnessed means seen."

"I know. We don't want to be seen."

Black Cloud shakes his head, "You'll understand later. Here, look."

Black Cloud gets out an old, tattered map of New York, fingers tracing paths through parks and open spaces, up into Westchester

County, over to Squantz Pond and Sherwood Island State Park in Connecticut, then down to northern New Jersey and Palisades Park. "Places to hide until the time is right."

"Hide out?" Tall Tim asks flatly. He drains his coffee, chair scraping back to stand. "Mmm, hmm. Mmm, hmm. Yup, that's stupid alright. Just wanted to make sure. Okay, see you for cards."

"You dumb old fool. There's gold in New York City."

Tall Tim looks at him.

"They said there was gold in the Black Hills, but that was a lie too," he says with a hand on the door.

"They'll be rewards, treasure. Just the other day you were talking about women...well, you'd be celebrated for decades. Women love a hero."

"Hero? Decades?"

"But we must be secretive, like James Bond..."

"And we get the girl?"

"You're married, Tim."

"Betty won't mind."

"That is true," Black Cloud says, nodding and laughing.

"Okay," Tall Tim says, sitting back down.

"That's it, okay?"

"Okay. Still stupid. But I'll drink your coffee."

"I was up all night for this. I hope it's not stupid."

"Need me to cut my hand and shake over blood? Because it'll take me weeks to heal. I'm anemic and old."

"Nah, your word is enough. Well, let's shake on it though." They stand in the cramped kitchen, hands clasped, sealing whatever madness this is.

They sit back down satisfied with themselves. Tall Tim smacks his lips after sipping more coffee while Black Cloud sits back in his chair crossing his hands behind his head as if they had just accomplished some great feat.

"Yep, we're gonna do something big."

"Yep. We sure are," Tall Tim echoes.

After crossing and uncrossing his legs and fidgeting with a pen cap, Black Cloud says, "Well, we better get started."

Tall Tim stares at him blankly, "With what? I thought we just did."

Black Cloud frowns and stands. "Let's go."

At first the two of them are left to their own devices and head out back. Unsure how to be seen on the national stage of the parade or what to train for, their first attempts at preparation involve sneaking behind trees, followed by ambushing kids with dried grass balls who are playing in the school yard. The kids—delighted by these crazy old men—return fire with enthusiasm. The elderly warriors retreat under a barrage of prairie ammunition.

Later, they attempt archery in Black Cloud's backyard, their arms shaking after just a few draws. By afternoon, they're sprawled on his couch with ice packs and beer, breathing like they've just run marathons.

"We're too old for this, Cloud," Tall Tim groans.

With an ice pack on his forehead Black Cloud responds, "No one will expect us. That's why it's perfect."

A knock at the door sends them scrambling to hide their ice packs like guilty teenagers as if they'd already broken the law. Bull Nose Pete stands at the door with his wide flat nose flaring.

"I've been watching you two, and man do you guys stink."

"Can you do better?" Black Cloud shoots back.

"A dead buffalo could do better."

Outside, Pete demonstrates proper bow technique, the arrows

singing through the air instead of wobbling like drunk birds. After thirty minutes, Black Cloud and Tall Tim still couldn't hit the red earth if they tried.

"Man, you guys do stink. What's this training for anyhow?"

"I told it to you yesterday."

"Having a float in the parade?"

"Yup…"

He looks at the two and shrugs. "I don't get it, but okay."

"So, you're in?" Black Cloud asks in surprise.

He shrugs, "I've got nothing to do anyways."

Tall Tim misses so bad with his next shot, his arrow flies off and hits Bull Nose Pete's redbone hound dog sitting nearby. The dog yelps and runs off. The arrow falls to the ground and the dog comes back and pees on it.

Bull Nose Pete frowns.

"You're half blind. Give me that. I'd piss on it too." He yanks the bow out of Tall Tim's hands.

"Sorry, Pete."

Black Cloud slaps Tall Tim on the back. "Need to find you a task you're better suited for. Like James Bond has Q, the operations person."

"In all fairness, Pete, I'm more like three quarters blind," he says, and they all laugh. The dog growls then licks himself in front of the fence.

"You okay, Jake?" Tall Tim asks the dog.

"Ah, that's nothing. He's been twice hit by cars, fought a raccoon once and had a hot frying pan fall on him." Pete scratches behind Jake's good ear. "Got into a scrap with a coyote last spring too. Won the fight, but the scars don't let the fur grow anymore on that side. Tough old dog, just like us." Looking up he says, "He can handle a dull arrow from a feeble marksman."

Tall Tim asks, "Indian dog, eh?"

Black Cloud watches Jake shake his scarred coat proudly.

"Takes more than a coyote to keep a rez dog down."

"You got that right." Bull Nose Pete smiles down at Jake and rubs his ear.

The next day when they finally drag themselves from bed, the three conspirators gather to practice horse rustling from their friend Samuel. Just following ideas that pop up in hopes it will direct them to the grand stage. Warriors first.

The sun stretches long shadows across the black and tan landscape as they crouch behind his corral fence, nursing hangovers and questioning their life choices.

Black Cloud and Tall Tim army crawl through the morning dust, their elbows collecting dried manure as they slide beneath the bottom rail. Bull Nose Pete, his sciatica causing him to scream every curse word known to the Sioux nation, gives up any pretense of stealth and simply rolls under the fence like a wayward log. The horses, used to far more dignified behavior from reservation elders, watch this display with what can only be described as equine disappointment.

They hear from the side, "What the hell you fools doin'?" Samuel walks up and shoots them dead with his fingertip. "Pow. Pow. Pow."

"Shh, we're practicing." They get up and tiptoe cautiously over to the horses.

"Fer what? And the horses can see, you fools," Samuel says, with hands on his hips. His sinewy muscles coil on his small frame.

The three men rise like warriors of old—if warriors of old had bad knees and lower back problems. They launch into what they imagine is a sprint, but looks more like a desperate hobble, aiming for a chestnut mare and two bay geldings.

Black Cloud reaches the mare first, his leap falling embarrassingly short of her back. Tall Tim manages to grab a handful of his gelding's mane before sliding down the horse's side like rain off a tin roof. Bull Nose Pete, showing more enthusiasm than skill, hits his mount's rump at precisely the wrong angle and bounces off, landing spread-eagle in the dirt. The horses, maintaining their dignity, simply step aside and continue their morning grazing while the three grown men lie groaning in the dust of their ancestors.

"Well, do it somewhere else. You're scaring the mare." She steps a few feet off chewing on hay, turning her head to stare at them as if witnessing the death of her last hope for human intelligence. The two geldings don't seem to mind, simply glancing at the men on the ground.

As they lay sprawled in the dirt, Bull Nose Pete clutches his lower back, moaning like a bleating goat, "Good thing this was fake and not some real-life horse thieving."

From his spot in the dust, Tall Tim says, "We're gonna get ourselves killed, Cloud."

"Maybe, but I ain't felt this youthful since like, well, never."

"Well, I ain't never felt this achy since my sciatica acted up this morning."

They all laugh with dirt on them—the soil and earth smelling sweet.

SIX

Shaking Off The Dust

The men sit with slack postures, hunched over while playing cards that evening. Doubts have grown and the weight of their failures settle in around them. Their enemies don't even know they exist, and they don't know what they're doing. Even with a year to prepare, they feel helpless. Everything they've tried—the horses, the bows, even their pitiful attempts at stealth—has only proven what they've known but don't want to admit: they're old men playing at being warriors. The fantasy felt noble in daylight, foolish by night. More like a retirement center than a center for protest.

Black Cloud knows they need a spark before this idea dies in darkness.

Bull Nose Pete stares at his cards without seeing them, his earlier bravado worn thin. "We can't pull this off," his nostrils flare with the admission. "We're barely hanging on as is. They're gonna take away all our land." His hand slaps the table hard enough to scatter the cards, a lifetime of frustration in that single gesture.

Samuel says, "Just deal, you idiot."

"Who's going to take our land? The Bureau of Indian Affairs?"

Tall Tim asks. "For what?"

"If we make them look bad or worse," Bull Nose Pete says deflated. "If word gets out, Old Whiteman himself is gonna come snooping around. You know, Cloud, your old buddy."

"He was never my buddy. But he did try to steal my girl." Cloud's jaw tightens at the memory: Whiteman showing up with flowers for Gloria after Black Cloud had left the Bureau, offering her a better life off the reservation, promising things a poor Indian never could.

"Bastard thought because he had money and a government job, he could take anything he wanted." He remembers her telling him this in the kitchen and how strong he felt knowing that she had chosen him.

"Well, you showed him. You got the girl." Tall Tim says.

"Forget him. It's bigger than us now…" Cloud shuffles the cards harder than necessary, remembering how Gloria had thrown those flowers in Whiteman's face, choosing love over comfort. Some victories you carry forever.

Samuel studies his cards and doesn't raise his eyes above them. "It ain't bigger than us. In fact, it ain't nothing at all but some old fools hurting themselves and trying to matter."

"We've never mattered to them," Pete adds.

"I'm sick of playing their game," Cloud says. "I don't want to win—I want to make them see. Just once."

"And then what? They clap and go back to ignoring us?"

"No." Black Cloud leans in. "Then they remember. That we're still here. And shoot, so we remember too."

There's a silence. A long one. Until Tall Tim mutters, "Got any threes?"

"Go fish," Pete replies.

"You're just mad cuz he took your job." Samuel stares at Black Cloud who nods.

"A job you would've had if he hadn't cheated on that entrance exam," Tall Tim adds.

Bull Nose Pete says, "Those white devil immigrants are always taking our jobs. But strangely, they won't take my bursitis or knee pain away."

They all laugh, but it's the kind of laugh that covers harder truths.

Samuel slaps the cards down and stands to leave.

"I ain't interested, Cloud."

"You never did have no sand in your back…all tough talk," Black Cloud challenges him. Tall Tim and Bull Nose Pete exchange glances, while Samuel's face darkens into something dangerous.

"I've got sand enough to whip your behind, you say that again."

"Great, then show us. Come on, we need you." Black Cloud doesn't back down, knowing a man's pride is the best rope to tie him with.

The hard man sits down.

"I've got more sand than all three of you combined. I just don't want to fight 'em. That's suicide. Life's hard enough," his voice carries the wisdom of old wounds and battles lost.

Black Cloud leans forward, "We're not fighting anyone, Sam."

"We're fighting the past, Cloud, and that's a fight you can't never win. Believe me, I've tried." He picks up his cards again, arranging them like he wishes he could rearrange the broken pieces of his past: decisions made, injuries not forgotten, relationships soured.

After a pause, Black Cloud's voice softens, "What we're fighting for is the future. I'm sick of the past, too."

Bull Nose Pete fans his cards closer to his face. "It's their game and we can't win. They set the rules. The house always wins, Cloud." He shifts and studies his hand.

"Well, I don't want to fight them either." He draws a card, and grimaces. "I'm just sick and tired of being a nobody, and well, a damned arti-fact, an antique. That's why we have to be clandestine like."

"Clan-what-who?" confounded Bull Nose Pete inquires. His nostrils flare and eyebrows rise.

"What clan?" Tall Tim asks, cupping his ears and leaning forward. "We talking about clans now?"

"It means a secret," Black Cloud sighs. "Don't you two ever read?"

The two men shake their heads. Samuel rolls his eyes.

"It's time," Black Cloud continues, his voice carrying the weight of generations. "It's time we do something 'bout this here Native America." He lays his cards face down, fingers pressing them against the table's smooth surface. "Cuz if we're so native, well, how come we ain't got no America?"

"The problem is," Bull Nose Pete says, and begins listing them out. "Well, we can't ride, we can't shoot, we're old, we're broke, you're ugly, and we're in terrible shape. How many fingers is that?" He squints at his own hand. "Oh, and we are damn antiques! Now can we just play cards and not speak about no revolution that'll get us all keeled." He grabs his lower back, face pinching. "You're causing my sciatica to act up."

Samuel lectures, "Maybe your sciatica acts up cuz you sit around all day and do nothing but complain."

"Hmm, could be." He throws down a card. "Go fish."

For a few minutes, they play cards in silence—each man lost in the maze of his own thoughts and history when a knock comes at the door to the open room. It's a woman in her late twenties.

Confident. A two-inch scar curves over her right cheek like punctuation: a story written in flesh.

The four old men freeze mid-hand.

"Hello," she says, her voice carrying more steel than deference. Multiple earrings climb her ears like silver stairs while a nose ring glints defiance. Her body is toned and brown, suggesting someone who's known hard work and survival.

The older men lower their cards and look around. No one, let alone a pretty girl, has ever interrupted their card playing.

"Howdy," Tall Tim says, nudging Black Cloud. He leans over and whispers, "I get the girl."

Black Cloud shakes his head at his friend's disjointed enthusiasm. "What can we do for you, miss?"

She walks into the mostly empty room, her boots echoing against the bare floors. The lone card table sits in the center. She waves, a gesture that doesn't match her warrior's build.

"Hi. Well, I'm here for…well I heard you men were doing some…training of sorts…and I was hoping to join you."

"Where'd you hear that?" Bull Nose Pete asks.

"Training what?" Paranoid, Samuel crosses his arms and asks, "Did Whiteman send you?" He glances past her into the hall.

"No. Who's Whiteman?" Confusion crosses her face. "I heard you were doing something important."

Black Cloud bites his lower lip, nodding slowly as he weighs risk against possibility, but knows they need that spark. "We might be. I mean, not at the moment." He glances at the card table.

Bull Nose Pete's chair scrapes back, "No, Cloud. I ain't training with no damn woman."

Her smile vanishes as she moves—one fluid motion that ends with Bull Nose Pete face-down on the table, his arm twisted behind his back at an angle that makes the other men wince. The cards hardly shift at the suddenness of the motion.

"I ain't some damn woman." Her eyes squint, peering down at him.

"Okay, okay." The three other men jump up, hands raised in peaceful surrender.

As she releases him and steps back, they help Bull Nose Pete up as he massages his shoulder.

"You broke him," Cloud says approvingly.

"Just his pride," she replies. "That grows back."

"You want to join us. Why?"

"Why do we get up in the morning? I have my reasons. I used to matter. Now I'm just surviving." She looks them over. Samuel meets her gaze and nods in understanding.

"Because sometimes you need to believe in something to get out of bed."

They pause. That, they all understand.

Pete groans. "Fine. But I don't want to spar with her."

Crystal cracks a half-smile. "I don't spar with men who whine, only men who go too far."

Black Cloud rubs his chin in approval. "Well, isn't this a most auspicious sign. Don't y'all agree?"

"Good sign, my bunions! She almost broke my arm." Bull Nose Pete rotates his shoulder, pride hurting worse than his joints.

"Well, she didn't, did she? This young woman is exactly what we need. Someone with a little fire in her belly." Black Cloud extends his hand. "Welcome. My name is Black Cloud."

She takes his hand; her grip is firm. The men notice how she positions herself to keep all of them, and the exit, in view, like someone used to watching her back.

"Why now?" Samuel barks.

She looks him over. "Because there's only so many years a person can sit in survival mode. At some point, you want to hit back at the demons inside."

Samuel nods approval.

"I'm Crystal," she says with a softening voice. "Sorry about that." She motions to Bull Nose Pete. "I get a little defensive. Trust issues." She shrugs. "I usually strike first, and if need be, apologize later."

"Understood," Black Cloud says.

Bull Nose Pete rubs shoulder, pride still smarting. "Maybe not the best way to introduce yourself."

She nods, considering the idea.

"Where did you hear about us?" Tall Tim asks.

"Morning Sparrow. She said she's been watching you and that you could use my help, and maybe, I could use yours."

"Ah." Tall Tim leans over to Black Cloud and whispers, but loud enough for all to hear, "I guess I don't get the girl. At least, not this one. She'd kill me."

Crystal raises an eyebrow as her mouth twitches toward a smile.

Black Cloud shakes his head at his friend and turns back to Crystal.

"Of course it was Morning Sparrow. Well, maybe you could you help us with hand-to-hand combat? Clearly, we're not very good at it." He looks at Bull Nose Pete,

"Are we?"

Bull Nose Pete frowns and looks away.

She looks them over, taking in Tall Tim's suggestive eyebrows and awkward wink, half at her and half at the table. Her gaze catalogs their beer bellies and bad knees with professional assessment. Five years as a bartender in the roughest bar on the reservation taught her how to read men like worn paperbacks: their weaknesses, their bravado, their desires, and the way alcohol can turn them to violence, sorrow, or amorous offerings.

The scar on her cheek serves as a reminder from her first week on the job, before she'd learned that lesson. Now she could drop a drunk cowboy twice her size without spilling his beer, a skill earned through necessity rather than choice. The reservation didn't offer many jobs to single women with trust issues and a talent for fighting.

"I can do that," she says.

"When do we start?"

She answers, "No time like the present. Those cards aren't getting the flab off them bellies or getting you ready none."

Black Cloud glances down at his belly and sucks it in. "I fold," he says and steps away from the table.

She surveys the empty room with purpose. "This is a perfect workout studio."

Tall Tim says, "Oh, I thought we were gonna ease into being superheroes…"

"There's no easing into anything." Her voice hardens with earned wisdom. "You want something, you go for it with every cell in your body." She doesn't mention the years spent training for her job at the roadside bar: the daily pullups, pushups, squats, and martial arts. But she wasn't always this way. Innocent once but hardened by men and what they took away from her.

Before the bar, she'd been working the register at the Gas-n-Go, eyes down, voice soft, letting men's comments slide off her back like rain. Then one night, a robbery went wrong. She watched her co-worker die as he tried to back to fight back and couldn't. The next day, she found the reservation's only dojo, run by an old Vietnam Vet who'd learned martial arts overseas.

"You're angry," he'd told her. "Good. Hold onto that. You're gonna need it."

She trained every day until her muscles screamed, until she could hold her own against men twice her size. When she applied at the Red Rock Bar two years later, she was ready. That anger turning into purpose.

Lining up on the hardwood floor, they look at each other and gulp. Black Cloud's eagerness did not seem to be shared by his comrades. After a few jumping jacks and jogging in place to warm up, all of them bend over gasping for air, except for Samuel, who keeps on going.

"What's the matter boys?" he says, lifting his knees higher.

She teaches them proper sit-ups and, again, only Samuel can do more than five.

"Okay, well strength isn't going to be our strong suit. But we've got time. Next Thanksgiving, right?"

They grunt "yes" in unison, collapsing to the floor.

"So, without strength, we've got to be secret."

From their spots on the floor, the men exchange glances, excited to hear that word uttered once again.

Black Cloud rolls onto his side, "We could really use you, Sam."

Samuel nods and half smiles enjoying the rigorous exercise. "Someone's got to save you from getting killed." The eyes of the two friends meet, something unspoken passing between them—like the embrace of soldiers in a war they didn't sign up for but can't walk away from. A war that started long ago. One that maybe they could help finish.

They all know this is so much more than a float in a parade. This will be a battle to be seen. Sometimes to stake a claim, elbows need to be thrown.

The training ends with sore knees, scraped elbows, and something close to hope.

After, Cloud leans against the wall. "We're still a bunch of misfits," he says.

Crystal shrugs. "That's what makes us dangerous."

And for the first time, they believe it.

SEVEN

The Team Forms

The next day they meet behind Black Cloud's trailer, where a half-acre of dirt and grass stretches toward brush and wood fencing like a training field that's been waiting all these years. The day is warm enough, in the mid-forties and dry.

Black Cloud still isn't sure how they'll get from A to B—how to bridge the dream with the doing. They're still stumbling through and figuring out the plan. At night the messages feel clear, like someone's whispering into his sleeping mind. By morning, the road disappears in the light. But he's learning to trust that if he shows up, so will the path.

So, they prepare for all battles that may come their way.

Last night he did some online research and found that getting a float in the parade costs hundreds of thousands of dollars.

"Well, we should steal one then." Tall Tim says while jogging slowly in place.

Samuel adds, "Stealing sounds better for all that's been stolen from us."

"Well, who do we steal a float from?"

They shrug.

"Okay, we'll revisit this another time. But they do have the initial lineup of floats that'll be there." He holds up the list.

His mother's trailer stands quiet now. The wailing has ceased.

Crystal's warming up, her body slices through the space like a blade. Every movement is precise, forged through necessity.

She demonstrates the moves that have kept her alive these past years. Each technique carries its own story: the wrist lock applied after a drunk cowboy grabbed her arm to pull her into a dark room, an ankle sweep perfected when her ex-husband thought he could control her with his fists and size, and ended up breaking a coffee table with his fall.

"Damn, woman. When I get up, I'm gonna…"

"No more," she stood over him ready to land blows, her hands clenched like granite.

Standing at five-foot-seven with short black hair, high cheek bones, and a dimpled chin, her tight blue jeans and long brown coat can't quite hide the fighter's grace and power in her movements.

"You could be a mixed martial arts star," Tall Tim says as she demonstrates a wrist lock and then an arm bar takedown that leaves him tasting dirt.

"Not too hard, Crystal. He's feeble and we need him. Well, we sort of need him," Samuel jokes.

Samuel's laughter is cut short as she puts him down next to Tall Tim. Both men lie on the ground, learning what countless bar patrons discovered the hard way: that treating Crystal like a cheap thrill comes with painful consequences.

At the property's edge, movement catches Crystal's eye—a lean man and a teenage boy linger at the fence line along the dirt road, watching.

"Can we help you?" she asks protectively, helping the older men up. They stand and brush themselves off.

"Hi, well, we were happening by and see that you're training over here," the man says, his hands clasped behind his back.

He has a well-trimmed beard, slender face, and intelligent brown eyes. The broad-shouldered boy hangs slightly behind him.

"We, ahh, were hoping we could join you."

Crystal sums the man up quickly and shouts, "No!" Her answer is curt and blunt, words sharp as a dagger. In their dismissal, she turns away.

"Pop, I told you we wouldn't be welcome." The boy turns to leave, shoulders sinking forward.

Crystal reminds Samuel of his daughter who doesn't speak to him, so he says, "Definitely not," and steps forward to stand with her.

"Now hold on. Hold on. Everyone's getting excited here." Black Cloud raises his hands to settle everyone down. He knows he needs a small army to make a big impact, and he believes whoever shows up has been brought here to help. He's learning to trust these coincidences, believing whoever shows up has been brought here for a reason. He doesn't know their background, but they were drawn here, and that is good enough for him.

"Who told you we were here?"

"Well, I'm Morning Sparrow's second cousin." The man steps closer at the inquiry.

Black Cloud rolls his eyes. "Of course, you are." He scowls, kicking at the dirt, not liking the source. He points and says, "He's just a boy. How old are you, son?"

"Seventeen, sir." The boy steps out from behind his father's shadow—brown parted hair, large brown eyes set far apart, and big hands like gloves.

"Well, we're doing hand-to-hand combat here. Probably no place for a child." Black Cloud turns away, testing them.

"I'm no child, sir," the boy says.

The man, no more than thirty-five who must have had his son when he was just a kid himself, steps forward.

"Please, sir. I'm an ex-convict. I've made mistakes, but I need to show my boy that there's something better than what I've done. It's not easy raising a son. But that's no excuse. I know that."

"Well, how can you help us? Are you sure you even know what we're doing here?"

"I know enough." The father nods to the boy, who steps forward.

"It's okay?" The boy glances at the bow lying near Black Cloud's feet.

Black Cloud nods and steps off so the boy can pick it up.

Snatching it off the dusty soil, he checks the weight in his hands, studying its length from end to end. He peers through the felt sight and runs his fingers over an arrow he pulls from the quiver.

Looking in the distance to find a target, his father points.

"Tommy, shoot that post tip over there."

"I can't see no post tip," Tall Tim says, shading his eyes.

"Fool, I bet you can't even see the sky above," Samuel mutters belligerently.

He peers up. "It's blue," he says, though it's overcast and gray.

"Show them what you can do, son." His father steps aside, giving him space. The fence post is four inches by four inches, fifty-plus yards away.

Checking the wind after licking his finger and sticking it up for direction and speed, he studies the distance again with the bow now wedged under his armpit for support. His right hand slowly pulls the tightening bowstring, then lets the feathered arrow fly.

Floom. Through the air it flies like an ancient missile.

Plunk. It embeds itself into the center of the post fifty yards out.

Dead center.

"I heard it, but I couldn't see it," Tall Tim stammers.

A roar of approval rolls through them. Black Cloud steps closer.

"How did you learn to shoot like that, young man?" Black Cloud checks the distance again. All of them are stunned.

"Archery team and hunting, sir."

"Nah, it's in his blood. He's always been a great shot. Since he was a child. He could shoot a star out of the sky if he needed to." Proudly, his father ruffles his hair. Tommy's face splits into a grin.

"His mama called him Eagle Eyes."

"And what does she think about all this?" Black Cloud asks.

His father shakes his head and waves a hand in front as if brushing the idea aside.

Black Cloud nods, understanding. He glances at the stunned faces of his crew then back to the father and son.

"Well, welcome aboard. The more the merrier." He looks back at each person in the group. "Looks like we've got ourselves a sharpshooter. We'll use him only for non-confrontational parts," Black Cloud assures. "Long-range distraction. No front-line work."

Tom Sr. nods his approval.

Samuel steps forward. "Now hang on, hang on. We can't take a kid without his father." Always in a surly mood, Samuel challenges the dad, "Now, how can *you* help? You know what we're up against. You say you're an ex-con; you steal cars or something? It better not be assault or stealing some old lady's social security money, because I won't stand for that." He gets close to the man's face and stares up at him, fists clenched.

The man looks away. "I ain't proud. But I…I used to break into stores. Couldn't find a job, so I guess, that became it."

Black Cloud steps forward. "Broke into stores, huh?" He nods at Samuel in approval.

"That's right."

Samuel's words deride him. "Well, you must not have been very good at it if you got caught. Why should we trust you?"

The man's voice tenses, he shoots Samuel a stern look, "I got caught because my driver fell asleep."

"How many stores?" Black Cloud asks, intrigued.

"Thirty-two." The man's eyes lower again.

"Thirty-two? Goddamn!" Black Cloud exclaims.

"The biggest was a bank in Reno."

"We got us here a regular Jesse James," Bull Nose Pete chimes in.

"That's not me anymore, sir…I'm redeemed." He nods to his boy who nods back.

"Mm hmm, I've heard that before," Crystal says under her breath.

Black Cloud continues, "Now we don't want you to be that no more. You see, we just need some technical help, if you will."

"I'm on parole." He looks around at their faces, then at the eagerness of his boy. "I can't do anything with you; they'll take him away."

"No, no, no, we don't want that."

The man looks at his boy then at everyone else. "But I sure can tell you how."

Black Cloud nods his head, rubs his cheeks then forehead, and says, "Listen, we need to learn how to attack clandestine-like and enter a float in a parade. Do you know what that means?"

"Sure do, means a secret. The only way to do it…"

Black Cloud extends his hand before he can say anymore, impressed by his willingness, and says, "Well I'll be. What's your name?"

They shake. "Thomas Calhoun Senior, sir."

"My name's Cloud, Black Cloud. And he's Junior?" He nods to the boy.

"Everyone calls me TJ," the teenager offers with a slight smile. "Easier than having two Toms around."

"Even Tim can remember that," Black Cloud says, and they all laugh.

"So, we don't want to rob, exactly. More like steal a float beforehand and somehow put it in."

"Well, it'd just be the reverse then. Since you are all new to this," he nods, "how 'bout we start with an explanation of some basic teamwork operations."

Black Cloud nods and steps off.

Crystal and the men sit. Tom Sr. grabs a stick and starts drawing out general plans and strategy in the dirt.

He traces a parade route and a circle around Macy's. "NYC is a different animal. You show up there without practice, and they'll eat you alive. Listen, you're about to walk into one of the most secure public events in America. It's not just about stealing a float. You need to be ready for crowd control, security cameras, timing, distractions. You can't practice that sitting around talking."

Black Cloud folds his arms, jaw tight. "We're going there to make a statement, not to rob people."

Tom Sr. nods. "Exactly. But in order to make that statement, you need to know how to move through a crowd, how to stay calm when things go sideways, and right now, you don't. You think you're going to steal a float, enter it into the parade, and get away with it? You need training."

Samuel raises a hand. "What kind of training?"

Tom Sr. locks eyes with him. "We're going to learn how to

move like them. Practice in controlled settings. Test our communication, our timing, our distractions. Better to fail here than fail in New York."

Crystal crosses her arms. "So, we're gonna rob our own people to practice robbing the white man?"

Tom Sr. shakes his head. "We're not robbing. We're training. You want to survive this? You need to get good at it."

"So, how?" Bull Nose Pete asks.

"We hit small places where we can test our tactics without getting caught. Places where we can fail and learn without losing our lives. You think you're going to walk into Manhattan and pull this off without real-world practice?"

Tall Tim frowns. "And if we get caught?"

"Then you learn from it," Tom Sr. says. "Better to get caught here than die out there. If you're serious about this, that is."

There's a murmur throughout the group…

Black Cloud stares at the ground, jaw clenched. "So, we're just playing at being robbers now?"

Tom Sr. meets his gaze. "No. We're training to stay alive. And without the cops, hopefully."

Crystal studies the man's movements, focusing on the patterns he's sketching in the dirt. "Ex-con, huh? Great. Just who we need to guide us."

He stares at her without response, studies the hard contours of her body and taut mouth, her scar and judging eyes. He accepts this judgment and does not return one.

"I ain't like that no more, ma'am. Ain't you ever made a mistake that cost you dearly?" He nods to TJ. "Judge not lest ye be judged."

Something in his gentle response contradicts the hardness she expected from an ex-con.

She glares at his challenge, yet there's none of the violence or anger in his eyes that she's known. Looking away, the answer to that question is never far from the surface.

With eyes lingering across the yard, she mouths the word at him, "Sorry" and blows hair from out of her face.

He nods with the slightest hint of a smile, their eyes locking briefly until she looks away.

"Now if I may continue. In general, you'll need a point man, a look out. You need eyes from above like a bird's-eye view scoping it all out in case something goes wrong. This way you can pull back without committing. Someone uninvolved."

"That could be you, Dad."

He shrugs, the stick pausing in his hands as he considers it. Crystal studies him. He continues marking the earth with practiced strokes, explaining each detail with the patience of a man who knows his craft well and learned his lessons the hard way.

"Driver here, and one or two guys with weapons, not to use but to control if anything or anyone gets out of line. Communication always depends on how many and how big a job it is. Scope the locations and understand the weak and vulnerable parts, time frames, when people come and go, when they're slow or employees take breaks. Know all this or you won't make it back out."

He steps closer drawing a few x's in the soil, accidentally brushing Crystal's knee as he leans forward. "Always know your exits."

Samuel chides him, and jokes, "And give your driver lots of coffee…"

"You've got that right, lots of coffee." He looks up. "It's an operation like anything else, and I was a good thief."

"So, it's strategic," Black Cloud says.

"It must be. Like moving parts in a clock. There's always an opening, an opportunity for it to chime. But that means there's also a time limit to that opening. If not, the clock stops. Everything stops. And let me tell you, you don't want that clock to stop. Because if it does, that means you're caught. You folks are going to New York City to stir up trouble and get an unauthorized float in the Thanksgiving Day Parade, right?"

"Among other things," Black Cloud says ambiguously.

"Look, the less I know the better." Tom Sr.'s voice is tight like country fiddle wire. "Well, you *cain't* start there. That's like saying I never played baseball before and I'm ready for the big leagues. We've got-ta start small."

It was decided that only the old men would participate. They didn't want the kid directly involved with this kind of task and risk him potentially throwing away his future. And better to have Tom Sr. and Crystal in the background training and laying the plans while remaining in the shadows.

Black Cloud decides, "Tom Sr. would go to prison and most likely never see TJ again. He will stay on the sidelines with advice and Junior will only be used as a sharpshooter out of plain sight—and only for distractionary purposes."

Tom Sr. speaks again, catching Crystal's eye as he delivers the harsh truth. "We will have to train in real time, or you will get killed in New York City. Their police force is the size of an invading army, forty thousand-plus."

All the men gulp.

"They still might get killed anyway." Crystal meets Samuel's gaze, something unspoken passing between them.

"Maybe, but we'll be standing tall and making a difference if we do." Black Cloud adds defiantly.

Tom Sr. asks, "Any friendly places around here with low risk?"

"We don't want to rob anyone…" Tall Tim protests.

Samuel asserts. "Well, ain't choo never been robbed before? Cheated?"

"You can give it back." Tom Sr. says softly, his eyes finding Crystal's again.

"I s'ppose."

"One way or another, you need practice. Taking or giving. Let's first work on taking. Then we'll figure out a strategy on giving or putting something in. I ain't never done that one before."

That evening, Black Cloud sits alone at the edge of the reservation, where the asphalt ends and the rust-colored dirt begins. The wind is dry and cold, whipping his black hair as he stares at the horizon.

Somewhere out there, past the brown hills and brittle trees, is the rest of America—busy, distracted, and mostly indifferent to his people's pain.

But not for long.

EIGHT

The Raiding Begins

Outback the next morning with an overcast sky, Tom Sr. and Black Cloud finalize their strategy for the first raid. Black Cloud pauses and looks up at him when they're packing to leave after reviewing timeframes and positions.

"It just dawned on me, Tom. You have the most to lose here. Nothing is worth losing TJ for. So why are you doing this? Why are you taking such risks, even if you're behind the scenes?"

"Why?" He pauses looking off to the hills. "A few reasons, I guess. When my sister was thirteen, she was raped, and the authorities didn't do anything about it. Everything was taken from her. Everyone knew it was this white man in town and did nuthin'… Then when I was in prison filled with rage, I saw more abuse by guards and, well, around this time I found Jesus Christ. The 'righteousness protects the innocent, and wickedness is the downfall of sinners.' Then my wife ran off. TJ's mom. At that point, I decided I would always do my best to protect the innocent and when I heard about this here, I felt like it was a calling to do just that."

"And what about TJ?"

"Well, I don't intend for us to get caught. You see," he smirks slyly, "just serve God's will. My boy TJ is a righteous innocent." He pauses. "That is what's in my heart. I have known wickedness and we must live with honor. If not, why live at all? And we ain't getting caught. Not ever again. I was called here to help. Like you. TJ wanted this too."

The first place they chose to get real-world practice on the reservation was a dilapidated plywood shack near Wounded Knee Memorial that sells blankets, necklaces, and jewelry. The wooden structure leans slightly, weathered by decades of prairie winds.

Tom Sr. had called it **"Phase One"**: test the team's composure under pressure, create a small public disruption, and retreat without causing harm. Just enough to simulate the chaos of the real thing. The point wasn't theft. It was presence.

They weren't robbing it, not really. It was a training exercise. But the stakes—pride, unity, resolve—were real.

They found somewhere safe, like being on stage for the first time or giving a speech they were practicing.

As Black Cloud and the men approach in their Ford pickup truck, they hear bickering over their walkie-talkies while pulling into the dirt parking lot. Crystal and the two Toms follow in their car from a hundred yards out.

Crystal argues, "No, I don't think it should be like that. 'Go' should be the pointer finger and 'stop' should be a closed fist."

Tom Sr. responds, "Look, 'go' is always an open hand and 'stop' is always a closed fist. Can we agree on that? Jeez."

Black Cloud clicks the button on the left side of the gray walkie-talkie. "Um, guys, guys, we can hear you. Let's just keep it simple. Open hand means 'go,' and closed hand means 'stop.' Okay?"

"That is correct, Cloud," Tom Sr. says.

"I don't think so," Crystal says.

"Let's just keep it simple."

Crystal says, "Fine. God. Why are all men assholes and never listen to me?"

"We're not *all* assholes."

"Sorry TJ, not you," she says.

"It's okay, Crystal." TJ says. "If you just get to know us, you might think differently."

"Why are *you* being so difficult?" Tom Sr. asks. "We're all on the same side here. Just give us a chance, okay?"

"We'll see."

The four men pull into the dirt lot. Dust rises up around the truck as if a great storm is brewing as they come to a stop.

Each wears a mask of a great leader: Samuel sits proudly behind the stern visage of Red Cloud, whose resistance against broken treaties mirrors his own stubborn defiance. Black Cloud chose Sitting Bull's dignified features, remembering how his father used to say the great chief died not fighting with weapons, but with wisdom. Tall Tim wears the famed Crazy Horse: the uncompromising and spirited war chief who played a pivotal role in the Battle of Little Bighorn, leading the Sioux resistance against the U.S. government. Bull Nose Pete sports a floppy-eared Snoopy mask pulled from the depths of his closet. On the ride over he said, "I swear, my grandson left it last Halloween." But they saw how carefully he'd dusted it off, and cared for it, how gently he'd positioned it over his face.

Samuel adjusts his Red Cloud mask, the rubber strap a little frayed, and says, “You look ridiculous.”

“Snoopy never looks ridiculous. You should try laughing a little more. What’s ridiculous is that sour disposition of yours.”

They enter single file, spreading out into the small shack like they’d been taught, taking up points at the four corners as if browsing. The wooden floor creaks beneath their feet as they finger stacks of shirts and trinkets with exaggerated interest. Samuel studies a dream catcher as if he hadn’t seen a thousand before.

Tall Tim pretends to be—or may actually be—fascinated by a rack of postcards. His loose-fitting mask bobs as he nods at each image. “Ooh this one is beautiful.” He smiles unseen, holding up a picture of the chiseled Badlands at sunset.

The proprietor, Sally, short and heavyset, carries herself enthusiastically but with the weary dignity of someone eking out a living. She’s helping a white couple fresh from the crumbling memorial up the hill; the man’s ponytail swaying as he examines a colorful blanket.

Black Cloud and Tall Tim draw their plastic yellow guns—the ones that say “Bang!” on the side—keeping them low like they’d practiced in Cloud’s backyard. They wait for Sally to return to the plywood counter, but she’s still explaining the blanket’s pattern to the couple. The two men exchange shrugs, then approach anyway.

“Stick them up,” Tall Tim whispers leaning over to the owner, while the white couple looks at something else along the wall with their backs turned.

“Excuse me?” She raises an eyebrow and looks at the silly yellow guns.

Black Cloud admonishes him. “It’s stick *‘em* up, not *them*.”

“Oh,” Tall Tim responds.

"Cloud? Tim? What the hell you two doing?" Sally peers in around the masks, leaning closer.

"Hi Sally," Black Cloud says, Sitting Bull's stern expression at odds with his sheepish tone. "We're holding you up."

"Yes, you're holding me up from helping these fine customers." She gestures to the couple still examining turquoise jewelry along the wall.

She looks at the yellow translucent guns that say *Nerf* on them and shakes her head. Mockingly she raises her voice.

"Are you going to rob blankets that local families have made—the same families that struggle to put food on their table? Or the seven dollars I have in my pocket?" She pulls it out to show them and moves behind the small counter. "You would rob your own people?"

"No, of course not." Black Cloud and Tall Tim look at each other through their masks, great chiefs reduced to scolded schoolboys. They both shake their heads. "We're just practicing for something," Black Cloud says.

"Training," Tall Tim says, and Black Cloud elbows him.

"Sorry, Sally."

She clears her voice. "You mean, Talks with Trees," she says raising an eyebrow and nodding as the white couple look at jewelry on the counter next to Tall Tim, who sheepishly lowers his gun and steps aside for them to look.

Sally pretends to pull a shot gun out from under the counter and shoots them dead while making sound effects to match.

"Pow. Pow. Pow. Pow. You're all dead. Now will you idiots get out of here before I call your sister? You're like children. Scaring these lovely customers of mine."

Black Cloud turned and raised a hand in apology. "We're sorry. Truly."

Sally nodded. "Just…whatever it is you're doing, do it for the right reasons."

The white couple finally registers the masks and guns.

"Oh my," the woman says, while her husband's phone appears like magic, recording the incident while his wife's hands fly up in surrender. She says, "Here, take our money," and reaches for her purse. "Are you this poor that you would rob someone with a plastic gun?"

"No, ma'am," Black Cloud answers like a caught child.

"You're sick. It's not your fault. You don't have to hurt anyone. We're here to help. Here's twenty dollars." She takes out a bill and extends her hand like she's feeding a stray. "We understand what it's like to struggle."

"Uh, thanks," Tall Tim smiles and reaches out to take it.

Black Cloud slaps his hand away. "This was just a prank. Please cut," Black Cloud does like a knife cutting across his neck so the husband will stop filming.

"Are you threatening us?" The woman cries out. "Oh my God. Donald did you get that?"

Bull Nose Pete steps quickly over, slapping Tall Tim and Black Cloud on the back saying, "Sorry, we're just practicing for a show."

Samuel stands near the exit shaking his head with arms crossed. Red Cloud's disapproval radiates through his plastic visage.

The woman clutches the money back to her chest and asks her husband, who's panting, "Did they just threaten us?"

"They're just kidding, ma'am," says Sally, who shoos the men out. "It ain't even Halloween!" she shouts after them as they leave the shack and walk out into the dirt parking lot. The great chiefs hanging their heads.

From outside, Black Cloud overhears the woman excitedly say,

"Honey, that felt so real. My heart is racing. They tried to steal from Talks with Trees. Well, we are going to buy everything she has to make up for it. You were so brave."

He turns to the truck, the weight of Sallly's words settling into his chest like stomach acid. This wasn't just a lark. If they were going to move forward, every move had to mean something.

It wasn't victory. But it was data. And Black Cloud knew even in humiliation—maybe especially in humiliation—you learn where your weaknesses hide.

One robbery down. Two more to go, he thinks driving out of the parking lot.

Inside the backup vehicle, "Well," Crystal mutters, "that couldn't have gone worse."

TJ laughs nervously. Tom Sr. doesn't. "This ain't playtime. If they're going to survive New York, they had better learn to make fewer mistakes. But that's why we practice."

NINE

7-Eleven - Rapid City, South Dakota

After additional training and honing their rough skills, they try again. The Wednesday evening air holds the bite of winter coming off the high plains at 3,200 feet above sea level as they gather for their second attempt at robbery. It's 9 p.m., and Rapid City's Main Street pulses with the tired rhythm of a small city winding down: headlights sweep past storefronts, neon signs hum their lonely songs, second-shift workers drag themselves toward home.

This isn't Sally's shop anymore. This is **Phase Two**: a real location, unfamiliar ground, with real stakes. As Tom Sr. had drilled into them, training meant nothing if it didn't hold under pressure.

Last week's debacle at Sally's shop had been embarrassing enough on their home turf, but here in Rapid City, where their people had learned hard reminders about the white man's double-tongued promises, the stakes are different.

The masks wouldn't protect them here. Not from police. Not from judgment. This is the first real test of resolve. Tonight brings new stakes. This is the real world.

Tom Sr.'s words echoed: "Train where it matters. Where fear lives."

This is the phase that taught control: of nerves, of breath, of timing. If they fail here, they'll fail when more it at stake.

Driving over, hoping to improve upon last week's failure, Black Cloud watches the oncoming cars, remembering how his parents' generation relocated here in the 1950s. The Indian Relocation Act encouraged many to move off the reservation in an attempt to terminate reservation life and force them into cities, effectively weakening community and tribal bonds. Often referred to as the Indian Termination Policy—which promised jobs and opportunities, but isolated and assimilated them into urban populations. His father called it assimilation. His mother called it capitulation. But all of them carried the same truth—displacement as policy.

Instead, they found "No Indians Allowed" signs in shop windows and their children shipped off to boarding schools which meant the continued erasure of their culture and their native tongues. Now these same streets welcome everyone's money, forgetting the hard history beneath the cracked pavement.

Crystal and the Toms had listened to last week's comedy of errors from the crackling walkie-talkie in Black Cloud's pocket. After their earlier argument, they couldn't help but laugh.

Afterwards, Tom looked over at her and said, "I know some men take what ain't theirs. But we ain't like that." He motioned to TJ in the backseat, who shook his head.

Crystal and Tom glanced briefly at each other, their eyes lingering like distant stars before she quickly looked away, afraid to stay in the moment any longer. She stared at the safe dashboard instead.

"Maybe," Crystal replied, finding the courage to look over at him again, though briefly.

"I swear, I'm not like that anymore," Tom's calloused fingers traced patterns on the car's steering wheel. "I spent five years behind bars learning there's a difference between taking what ain't yours and fighting for what is." He'd motioned to TJ, who sat studying topographical maps of New York City.

"Prison teaches you real quick what matters, and it ain't other people's money." The boy's head had snapped up at his father's words in nodding, fierce agreement, too familiar with the cost of his father's past choices and their time broken apart by them.

"Maybe," Crystal repeated, finding the courage to look over at him for longer, finding a hint of safety there. For a moment, her guard dropped just enough to let Tom Sr. see past the scar, and the careful distance she's kept others. Something in the way he spoke about redemption made her wonder if people really could change. Remembering the part of herself she's kept locked away in a safe place that no one has seen for a long time, including her. She'd fought so long to survive, she'd forgotten it was there at all.

But tonight brings new stakes. This is the real world. It's off the reservation, where tribal police can't look the other way, where every movement carries weight. This isn't Sally's shop with its familiar creaks and hometown mercy; this is Rapid City after dark, where Native faces draw second looks, where squad cars slow down when they spot brown skin. Here they'll learn if their hearts can steady when real fear hits, if their hands can stay firm when every instinct screams for them to run. It's one thing to play warrior on home ground, in your backyard; it's another to step into white man's territory where toy guns can be misconstrued as real danger and dealt with swiftly.

They must be able to act with racing hearts and deal with real fear. *Control the fear,* as Tom had taught them. They settle in to watch for Black Cloud and the men to arrive.

Crystal watches without blinking. Tom Sr. without judgment. TJ without speaking. This was their battlefield now—neon and linoleum, not buffalo hides and blood. The terrain had changed. The war hadn't.

Crystal and the Toms park their borrowed Pontiac Fiero across the street at the 76 Gas Station. The car—a temporary loan from Tom's sister until his plumbing business can put enough cash in his pocket—protests each turn with squealing belts and a rattling dashboard.

They settle in to watch for Black Cloud and the men to arrive, the car's worn engine ticking in the night air as it cools. There's no bickering this time, no chatter at all. Even the static from their walkie-talkie feels too loud in this foreign territory, as if the smallest crackle might draw unwanted attention and give them away. All three focus on the 7-Eleven and wait for Black Cloud's truck.

TJ's fingers drum silently against the door's armrest with his bow next to him, while his father's eyes scan the street with the practiced wariness of a man who once made his living studying exits, until the last one closed off like a sealed prison gate. Crystal sits perfectly still, her fighter's instincts cataloging every car that passes, every shadow that shifts, every twitch of her skin.

All are focused on the 7-Eleven's harsh fluorescent glow cutting through the darkness like a spotlight, watching and waiting for Black Cloud's truck. Minutes later it crawls into view, moving slowly and deliberate as if trying not to draw attention to itself. The great chiefs' masks catch the neon light as Black Cloud and his crew park near the storefront, their engine settling into nervous silence.

Through the plate-glass window, the men see the Slurpee machine's endless turning. The green, white, and red sign throws colored shadows into the dark truck cab. Only one customer remains inside: a young white man in a cowboy hat browsing the cigarette selection behind the counter.

"This is real now, guys," Black Cloud says to the men.

"This is our city. We can raid it, right?" Black Cloud declares, wanting to sound more confident than he feels. All the men gulp, including him.

They wait for the young man to leave, taking his time selecting Marlboro Reds.

"We could go to jail," Bull Nose Pete worries under his breath, fogging the window he looks out upon. Snoopy's face looks scared in the shadows. It's the first time anyone says it out loud. The risk. The real-world cost. The great chiefs' masks catch the neon light looking more like ghosts than warriors now—shadows of a history that refuses to be forgotten.

Black Cloud encourages, "Yes, but if we can do this, we'll be unstoppable."

They watch as the cowboy pays for his cigarettes and hops into his Ford Mustang one spot over, leaving them alone. Their moment of truth hangs heavy upon them.

After a final moment of pause, they step out of the truck and into the store. They use the same tactics and spread out to watch the corners, boots squeaking against the freshly mopped linoleum. Tall Tim pretends to browse magazines. His Crazy Horse mask nods at articles in *Better Homes & Gardens*. Snoopy studies the ingredients of Funyuns while standing in the chip aisle.

On edge, Black Cloud and Samuel walk up to the counter, the plastic guns feeling heavy in their hands. Control. Communication.

Don't escalate.

"Stick 'em up," they say in unison, more seriously than intended, as they raise the yellow water guns at the pimply-faced clerk. The moment is so absurd they realize how hollow the threat sounds. But it's not about threat—it's about nerves, roles, discipline.

The young man, barely in his twenties, doesn't look up from his *Archie* comic book.

Standing a couple feet from the counter, Black Cloud leans in, his voice dropping to a whisper. "We're just practicing for a play. So please don't hit a button triggering the cops."

Samuel adds, "We promise to return the merchandise. We're just here to steal a few bags of chips and this." He grabs a Slim Jim from the display and throws it onto the counter. Black Cloud looks at him through Sitting Bull's disapproving features. Samuel shrugs, rubbing his stomach. Both men stand with water guns extended.

Tom Sr.'s rule: Always know your line. Always know your exit.

The kid still doesn't look up from his comic, as if being robbed by Native Americans in historical masks wielding plastic water guns is just another Wednesday night in Rapid City.

"Um, young man," Black Cloud looks at Red Cloud for support. His plastic water gun lowering. "We are here to rob you. Hold you up. This is a heist, if you will. Really just a play we're practicing for, so please don't shoot us or call the cops."

"Okay," the kid squeaks indifferently, flipping another page. He laughs, pointing at the comic. "Blockhead."

"Well, don't you care?" Black Cloud can't let it go, feeling their attempted heist sliding into farce once again.

The kid finally looks up, does a double take at the assembly of great chiefs and one cartoon beagle gathered in his store. After a moment's consideration, he simply shrugs and returns to his usual bored tone. "Mister, this place has been robbed so many times I don't sweat it no more. Just don't hurt me and we're good."

He lowers his comic. "Everyone steals from everyone: the insurance companies steal with their high premiums, robbers steal our stuff, insurance pays us back, then we pay the insurance companies again with even higher premiums." He shrugs, the wisdom of a hundred-night shifts in his voice. "Circle of life."

Satisfied with his convenience store philosophy, he returns to laughing at his comic book. In this kid's deadpan, Black Cloud hears something truer than fear—indifference. And in that, a lesson: the world isn't always watching. Which is why they must make it.

Black Cloud nods, squinting his eyes after receiving this strange, unexpected lesson in late-night capitalism. "I see." He raises the plastic water gun and squirts the kid, the stream catching both his face and his precious comic book.

"Aw, come on. Now that's never happened!" The kid shouts wiping his face with a napkin as the men leave with their stolen goods.

Samuel clutches his Slim Jim like a trophy as they file out. The masks of great leaders reflect in the store windows, somehow feeling more ridiculous and more appropriate than before.

In the truck the silence feels different this time. Not shame. Not exactly pride. More like a glimpse of something working. Black Cloud says with a grin, "Now we're getting it!"

He says placing the stolen goods on the passenger floor while Samuel tears into the beef jerky.

All the men high five except for Samuel. "That kid didn't care, Cloud." He says between bites. "What happens when we go into a store that does?"

Black Cloud ponders this as well. The masks hadn't protected them. But their plan—flawed, fragile, absurd—held together. Barely.

"Let's just enjoy our victory for now."

Because for the first time, it felt real.

Black Cloud gives a thumbs up to Crystal and the Toms across the street as they pull out of the parking lot. They drive down the road heading home, leaving the city's lights behind for the darker safety of reservation territory.

TEN

Jewelry Store - Sioux City, South Dakota

Tom Sr. had warned them: "You have to feel real danger before you'll know what to do when the cops come." During training, Tom Sr. said they needed to hit a high-risk shop. Something to steel their nerves. If they were serious about New York, they'd need to walk into a live fire zone—one where mercy wasn't expected.

If not, they would most likely fold under the pressure of dealing with cops in NYC. They debated beforehand and agreed.

This would be their final test **Phase Three**: surveillance, response time, nerves under fire. Tom Sr. had stressed it again and again—if they couldn't operate in real-world tension, they'd fall apart on Sixth Avenue.

A few weeks later, riding the wave of their convenience store success, they set their sights on a bigger target: a jewelry store in Sioux City. The city itself sits on what was once ancestral hunting grounds of the Yankton Sioux tribe. For generations, Chief War Eagle and his people had roamed these bluffs overlooking the Missouri River, tracking the seasonal migrations of bison, elk, and deer. But those days are long gone; the bluffs now bear the names of white settlers. Their history erased.

Black Cloud chose this particular jewelry store for a reason. Word on the rez was the owner overcharged Native customers—charged twice as much for less and treated them like second-class citizens. They had been keeping an eye on it, noting the comings and goings of the white proprietor and the type of customers that frequented the establishment. It was clear this was a business that catered primarily to the city's wealthy white residents, a stark contrast to the poverty and disenfranchisement faced by the local Native community.

This only fueled Black Cloud's sense of right and wrong as they plotted their next move. It was time to take back what was rightfully theirs: justice.

There was no delusion about stealing riches. They weren't robbing for money. They were robbing for muscle memory. For nerve. For the ability to walk into the belly of American and not flinch. But none of them anticipated the belly biting back.

With their masks in place, just before closing time, the group strides into the store, ready to put their plan into action.

"How can I help you?" the proprietor asks. Tufts of white hair sprout from his ears, bushy eyebrows matching the color of his suspicious stare. His hands remain hidden beneath the glass counter as he watches them spread out. Normal customers don't spread out or wear masks for that matter.

Black Cloud insisted on the water guns—said it made them harmless, just enough to simulate fear without causing real damage and hopefully disarm an unsuspecting owner.

Black Cloud strides in with his newly found confidence. "This here is a stick up," he declares, raising his yellow squirt gun.

At those words, the proprietor's demeanor shifts dramatically. He pulls his hands from under the counter holding a double barrel shotgun, the weapon clicking as he cocks it.

"Oh, is it now?" He levels the gun at Black Cloud's head less than a foot away.

Black Cloud freezes, the yellow squirt gun suddenly feeling like a foolish toy in his hands. He quickly realizes this is not a game or a practice session for others, but daily life and the stakes were high.

The room freezes. Black Cloud feels the sting of sweat under his mask, the toy gun a joke in his trembling hands. The air dries up. He swallows hard, all traces of bravado evaporating in the face of this very real threat before him.

Bull Nose Pete shouts from the corner stepping closer, hands raised in a placating manner. "Now take it easy, we're just practicing for a play." He calls out, his voice betraying a tremor of fear.

The proprietor's grip on the shotgun doesn't waver as he glares at the group. "It sure doesn't look like a play to me."

From behind a swinging door, a young woman suddenly appears, her face etched with alarm. "Daddy! No! Don't do nothing crazy. Remember what happened last year when you shot those men?"

"What men?" Tall Tim panics raising his hands in surrender, and they all start shouting, trying to get the old man to lower his gun.

"Too many of your kind robbing me of late. I ain't that handy with this gun but handy enough to kill one, two, or three of you." He sweeps the double barrel across the group, their raised hands casting shadows on the glass cases of glittering diamonds. "I suggest you walk right back out of my store. Unless you want your guts spread out on them diamond stud earrings behind you."

"Now take it easy. We're just having a little fun, practicing for a play," Black Cloud urges, his voice steady despite the shotgun's dark barrels staring him down.

Their hands stay up as they back towards the door. Bull Nose Pete bumps into a wall display, catching it before it falls over.

Samuel says, "We ain't even got no real guns."

"That's good. Easier for me to *keel*. Now get the hell out of my store."

"Yes sir. Yes sir." They run out, and the bells of the door chime as it closes behind them.

The great chiefs retreat and their revolution folds under the weight of one trembling trigger finger. There are no dress rehearsals in the real world. Only consequences.

They quickly pile into Black Cloud's pickup truck and tear out of the parking lot, tires squealing against pavement as they head for their rendezvous point two miles away.

Breathing becomes shallow. Their hands shake against knees and armrests, the adrenaline crash hitting them all at once.

Horror settles in during the drive, the masks of great chiefs now feeling like the hollow plastic they are against their sweating faces. Every red light makes them jump; every passing car becomes a potential threat as they look for the flashing lights of police cars.

In the night shadows, no one notices that Tall Tim has peed his pants, the sharp smell of fear masked by the truck's heater and their own thundering heartbeats.

They mill around the parking lot of a Hy-Vee Grocery store, their masks left on the truck seats to get away from the evidence of their foolishness. Samuel breaks the heavy silence. "Does robbing a store equate to entering a stolen float in the parade? I mean, what the hell are we doing here?"

Bull Nose Pete's voice trembles. Even though it's a cool night, his clammy hands are clasped together. "I ain't no thief and we bungle it every time. Plus, hunting birds is one thing. A standoff with unpredictable white people is something else." His nose doesn't flare but sucks in as he hyperventilates. "This ain't practice anymore; this is how people end up dead."

Samuel says, "If we bring guns to New York City, we are gonna get killed. Cloud, we gotta rethink this. Your plan ain't gonna work."

The fresh night air is not enough to stop him from shaking. The word *killed* hangs between them, real now in a way it hadn't been before.

"It's stupid." Tall Tim looks down at his darkened pants and walks off into the shadows of a tree so no one can see.

Samuel walks over to Black Cloud who had wandered off to sit on a parking lot curb, the weight of responsibility visible in his hunched shoulders.

He places his hand on his friend's shoulder and says, "We could be dead." The words are simple but carry everything—their families, their dreams, the cost of failure.

Crystal and the two Toms run over from the Pontiac, their faces tight with tension. They'd heard it all over the radio.

"Are you guys, okay? That was so scary." Crystal's voice is filled with compassion, understanding what it's like to face down violence.

Black Cloud is shaking and understands for the first time that their real mission might require more tact than masks and toy guns can provide.

"Well, what did we expect?" Bull Nose Pete demands, his words carrying a heavy truth.

The boy had his sites on the target, but arrows don't fly through plate-glass windows and bullets move a lot faster. "You'd be dead already, Mr. Cloud," TJ says quietly, his voice carrying the weight of an adult's understanding.

Black Cloud stands up and surveys his crew: from Samuel now on the curb to Tall Tim hiding in the shadows, each face showing the same dawning realization.

"We ain't no raiders. I'm sorry. This was a bad idea. But how do we practice in live situations without risking our lives or getting shot? It's stupid. Impossible." He's angry at himself for putting everyone at risk.

"Maybe we don't," Bull Nose Pete says, voicing what they're all thinking.

Tall Tim says, "Well, shoot, we ain't trying to steal stuff. Well maybe a float. But I thought we was going to New York City to be in a parade."

Black Cloud lowers his head, rubs his chin, and begins pacing back and forth in the parking lot.

Near a green dumpster that reeks of spoiled produce, he stops and says, "No. No. No. You're right. We're not going there to rob things or even to steal a float." He wags his finger in the air while continuing to pace, energy building with each step. "Hmm," he says pacing some more.

The others watch him, recognizing the look that comes over his face before a big idea—the same look he had when he first mentioned the parade.

He continues as if speaking to himself, some new realization occurring. "Small thinking gets you killed. But big thinking…big thinking might just win the day." Energized by some new idea, he starts walking briskly toward the truck, then stops and turns. "We're not going there to steal things. No. We're going there to steal the whole darn show."

Samuel bolts off the curb. "What? That's how you get caught. Killed. I don't know much about anything, but I do know that." They all look at each other.

"Oh yes," is all Black Cloud says, with newfound purpose.

Bull Nose Pete chimes in, to no one in particular, "Whiteman took your job. Now he's gonna take our land and throw us in jail."

Black Cloud walks past Tom, their eyes meeting with shared understanding. He speaks over his shoulder, his voice carrying renewed confidence. "Clandestine, right?"

Tom Sr. nods, looking over at Crystal, then mutters, "Clandestine." The word hangs in the night air like a prayer or a prophecy. "Righteousness."

Later that night, long after the others had gone home, Black Cloud sits at his kitchen table with a beer gone warm in his hand. He whispers aloud, "I thought I could take something back. Not the jewelry. Not the money. Just…dignity. Presence. Our place in that world. But maybe you don't take that by force. Maybe you show up and dare the world to look you in the face."

ELEVEN

WHITEMAN

A few days later, they stand outside the recreation center in the fading afternoon light, Samuel checks his watch.

"I gotta check on the horses," he says, knowing they haven't been fed since morning. The old bay gets a little ornery if her dinner runs late.

Crystal asks if she can join him. She always loved being around horses as a girl and dreamed of becoming a bronc rider.

As they're leaving, three black sedans drive up at a fast clip, kicking up dust against the afternoon sun.

"Shit feathers, it's Whiteman," Bull Nose Pete says quietly but loud enough for everyone to hear, the name carrying weight, history, and warning.

The sedans bounce to a stop on the uneven ground and federal agents emerge from their cars like suited dark knights. Only one steps forward, removing his sunglasses with practiced authority. Good looking, in his fifties though youthful, fit with beady eyes that catalog everything they see. He carries himself like a man used to having his orders followed, like someone who's spent years making

Native people feel small on their own land.

"Ahh, if it isn't the Bureau of White People," Black Cloud says, the words carrying an old bitterness.

"Hello Black Cloud. How have you been? Still kicking around here, huh?" The man studies the dirt-poor conditions with disdain. "You could have done so much more for yourself." He spits through his teeth hitting a small stone, then kicks it. His frown deepens as he looks around at the decaying town, then back at Black Cloud. "Know anything about these raids we're hearing about?"

"Raids? What kind of raids?" Black Cloud shakes his head and shrugs, feeling sweat begin to form in his armpits.

Staring at him, Whiteman steps closer. "You always had that fire in you. Came from your mother dragging you to those AIM rallies as a kid. The files said she made you carry signs too big for your arms." He chuckles without warmth. "Leonard Peltier posters on the rez school lockers, if I remember right. And when you lost the job to me, you got even angrier and more defiant to this great nation of ours. If it's you or your friends," he looks around at the group, eyes lingering on each face like he's taking mental photographs, "I'll bust every one of you."

They all knew this went deeper than a job. This was the weight of history between these two men. And now, the government was watching.

Black Cloud's jaw flexes, but he says nothing.

Whiteman stares for another moment at Black Cloud who doesn't flinch then pulls out a lined notepad from his back pocket and flips through a few pages. "A clerk heard someone say, 'Not to worry, it's a training drill. We'll bring the stuff back.'" He flips to another page with deliberate slowness, licking his fingertips between each turn of the page.

"A jewelry store owner said about the same. One last raid, perhaps?" Whiteman peers around with his beady eyes and spits chewing tobacco, staining the red dusty soil. "All wearing masks, too. This ain't some American Indian Movement, Leonard Peltier shit, I hope."

"What raids?" Black Cloud asks again. His Adam's Apple bobs and a bead of sweat develops on his forehead under his thick black hair, ready to drip.

Whiteman refers back to his notes again, making a show of studying each page.

"A blanket stand outside Wounded Knee, some kooks on social media posted. A jewelry store in Sioux City, a 7-Eleven in Rapid City, yet strangely, all of the items were returned. Except for one beef jerky, paid for with exact change left in a box." His mouth twists into a small smile. "Forensics are taking fingerprint swabs now."

Black Cloud forces his face to stay neutral knowing that the swabs would fail, as the Great Spirit—through Samuel—told them to wear latex gloves.

"Why would someone steal something to return it? Sounds like kids to me. You know, some prank."

"What's the crime if it's returned?" Tall Tim ponders aloud.

Whiteman shoots him a look, then surveys Black Cloud's associates outside the rec center. His eyes stop on TJ, who's holding a bow in his hands. The boy quickly lowers it behind his back, but not before Whiteman's eyebrows rise slightly as he takes the information in. He doesn't know about the parade, but he does know Black Cloud comes from a line of "troublemakers," and Whiteman sees it as his job to suppress that legacy before it starts up again. He wanted to say, *When will you people stop already when you've been beaten time and time again?*

Black Cloud steps forward, drawing the attention back to himself. "How do you know they're from the rez? Probably white kids dressing up and pinning it on us."

Whiteman nods rubbing his chin, then shouts back to one of the cars. "Agent Malory, didn't we get a lead on a pickup truck?"

Agent Malory stands next to her car nodding. "Yes sir," she says stepping forward.

Black Cloud lets out a laugh hoping to sound genuine. "A pickup truck spotted around here? That's like saying someone saw leaves fall or blades of grass. They're everywhere, man." He swallows hard, knowing it had been his truck. Though only fifty degrees, sweat is about to drip down the side of his face and reveal him when three pickup trucks drive past. Two drivers honk and wave. Black Cloud waves back smiling. Luckily, his sister borrowed his truck today.

"So, no uprising, the American Resistance Movement, or Leonard Peltier and all of that, thinking he's Crazy Horse?"

"Oh no, of course not. We're beyond that. Just happy and snug as a bug on our rug." Black Cloud offers up his falsest smile, the one he's perfected over years dealing with government men who only hear what they want to hear.

Whiteman nods and retreats to his car, each step measured and deliberate. "You'll call me if you hear anything?"

Black Cloud nods, the fake smile still plastered on his face. "Oh, of course."

Whiteman stands at the car door, fixing Black Cloud with one last stare, as if trying to peel back any layers of deceit. Finally, he gives a short nod, as they turn the vehicles around.

Black Cloud waves as they drive off. His heart pounds against his ribs, and the back of his shirt is soaked. The group watches the three black cars turn around, government tires kicking up reservation dust. Only when they disappear over the horizon does Black

Cloud release the breath he's been holding.

He kicks at the dirt, sending a stone skittering across the red earth. "That son-of-a-bitch stole my job."

Bull Nose Pete and Tall Tim look at each other.

TWELVE

Planning - Late Spring

The planning session at the rec center runs late into the night. Time frames, personnel at locations, the when and where, with diagrams and maps spread across the card room table until Bull Nose Pete starts nodding off mid-sentence. One by one, they filter out into the night: Crystal and the Toms first, then Samuel muttering about his horses, finally Tall Tim with a promise to bring coffee tomorrow, heading home to his wife, Betty, who he surmises must miss him terribly.

The air hums with exhausted resolve, but something deeper too—a feeling they've crossed into new territory, where dreams risk becoming consequences.

Black Cloud stays behind, methodically reviewing their notes and final paperwork one last time. All of this is on handwritten pages. No internet, no computers, nothing traceable except for paper he intends to burn in a ceremony releasing it to the world. Each scrap of paper feels sacred, dangerous, inked with vision and treason in equal measure. Unbeknownst to him, Whiteman is surveying the building from his car out front, taking note of the crew filing out.

Once quiet, the beam of Whiteman's flashlight cuts through the darkness of the rec center, casting long shadows down empty hallways.

"I know these guys are behind it," he mutters to himself, looking into rooms, the words echoing off cinderblock walls. "I could see Black Cloud sweating."

Black Cloud leaves the card room, shutting off lights behind him, when movement catches his eye—a bobbing flashlight beam approaches through the dark hall. He recognizes that purposeful walk, even in the shadows.

He flicks on the hallway light, the fluorescents humming to life as he quickly folds up the paperwork and slips it into his back pocket.

"What are you doing here?" he tries to ask casually, hiding his sudden burst of anxiety and shortness of breath.

"What do you have there? I want to see it." Whiteman's beady eyes fix on the papers sliding into Cloud's pocket, thirty years of distrust packed into his stare.

"It's personal. I come here to think and write my thoughts down." The lie tastes bitter, but necessary. Black Cloud's fingers press against the papers that could give everything away.

"With all your pals? Don't make me do this the hard way."

"Piss off, Stanley," Cloud says and begins walking away. His heart pounds knowing the concealed, folded truth sits accessible in his back pocket.

"I know you're behind this."

Black Cloud turns, his own three decades of anger rising in his throat.

"Behind what? You don't know shit, Stan, like always. That test you cheated on? You don't think I knew? Everybody knew. I should have had that job."

"Well, you stole her from me. I would have taken better care of her. And you know it. She died because of you." He points his finger at Black Cloud's chest, "And you're going to pay for it."

Black Cloud shakes his head, his own grief turning to rage, clenching his fists.

"Fuck you, Stanley," he says and walks down the hallway.

"You get that look, Cloud," Whiteman shouts after him, "the same one you had when you walked away from everything. You get that look and people end up marching… or hurt."

Black Cloud walks out of the building, leaving Whiteman alone with his poisoned memories.

After this encounter, Whiteman is determined to catch him and starts watching the rec center nightly from down the block with a long-range, infrared zoom lens camera trained on the building like a sniper—dead set on catching his man.

Each night he sits in his black sedan, logging comings and goings, noting patterns. He watches Crystal arrive with the Toms, catalogs how long they stay, documents every scrap of paper they tuck away. The locals eye his car suspiciously as they walk past it into town, but he doesn't care anymore about maintaining cover. It's justice, he tells himself. But in truth it's something darker, vengeance baked into bureaucracy.

Three decades of obsession have taught him patience, leading up to this point. These same decades have taught him about the abuse of power and callousness. Night after night he waits intent on proving that this time, Black Cloud is the one breaking the rules. This time, he tells himself, justice will look different than a silly stolen exam or a silly woman's choice. This time, he'll have his revenge served with a side of federal charges.

THIRTEEN

A Revolution Begins

Weeks pass and whispers spread across the Indian Nation: stories carried on the evening winds from one reservation to the next. It starts with a Comanche elder at a gas station in Oklahoma.

"You hear what they're doing up in Pine Ridge?" he says to the attendant who shrugs. "Well, you're gonna."

A Blackfeet grandmother in Montana passes the tale over coffee.

"Those Sioux boys, they're waking something up." She does a jig in her seat, shimmying back and forth. "It's time we all wake up. Those whites used to divide us. Not no more. Now *we* can unite us. It takes just one spark to start a fire."

The Iroquois hear it in New York from a hiker. Cheyenne cowboys discuss it at a fence line in Wyoming. The Nez Perce whisper it across the Sawtooth Mountains in Idaho while hunting deer. Apache runners bring word from Arizona, while Seminole fishermen in Florida pass it between boats in the Everglades, alligators watching them with prehistoric eyes. The Kiowa speak of it in hushed tones at tribal council meetings.

"They say Black Cloud's leading it," a Navajo teenager tells his uncle outside a convenience store in New Mexico.

"Who?" the man asks with the door open.

The teen shrugs. "I don't know. But they say he's got big plans for the next Day of Mourning. *Black Cloud's Uprising* some are calling it."

"Hmm," the man looks away. "About time somebody did. Good enough for me. Let us send a scout," he says as they walk in.

Each tribe carries the story in their own tongue, but the message remains the same: something is stirring in the heartland, in their hearts, something that tastes like hope and unity.

Some call it a rebellion, others call it justice, but everyone agrees: Black Cloud's raids are just the beginning of a growing storm within the Native community, and there is strength in storms as they become unstoppable.

Many also think he's a fool and will get killed but send a scout anyway to find out more about this big plan.

Tribes of the southeast to southwest to northeast and northwest, reservations near and far hear about Black Cloud's raids and want in. Runners and scouts from across the country begin showing up at cards, and while they train and practice.

They came in ones and twos at first—runners and scouts from reservations near and far, appearing like shadows at the card room door.

Wednesday brings an Apache trucker who drove straight through from Arizona. By Thursday, a Cheyenne elder arrives on horseback, a traditional medicine bag hanging from his saddle as cars drive past him.

"We have heard that you are planning something," the Cheyenne elder says to Black Cloud, his weathered face serious beneath his hat. "Something that'll make them see."

"What exactly did you hear?" Black Cloud asks carefully.

The old man's eyes crinkle, "Enough for me to ride three days."

Black Cloud smiles at his response and pulls out a chair for him.

Each brings stories from their people: tales of broken treaties, hardships, poisoned water, sick relatives, and stolen lands. But they bring something else too: skills, contacts, and knowledge passed down through generations.

A Navajo Code Talker's grandson offers communication strategies. A Hopi woman who works security at casinos brings blueprints of crowd control.

The movement grows like prairie grass after rain, quiet yet implacable.

While sleeping, Black Cloud's unconscious mind buzzes with information and possibilities. Ancient wisdom mixes with modern tactics as the momentum builds and plans formulate.

He wakes in darkness to find his hands already reaching for paper, ancestral voices urgent in his ears. The kitchen table has become his war room: maps spread across its scarred surface, lists of personnel growing in his hurried handwriting. Sometimes he doesn't remember writing the plans, as if the spirits themselves guided his pen. Then once his mind is spent, he stumbles to his blue recliner and falls back asleep, exhausted. In the morning, they review, train, and prepare.

Each person adds their own expertise to the growing plan. Samuel mentions wooden diversions. Bull Nose Pete seconds that with mechanicals and diversions. Crystal marks potential escape routes and possible areas of hand-to-hand combat if things go sideways. Tom studies entry points with the careful eye of someone who once made his living finding weak spots.

"You really think we can pull this off?" Bull Nose Pete asks one morning, standing over his shoulder in the kitchen, watching Black Cloud add another page to their growing stack of plans.

"Have to," Black Cloud answers without looking up, his pen never stopping. "The ancestors aren't giving us a choice."

Later that afternoon, White Feather notices dark circles under his eyes. "You're wearing yourself thin."

"Can't help it," he says, rubbing his face standing outside of her trailer after visiting their mother together. "Every time I close my eyes, I see another piece of the puzzle."

"I don't like it. It's trouble."

Every night it happens—he bolts upright at 3 a.m. in a sweat that cools on his skin as he scribbles diagrams of tactics needed, parade routes and security patterns.

Around town, they've become something between celebrities and omens. The diner's morning regulars fall quiet when they enter, conversations shifting to whispers over coffee cups. Some people smile, offering subtle nods of support—an extra piece of pie appears with Black Cloud's lunch, "On the house" murmured by a waitress whose grandfather told her stories of Wounded Knee. Others turn away, fear of change and trouble written in their stiff shoulders—an excuse for the government to intervene, blame them, and take more rights away. Shaking their heads in judgment as they walk past.

Disapproving, his sister frowns and drops his plate when he eats with them, often not speaking to him at all during dinner. She thinks it's a mistake and dangerous and will set them back a hundred years. Her disapproval cuts the deepest.

"Your uncle can't stay for dessert," she says to the children while glaring at him, each syllable sharp with warning.

"No..." Little Wonder and Lilyanna sigh, too young to understand the weight settling over their family.

Black Cloud watches his sister's face, sees their mother's same stubborn worry in her frown. She thinks it's a mistake, that it's dangerous. He understands that she has more to lose than he does. Her children's future stretches out before them, and she's learned to navigate the world as it is, not as it should be. This could affect their self-determination as a people.

Though few know the facts of the actual plan, Black Cloud is surprised by all this—the sides taken and lines drawn across dinner tables and store counters, through families and friendships. But looking back through history, he realizes it's always been this way.

Ideas and actions cause opinions and reactions, sometimes violently, even among loved ones. Even the Great Wars saw brother fighting brother, and friend fighting friend. All for a cause they believed would change everything. All for a cause they thought was just.

"Excuse me," he says softly, rising from his sister's table. He kisses the children, their faces still bright with innocence, untouched by the weight of what's coming.

Walking past his mother's darkened trailer, he remembers her words from last Thanksgiving about doing something big. The ground is still hard from winter, zippers are raised, and most training occurs inside the card room. More sit-ups and burpees, though still only Samuel can muster more than a handful. Fewer cards are played as they've traded playing hands for fighting hands, even if most of them aren't ready to fight.

After Black Cloud talks it over with his gang, his response to each new person who shows up becomes the same: "The more the merrier." But the words carry more weight now as it spreads, heavy with responsibility.

He receives messages from tribes who want to honor their fallen chiefs and ancestors, each one a reminder that this has grown beyond the Sioux, beyond Pine Ridge, and beyond his own vision. The truth hits him one afternoon while sitting on a sun-warmed rock while taking a break from training, catching his breath in the winter air.

It has always been about all First Peoples from the very beginning.

The notes come daily now, often with donations that he sets aside. Many tribes simply write, "Thank you for doing this" or "We're with you, our red brother." Some arrive from lesser-known tribes, ones with only a handful of members left, their names nearly lost to history. Some tribes he's never even heard of reach out, their existence itself an act of resistance.

Each evening, he sits at his kitchen table, reading glasses perched on his nose, carefully opening these messages. Then he performs his own ceremony, burning each letter out back, watching the smoke carry their words on the wind. Partly it's security—nothing for Whiteman to find—but mostly it's ritual, sending these promises skyward so they'll be heard across the earth.

A sharp knock echoes through the rec center room. An Arapaho scout stands in the doorway, early morning light at his back, watching them grunt through their daily sit-ups on the hardwood floor. The room smells of sweat and determination.

Black Cloud says through strained abs, "Yes? What. Can. We. Do for you?" He lets out a final gasp then stops, dropping back to the floor, chest heaving.

The young man stands in the doorway and says, "Word travels fast on the prairie wind. A wind that carries our names and past like a river." He shades his eyes as if looking into the sun, gaze fixed upon some distant point beyond the cinderblock walls.

Halfway through a sit up Samuel barks, "Cut the crap, son." Then barks again while shifting upright from the floor reaching his elbow to his opposite knee, "What'd you hear and what do you want?"

"Seriously?" the young man asks stepping in. "My uncle works at a tire store down in Jackson and can't keep his mouth shut. He heard it from his cousin, who had coffee with someone who said they heard it from a fat salesman out of Lincoln who said it wasn't no white kids and that it wasn't no great leaders neither. So, is it true?"

Black Cloud shakes his head trying to follow the logic, sweat dripping from his morning workout. Exchanging looks with Bull Nose Pete beside him, he tells the scout to report to him—pointing at Bull Nose Pete—the following morning.

Protesting, Bull Nose Pete looks over at Black Cloud, and demands, "What? Why me?"

"Sounds like you," Black Cloud laughs, slapping him on the shoulder as they both fall back to the floor panting.

Each group is beholden to their group leader, assigned with tasks and responsibility, the information flowing like water through carefully constructed channels. Only the group leaders interact at the top, a structure Tom Sr. had suggested from his past experience.

"Information is like money," he'd told them one night over the plans. "The more hands it passes through, the more likely it is to get lost or stolen."

This way only small bits of information leak out, and only a few key figures know the full scope of what they're planning. Each person learns only their specific tasks, everything else is strictly need-to-know. If something falls apart, if someone gets caught, they can't reveal what they don't know.

Plausible deniability.

Over the months, it grows into a network of scouts that would have made their ancestors proud. They travel like shadows across the country—by horseback, car, and motorcycle, each carrying a piece of the larger puzzle. The new pony express rides again, this time with USB drives and burner phones.

As early summer warms the earth, one dedicated soul even skateboards two hundred miles, camping along the way. Instead of phones and internet that the FBI and Homeland Security can track, they meet at interstate rest stops and late-night Denny's restaurants, passing information in whispers over coffee cups and Grand Slam Breakfasts. Each movement is calculated, each gathering small enough to avoid notice.

This wasn't just another protest or march. It was something entirely new. No hashtags. No permits. No press releases. Just silence, sweat, and shadows moving toward the heart of America's biggest stage.

The groups expand like ripples in a pond while the training and practice intensifies. Most focus on logistics, learning to drive delivery vans that will drop items and disappear, practicing routes that look innocent to watching eyes.

It is now in full motion. A photocopied message is distributed throughout their channels reading:

Let's make this big.

Little Big Horn BIG!

The note remains deliberately cryptic: a reference to the Battle of Little Bighorn in 1876, when the combined forces of Lakota, Northern Cheyenne, and Arapaho defeated Lieutenant Colonel Custer and his 7th Cavalry. It was a day when Native people stood together and proved the impossible possible, when Sitting Bull and Crazy Horse led their warriors to protect their way of life against those who would destroy it. Now, generations later, the words carry the same weight: unity, resistance, and victory against overwhelming odds. The bones of that day still rattle beneath the grass.

Without knowing the who, where, and what waiting on the other end, they're just words on paper to outside eyes. But to those who understand, who grew up hearing stories of how their great-grandparents fought that day in Montana, it speaks volumes of another such coming moment.

They practice across the land where their ancestors once roamed free—from the plains to the mountains and sea. From Canada to Mexico, Atlantic to Pacific.

Every kind of person joins the training, getting ready for the big push east: fat and skinny people, people with limps and glass eyes, the old teaching the young forgotten skills. Even dogs workout alongside their owners, creating pride and a glimmer of that distant mountain called hope growing ever clearer on the horizon.

But they all understand the truth: only a handful will be chosen to complete the mission.

Most will serve in a support capacity and fewer still will make the trek. Their hands are needed for building, cutting, painting, and designing. These are people who know hard work, who've made their living with calloused hands and aching backs. Now those same hands will shape something bigger than themselves.

One day a note arrives from an anonymous tribe and is delivered by a short kid with long hair riding an equally long skateboard held together by duct tape. It was known they needed a computer whiz.

Alex is our best computer hacker and can get you into Fort Knox if need be. Just let us know when and where.

—Anonymous Red Believer

Cloud scribbles the answer back. The kid looks at it and says, "Righteous," then folds it up and puts the note into his backpack and skates off.

Walking in town later that day, Black Cloud feels a presence behind him before he hears the voice, "You Cloud?"

"Yes." His hand tightens around the grocery bag he's carrying, and his eyes start to shift.

"Don't turn around. Not in public." The voice carries the quiet authority of someone accustomed to being listened to. "You need help or this isn't going to work."

His instincts urge him to turn, to face whatever threat might be behind him. He starts to pivot.

"Don't turn around." The voice is right behind him.

"Uh, okay," he stutters. "Let's umm, meet at the rec center in an hour."

There's no response. The presence vanishes. When he finally turns, the street holds nothing but afternoon shadows and passing cars.

The man turns out to be Ben Blackfeather, ex-Army intelligence from the Apache Tribe. His people were legendary for their resistance against both Mexican and American forces, with warriors like Geronimo and Cochise holding out against impossible odds for decades. The Apache had mastered the art of guerrilla warfare, using the land itself as a weapon, appearing and disappearing like desert spirits. Ben carries that legacy in every calculated move.

But Ben has his own history with broken promises. After serving three tours in Afghanistan, using his surveillance skills to protect American interests, he'd returned home to find his tribe's water rights being stripped away by the same government he'd served. His attempts to work through official channels had been met with silence, then threats. He'd learned the hard way that some battles can't be won by following the rules.

"I tried doing things their way," he tells Black Cloud later at the rec center, his voice carrying the weight of lessons learned. "I filed paperwork, went to meetings, wrote letters. You know what they told me? 'Thank you for your service, now sit down and be quiet.'" He shakes his head. "I'm done being quiet."

He and Alex, the computer hacker, will work together in New York, but only when necessary. No prior communication. Like pieces of a puzzle slowly finding their way to the table, each person brings not just skills, but their own reasons for joining the fight.

FOURTEEN

The Ties That Bind Us

As the sun rises higher in the sky and the summer heat settles in, the team is finally finding its rhythm—some more gracefully than others.

Tall Tim, to everyone's surprise, has a knack for urban layouts. Maps, routes, alleys, the very veins of a city all lit him up like a pinball machine. "Look at all these alleyways!" he shouts one morning, jabbing at a map spread across the rec center table. "Perfect for sneak-outs, ambushes, backup plans!"

The group looks at him sideways, a few questioning his sanity.

Bull Nose Pete mutters, "I've never once been excited about an alleyway."

Pete will handle electronics, mechanicals, and explosives. Afterall, he owns a CB radio and works on old stereos for friends and relatives. He always gets the colored wires correct, the ground wires set properly, and hasn't burnt anything down yet.

The friends smile at each other enjoying the playful banter while doing something meaningful instead of just sitting around, and well, doing nothing but pass time.

"It sure feels good having a reason to wake up in the morning." Samuel will handle anything requiring actual skill: woodworking, design, the art of not accidentally hammering his own thumb. Years of fixing his own property and having built his horse barn.

Crystal will train scouts from each tribe with basic self-defense: blocks, pressure points, wrist and arm locks—then he or she will bring these moves back to their tribe to train, so all can use the same methods.

"My instructor taught, when you master the basics, you can master anything." She teaches them how to turn bar moves into warrior skills. "This wrist lock works great on drunks," she demonstrates on a wincing Lummi volunteer, "and even better on anyone daring to stop a revolution."

Tom Sr. keeps the timeframes tight. He is the quiet watchman, managing risk, and coordinating moves like a chess master. He keeps to the shadows, planning in private so no support staff will ever learn of his existence.

He often meets up with Crystal at the diner to unwind. He says to her, his hand placed close to hers on the counter, "Because you can't have a surprise party if everyone knows you're coming. Pie?"

She nods smiling as they share a peach cobbler. Their banter is more at ease and playful.

One day, while finishing dessert alone, Whiteman enters.

"Hey Betty," he says to Tall Tim's wife who works as a waitress there. "Coffee to go." She nods taking a pencil from behind her ear. Waiting, he stands two stools over then says to Tom, "Pretty girl," and nods to the door Crystal just walked out of. "I think she works at the local bar. Hey, can you pass that sugar and creamer?" though Tom glances at a sugar and creamer in front of him.

Tom slides it over as Betty drops off his coffee and check.

Whiteman looks, "Much obliged,' he looks at him. "Now ain't your boy into archery?"

"Why, yes he is."

Whiteman nods sipping from his coffee. "It would be a damn shame if he and you got wrapped up with some bad people and things didn't go your way. You'd lose him, you know?"

Tom's hand tightens around his coffee mug. "Mister, I don't know who you are, but if you talk about my boy again. I'm gonna…"

"Whoa. Whoa." Whiteman puts his hands up. "I'm just saying, if he or you got yourselves into trouble. Well, you get my point. Be careful who you spend time with. Friends can be our worst enemies. Thanks for the coffee, Betty." He throws money on the counter.

"Sir," he locks eyes with Tom, nods, then sips his coffee and walks out.

Meanwhile, TJ works with sharpshooters launching arrows and diversions, after gathering twelve of the best archers this side of the Pacific, many of them he met at shooting competitions across various reservations that his father took him to. They practice daily, their accuracy growing tighter.

One morning, a recruit shows up painted green like the Statue of Liberty and stands there unmoving so passersby will think he is a sculpture.

"Am I art…or on a deadly mission?" They all laugh, but nod taking notes and begin discussing what disguises they will wear.

Disguises will be their new war paint and camouflage. One guy shows up as a construction worker wearing a hard hat and a tool belt full of arrows, another is dressed as cabbie with a newsboy cap and a cigar in his mouth. He uses his best New York accent, which is awful.

"Eh, where you wanna go, bub?" The sharpshooters howl.

The twelve sharpshooters train daily at the furthest field behind the school, their arrows finding smaller and smaller targets.

"We're either going to make history," TJ tells them one morning, "or end up with the best archery club ever."

They fist bump as they break and begin packing up for the day. The sun slowly sets over the rusty green hills.

Denni, an Ojibwa girl and the best archer in her tribe's age group, waits for the others to leave. The Ojibwas were sworn enemies of the Sioux for hundreds of years, and yet here she stands off to the side with her green, spikey hair wearing her lucky Ramones T-shirt.

She pushes off the tree and strides closer.

"You're doing great, TJ. Everyone believes in you." She flashes her eyes at him as she steps past to leave. "Hey, what does TJ stand for anyway?"

He looks up at her while packing a bag.

"Tom Junior."

"Mmm," she shakes her head not liking it. "Nah, you're not a TJ. That's a boy's name. You're a leader and this is the cavalry." She looks up at him. Her eyes almost move him backwards. "You're a Thomas. I'm going to call you Thomas." She points at him. "That's a man's name and a man needs to lead—or a woman, of course."

Mesmerized by her, he says, "Oh, of course. My grandmother used called me that."

She nods. "Smart lady. She saw it too. Well, see you tomorrow, Thomas," and she flashes him a quick smile.

He watches her walk across the field to a waiting car.

Black Cloud—the ringleader, the mastermind, the unlikely conductor and maestro—coordinates the growing chaos like a man directing traffic with a flare gun that's seen across the nation. A need develops; a need that is filled by a new volunteer.

Intel flows through him, each piece filtered and passed along to whoever needs to know. He's the center of their web and is hopefully setting the trap and not the one getting trapped by the very web he's weaving. Some days he can't tell which is which. But the voices keep guiding him and he keeps listening: to bring the past into the present to set it free.

Putting bygones and old struggles aside proves easier than anyone expected; it turns out having a common cause works better than centuries of old squabbles.

Denni's father and Tall Tim share coffee and strategy sessions, their tribes old blood feuds dissolve into friendly jabs about who has the better archers.

Apache scouts trade tracking tips with Blackfeet warriors, while Iroquois elders share ancient hiding techniques that even Tom Sr. hadn't thought of.

Whiteman would want to know what's going on here and why so much unusual interactions with other tribes. But most of what's heard on the scanner is archer competitions among kids.

One evening, after practice, they gather around a fire at the local campground. Stories flow like the coffee they pass around: tales of their grandparents, of battles long past, of lessons learned the hard way. A Kiowa elder pulls out his pipe, passes it to a Sioux chief's grandson.

"My grandfather would roll over in his grave," he chuckles, "but things change, so can people and old wounds. Let us smoke." He puffs and releases the sacred smoke then waves it over his face in a cleansing ritual.

"Who knew planning a revolution could feel like a family reunion?" Bull Nose Pete quips one night, watching a Cheyenne warrior teach his traditional dance steps to a young Crow scout. "A weird, slightly illegal, and totally secret family reunion, but still."

The bonds grow stronger than any treaty could forge, built on shared laughter, shared purpose, and the shared understanding that they're probably just crazy enough to pull this off.

One tribal leader says over the phone, "This gives me hope, and people with hope are unstoppable."

The words spread through the reservations like wildfire, reaching into places where hope had been rationed like winter supplies.

Soon messages pour in from tribes they didn't even know still existed—some down to just a handful of members, their languages hanging on by threads, but their spirits burning bright as ever.

"We're with you," they say, "even if we're too few to send warriors, we're sending our prayers and a small donation."

"Getting kinda poetic there, aren't you?" Tall Tim teases Black Cloud one morning, catching him mid-ceremony after burning the letters out back.

"Maybe," Black Cloud grins, watching the smoke rise. "But hope's funny that way. It starts with a spark and next thing you know, you're planning to crash the biggest parade in America. Hope is that powerful. I just hope we're not wrong."

"How could you be wrong about being right?"

Black Cloud double takes looking at his friend thinking he understands, but isn't quite sure.

Now a couple months away and hammering out the last details, they are a well-oiled machine—at least in practice.

They train even harder on Columbus Day, using their anger as fuel. The weight of history sitting heavy on their shoulders. When smallpox ravaged groups across North America faster than bullets ever could and killed millions of them. They channel it into purpose rather than rage. This isn't about revenge anymore; it's about being seen, about making sure their children won't have to learn their history from people who tried to erase it.

After the raiding had stopped, no more visits came from Whiteman. But they knew he was never far away.

Meanwhile, the movement swells behind the scenes. Black Cloud—the reluctant conductor, part tactician, part prophet—holds it all together. Information flows through him like wind through canyon walls.

They will infiltrate New York as tourists, float workers, marchers, and street vendors. Each need is met with a volunteer. Each new contact passed into the proper node. The command structure—conceived by Tom Sr.—is holding: no one person knows the full plan except him. No one can betray what they don't know.

And beneath it all, a sacred framework begins to take shape.

Operation Sunup.

The name came in a dream—first to Black Cloud, then later, in uncanny synchronicity, to Crystal. "Sunup," she said the next morning, stirring her coffee slowly, "because it ends the darkness."

Proud of himself and ready to share everything with his mother—how their plan has grown beyond his dreams, how tribes across the nation have joined their cause—Black Cloud hurries over to her trailer in his truck. But something's wrong. People gathering outside freezes his blood: tears sliding down familiar faces, people hugging like they're trying to hold each other up. A sharp chill spikes down his back.

"No...no, no, no," he mutters, slamming the truck into park and bolting toward the crowd. Leaving the truck door open, his feet barely touch the ground as he runs to the front steps. White Feather intercepts him, her eyes red and swollen, her body trembling.

"Mama's dead." His sister's voice breaks, the words falling like rocks.

"She called out for you."

His knees buckle. Her words keep coming, jagged, painful.

"We tried to find you, man, but you were too busy with your ridiculous plan. Your stupid training was more important than your own mother."

She turns her back, walking away with grief's sharp edges in her voice, leaving him alone with the weight of her absence.

Inside, her trailer feels wrong. It's too quiet, too empty while chaos and sorrow press against the windows. He cracks open her bedroom door out of habit, checking for one of her rituals, half-expecting to find her in the middle of a ceremony. But when he pushes it fully open, he finds only emptiness: a made bed and sage burning down in a bowl, as if someone had tried to cleanse the space of death itself. Her body already gone, like she'd slipped away between chants and walked into the hills.

She had been so vibrant just days ago, her hand warm in his, her eyes bright with that knowing look she'd always had, like she could see straight through to his soul.

"You are becoming a warrior, my son," she had said. "I can see it in your eyes. They are focused."

"No mama. I'm just a middle-aged guy with a belly," he said rubbing his protruding stomach, trying to lighten the mood like he always did.

She fixed her stern gaze that could silence a thunderstorm, shaking her head at his attempt to hide behind humor.

"Sorry mama, no jokes. Yes, I am trying to do something meaningful with what's left of my life. We *are* doing something meaningful, but I'm not quite ready to tell you about it just yet." The words felt heavy, loaded with everything he was holding back.

She nodded weakly. "I will be leaving soon. Our ancestors reach for me, but I will be watching."

Following the old ways, he removed a piece of hair from the left side of her head, then kissed her, tucking the strand into his jacket pocket like a talisman.

"Our ancestors are proud of what you will accomplish. They have whispered this to me."

"No pressure, mama."

"Only truth, Abraham. Truth and fire." She gestures for him to lean closer, and whispers with shortened breath. "Saving your people includes saving the whites, the *Wasi'chu*, who are trapped inside the same brutal history." She pauses taking several short breaths, "Many try to whitewash and forget. Do not let them forget." Her eyes close just as a hawk lands on the windowsill, its sudden appearance making him jump. It squawks when they lock eyes.

"Look mama," he says, looking down at her, but she is asleep and faintly snoring with weak shallow breaths.

The memory fades as he stands alone in her room.

Above her coffin at the burial, he sees something that catches his breath: thousands of hawks, usually solitary hunters, pecking at the sky like they're trying to open it up. A sight that shouldn't be possible. The birds move in patterns that remind him of the coordinated dances his mother used to describe from her youth, before the government tried to ban their ceremonies and beliefs. But beliefs are spoken and held in one's heart and memories, not in history books that can be eradicated by harmful government programs.

"Look," he points, trying to show his sister this miracle. The hawks rise into the blue, their wings catching sunlight, then soon disappear behind clouds, closing behind them like curtains to the other world drawn over a sacred moment.

"What, at the clouds? Sniffing glue again?" She glares at him, grief making her words sharp enough to draw blood. It's the same look their mother would give him when he was being foolish, now reflected in his sister's tear-stained face.

Morning Sparrow chuckles too, covering her mouth. "Cloud looking at the clouds."

Then an older cousin mocks him, "Head in the clouds again, huh, Cloud?"

He's heard that one since birth—at school, at work, at every family gathering where he dared to dream bigger than the minds of others would allow. But today it doesn't sting. He thinks of it proudly, knowing the purposeful work he's a part of.

He refocuses on the burial of his mother, who has died on the same day Crazy Horse was born—almost two hundred years apart. The circle continuing its endless turn.

FIFTEEN

Divided Among Us

A few weeks later, with New York City and destiny awaiting like storm clouds on the horizon, they're as ready as they'll ever be for this outlandish act of rebellion. The tribal coalition is tighter than family now, forged by urgency and shared purpose. And yet, the distance between Black Cloud and his sister has widened into a chasm. He hasn't seen the kids. Not since the funeral.

His mother's spirit, as promised, watches over their preparations—he feels her in his dreams, in the wind, in the whispers of pine trees. But her death and his single-minded focus has cracked something closer to home.

A message comes through Morning Sparrow one morning during training, who delivers it with an apologetic shrug.

"Your sister says to come over tonight. And Cloud? She's got that look." He nods knowing that look—the one their mother used to get before laying down law that even the federal government wouldn't dare to challenge.

That evening, the fall wind blows red dust that cakes like a fine silt onto cars and staircases. He walks the short distance between their trailers, dragging his feet.

Through the window, he can see her pacing, rehearsing whatever speech she's been holding back these past months. He takes his time climbing the metal steps, and sighs at the door prolonging the verbal buzzsaw he anticipates from his sister.

He steps inside, and she stops pacing.

"Thank you for coming. Now please sit down," she tells him, using that same tone their mother perfected—the one that could make warriors think twice about their life choices.

"Where are the kids at?" Black Cloud asks, looking to escape her glare with the neutral loving territory of a child.

"In their rooms. Now sit."

She points to the couch like she's directing traffic. Once his butt touches the seat, she rips into him.

"You are going to attack the Macy's Thanksgiving Day Parade. You are going to get yourself killed and make us look like fools."

Her hands plant on her hips, eyes drilling into him from above—their mother's stance, their mother's fire.

"We already look like fools," he counters, looking up at her, tired of the centuries old battles that need to be put to an end.

"No one thinks you can pull it off."

"Tall Tim does."

"Tall Tim is an idiot. He can't shoot an arrow straight or ride a horse, let alone tie his shoes."

"Well, that is true."

"This isn't funny."

"No, it isn't."

"They're gonna kill you and strip more of our rights and land away. We already have so little."

He weighs her words and responds carefully—the way their mother taught them to consider positions other than their own.

"We have so little because we haven't done this before. I ain't some antique and neither are your kids. Neither are you. They don't even know what being Native means. Half of them think they're damn Disney characters."

"No, they don't."

Just then Little Wonder walks into the room wearing Teenage Mutant Ninja Turtle pajamas.

"Hi, Unca Cloudy," he says with sleep in his eyes rubbing them. "Did sumthin bad happen? I heard shoutin'."

"No, sweetie," White Feather's voice softens like melting snow.

Black Cloud curls his mouth and raises an eyebrow looking at his sister. The living proof of his point stands before them in cartoon-character glory.

"Little Wonder, go to your room. I need to speak with your uncle. I'll tuck you in in a minute."

He nods and turns around, feet dragging.

"Good night, Little Wonder. I love you."

"Love you too, Unca Cloudy," he says, shuffling back to his room in his onesie.

He leans toward his sister, his voice low but carrying the weight of everything they've been working toward.

"I love that kid and want him to feel pride. I want all Native people to feel pride again, and if I have to die to do it then so be it." He stands up, his shadow stretches across her living room floor.

"You ain't Crazy Horse, Cloud, or Sitting Bull or none of 'em. You read too damn much."

He straightens his back and pulls in his chin, looking more like his father when he was still young and full of pride.

"I am Black Cloud of the Oglala Sioux, and they won't see us coming. Too busy with their war on terror, war on drugs, war on people, war on the environment. Not too busy worried about us savage natives locked up on our dirt-poor reservations. The Trail of Tears ends now, cause I'm tired of crying." He steps toward the door.

She lunges after him grabbing his arm.

"You're my only brother. I don't want to lose you to revenge and bitterness."

His anger flares. "It's not bitterness but hope damn it."

"There will be cops everywhere. They'll have sharpshooters. You are *witkotkoke*. Nuts." Pleading, she squeezes his arm. "Please don't."

"So will we," he says, shaking his arm free to walk out.

At the door he turns to her. "It ain't getting better, sis. Kids are dying here. Babies are dying. The people are sick. The land has been stolen and polluted. And not doing anything about it? That's what's *witkotkoke*."

"You'll get killed."

"Maybe. But just maybe someone will see we're still here and deserve their respect. But more importantly, we deserve our own, instead of asking the white man for his."

She looks away, anger melting into some softer truth.

"Damn I hate when you're right. So many people are looking up to you. Some even think you are Crazy Horse leading us home. But this isn't the way."

They stand a few feet from each other with love and fear filling the space between them.

"Well, what is? All I know is people are hurting, cheated, confused. Pursuit of happiness? Well, I'm pursuing mine. Ghost dances, sun dances, it's all in the past. But what is our future, casinos? No. No. No," he says and walks out.

They don't see each other for weeks after that night, pride and fear keeping them apart like an invisible wall. Uninvited to the family dinners, he doesn't stop by to watch cartoons with Little Wonder and misses Lilyanna's attempt at traditional dancing. But many nights, he stands in his doorway as the reservation settles into darkness, watching the lights in their windows blink out one by one. First the kitchen, where he knows White Feather is finishing the dishes, humming their mother's songs to herself. Then the kids' rooms—Little Wonder is probably still wearing those turtle pajamas, while Lilyanna brushes out her long black hair in front of a mirror like some fairy princess. Finally, his sister's room, the last light to go. He imagines her staring out her own window, maybe wondering about him, as they had always been so close.

He doesn't come by for dinner or see the children. The distance grows as their departure date approaches. They won't see each other again until the morning the caravan heads east several weeks later, when everything they've left unsaid will have to find its way into whatever goodbye they can manage.

Some wounds need time to heal, their mother used to say, and some need the medicine of distance to fully understand what is in your heart.

SIXTEEN

Heading East

The caravan is set to leave at the break of dawn four days prior to Thanksgiving, but the plan has been in motion for weeks. Like tributaries flowing toward a mighty river, tribes from across the nation have been converging on New York City—never more than two or three at a time, nothing to draw attention. Navajos arriving as tourists in Times Square, Crow members setting up carts as street vendors, Hopi scouts blending in as construction workers on sites overlooking the parade route.

For weeks they've been moving into position. A Cheyenne family opens a souvenir stand near Macy's. Two Blackfeet warriors take jobs as window washers on buildings along the route. A group of Seminole youth join a local cleanup crew. Each day, more pieces slide into place, all of them carrying components of what's to come. Equipment is stashed in rented storage units, supplies cached in plain sight.

Back on the rez, people spend their final days preparing in ways only they understand, and to possibly say goodbye. Samuel spends hours in the paddock with his horses, brushing their manes, whispering to them like old friends. He tells them everything—where he is going, what they're fighting for. The horses listen, the way animals do when they sense a change coming.

The night before their departure, Bull Nose Pete kisses his wife with quiet intensity, then bends to scoop his grandson into his arms. The toddler's cheeks are warm from sleep. Pete presses his nose to the boy's temple and inhales deeply.

"We're doing this for you, baby boy," he murmurs.

When the doorbell rings, Pete passes the child to his wife and opens it. A Shoshone man and a Pawnee girl stand in the frame, bundled against the cool night. They nod, and Pete hands over several wrapped packages—electrical and mechanical components to be embedded into Samuel's woodwork.

Tom Sr. and Crystal are finishing one of their endless "planning sessions" in the back booth of the diner. Their coffee has gone cold. They lean over maps, their shoulders touching occasionally—though neither mentions it. Outside, light snow filters down in lazy spirals. He mentions the visit he received from Whiteman that keeps replaying in his mind.

"What are you going to do?" she asks with worry in her eyes while sipping coffee, wondering if Whiteman will return.

"TJ and I spoke about it. We're moving forward cautiously, making sure we don't leave any crumbs for him to follow. We'll see if he shows up again. That means he has something. Other than that, it's just a fear tactic."

She nods wondering about this man she's grown fond of. "Just be careful." He nods looking into her eyes.

Even TJ noticed this change in his father. He smiles more now and takes extra care with his appearance, trimming his beard and picking out the right shirt before these meetings.

"You're not fooling anyone, Dad," he teases one night, earning a playful swat on the shoulder and a rare blush from his father. Crystal, for her part, has started wearing her hair down, something the bar patrons would never have believed.

Tall Tim practices navigation with his wife and grandchildren obsessively, having them act like buildings, tracing routes on maps until the paper wears thin.

"I don't get it either," he admits to her when asked about this strange talent. Betty is still proudly crazy about him.

"A while back, Stan Whiteman was in the diner harassing some customer minding his own business."

Tall Tim files this away and kisses her on the forehead.

"You be safe, Timothy."

Now, at the dawn of their departure, Black Cloud and Tall Tim finish loading the camper onto his truck. Once secured, Tall Tim and Black Cloud nod to each other, then hop in. The engine fires up at the turn of the key. The dark night yields reluctantly to a blue hint of morning light.

White Feather emerges from her trailer wrapped in her burgundy robe, clutching something in her hands, while others pull into the dry grass and brown dirt lot.

Some from other reservations had camped the night prior. There are six support vehicles scattered around the property like fallen leaves, their occupants doing last minute checks by flashlight, ready for the push east.

Taking inventory of the other vehicles, White Feather walks over and knocks on the window of her brother's idling truck.

Black Cloud rolls down the window while more pull into the lot, engines humming in the morning quiet. She holds out a thermos, her hands trembling slightly.

"I was up all morning making this invincibility tea. You'll need your strength," she says.

He nods, setting it next to him and places his hand on the black steering wheel, looking ahead.

"You're my red brother and I love you. Mama's gone, but you're as stubborn as she ever was." They peer over at the empty trailer next door. White Feather stands straight and takes a deep breath, looking around at the shadowy landscape and low rolling hills.

She refocuses on him. "There's no going back, you know."

"I know." He stares out the front window, watching the sky slowly paint itself awake.

"Don't let this be another Wounded Knee. Don't break our hearts…"

He quickly glances at her. "I won't."

"There's real danger and real consequences ahead. This isn't some TV show or book," she sighs. "If you're going to do this, win whatever it is you need to win. Strike in the morning. Have the sun at your back." She smiles cautiously. "You have always been a bit of a Crazy Horse—and a jackass too."

Tall Tim sits next to him, leans over smiling and says, "I'll take good care of him."

"That's what I'm afraid of, Tim."

Black Cloud looks at her and smirks, teeth yellowed from too much coffee.

"I may be stubborn, but you've always been tough. I wouldn't want to mess with you."

"More wiggle than jiggle, but I'll still whoop your butt." They slap a high five, the sound sharp in the morning air.

With this, he raises his fist high above the truck roof and honks. Honks are returned from cars and RVs idling around the property: a chorus of metallic war cries and hand waving as wheels begin rolling slowly toward the awaiting battle.

A small crowd gathers at the property's edge to send them off: elders in wheelchairs bundled against the morning chill—some half-blind with cataracts—mothers holding babies wrapped in woven quilts, with teenagers trying to look cool while their eyes shine with interest.

Dogs run alongside the vehicles, their barks mixing with war whoops and shouts of encouragement that carry across the reservation like thunder rolling through the hills.

Old Jimmy Two Bears, who hasn't left his porch in years, stands at attention in his faded military jacket, offering a crisp salute as they pass.

Miss Sue from the school waves her lesson plans like a flag rustling in the wind, while three of her students perform a traditional dance they've been practicing in secret.

Someone starts drumming—probably Henry White Horse, though no one can spot him in the growing crowd—and the beat follows them along the driveway like a warrior's heartbeat.

Morning mist now falls like a gentle cleansing, people emerge from their homes like spirit guides drawn by the sound and the movement, not understanding the unfolding event. Yet they line the reservation roads spontaneously, as if the ancestors themselves had called them to witness this departure.

"I want to go with you, Pop Pop." Tall Tim's granddaughter runs alongside their slow-moving truck. Her braids bounce with each step, beadwork catching car headlights. Tim reaches for her hand and touches it briefly as they roll along.

Many who do not understand the purpose of their trip run along the fence line.

"Are you going to see the Statue of Liberty and Empire State Building?" one girl shouts.

Black Cloud and Tall Tim roll toward the properties edge, where Tom Sr. and TJ wait in their sedan.

Black Cloud overhears TJ say, "It's okay, dad. I like her," as Crystal walks up to their awaiting vehicle.

Tom sits at the wheel of his new to him used gray Toyota Camry, trying to look casual and failing completely.

Crystal reaches for the rear door handle and says, "Good gas mileage," and nods approvingly. "You're smart and practical. I like that in a man. Too many guys with big trucks and little peckers. Sorry Junior, I mean small minds."

She hops into the back and closes the door. Their car rolls five feet, then stops. TJ gets out of the front and moves around to the rear. Crystal climbs into the front seat from the back, the dance of it all making everyone pretend not to notice.

While passing slowly, Black Cloud gives them a thumbs up and receives one in return. Through his mirror, he catches a snapshot of their makeshift army and a revolution in motion.

Armies can be comprised of anyone, he thinks, as long as their soldiers are dedicated to a cause. He honks the horn one last time as they turn onto reservation road, soon to split up and meet next in New York City.

To not attract any attention, Samuel and Bull Nose Pete are set to leave a few minutes later. Bull Nose Pete pulls up to Samuel's in his green Chevy Trailblazer, a picture of his grandson hanging from the rearview mirror.

Samuel's out with the horses, hand grazing the mare. He is divorced; anger once consumed him as he pushed people away with bitterness: the ones he didn't know how to love and a daughter who won't speak to him now. The mare never complains or judges.

When leaving, his wife had shouted from the door, "Keep that dumb horse of yours." She left with her new boyfriend waiting in a van outside.

He lives alone with the animals, the only ones he gets along with. "The only things you know how to love," she said to him once.

"Yeah, because she doesn't talk back," he said harshly, knowing the words would sting. He later regretted saying them.

But the mare's been with him for twenty-three years and often stands near him when he's lost in thought, nudging him gently with her head.

At the fence line, Bull Nose Pete urges, "She's fine Sam. Your niece will take good care of her and the others."

Samuel strokes the mare's neck. "Huh? Oh right. Okay."

Switching subjects, Pete asks, "Did the guys pick the stuff up?"

"Yeah, two days ago. Some scrawny Chickasaw girl and a burly Iroquois guy who could bench press my barn."

Pete nods waiting for him to finish haying them.

Samuel and Pete sit in the truck watching the horses eat.

"We've got to get on the road, Sam. We do this for them." Pete nods to them. "For my boy, too." He grabs the picture into his hands. "We don't matter anymore. We're the dust of history. We ain't the future. They are. The animals, the land, the people. But we can still make a difference."

Samuel nods, giving Pete permission to drive. "You sound like Cloud for Christ's sake." He half smiles. Tough words were never far away. "I ain't got nothing but that mare, two geldings, and a few chickens." The ornery wall is lowered, a rare moment where he lets his underside be exposed. All of his life's choices found in that comment. Sitting in the idling truck with the heater blowing, he looks at the pens and small dusty pastures.

"We'll be back. I promise." Pete says and begins backing up, then pauses.

"That's a promise you can't keep." Samuel glares at him with hard black eyes.

Pete weighs his words, "You've got friends, Sam."

No reply. Just a nod.

The nod gives Bull Nose Pete the green light to drive into an unknown future that will put all of their lives at risk.

A few miles outside the reservation, the caravan begins to peel apart—just as planned. No dramatic exits. No rally cries. Just subtle turns at predetermined intersections, headlights flicking off and on, each vehicle heading for a separate route east. Like deer vanishing into different parts of the forest, they disappear one by one onto waiting county and state roads.

Other tribes will meet at rendezvous points around New York City, having set the plan in motion across the Indian Nation that now buzzes with anticipation, fear, and long-lost hope. From pine forests to deserts, from mountains to plains, a unified excitement is felt for the first time in more than a century. For the first time ever, they move as one. Not split up by empty promises from different European nations vying for their hunting, fighting, and tracking skills. And not for a nation that has deceived them with treaties and false promises.

As they speed up to the highway, Black Cloud and the caravan kick up early morning dust that mixes with the first light of day, their course set toward the Eastern Seaboard. Soon they will be absorbed into what history will say about them, about those American Indians who dared to dream big and take risks. The wheels of time are now in motion as is the fate of these daring souls.

A few miles later, the first billboard looms: **"Experience the Majesty of Freedom—Visit Mount Rushmore!"** Beneath it, smiling white tourists wave in generic stock-photo glory.

Black Cloud scowls.

At the interstate exit, RVs and tourists get off the highway.

Angrily, Black Cloud says, "Everything that's wrong planted smack in the middle of our sacred land."

"I've heard some folks call it the Shrine of Hypocrisy," Tall Tim offers.

Black Cloud turns to him, surprised. "Where'd you hear that?"

"Betty." Tall Tim smirks. "She reads more than me."

Black Cloud laughs.

Another sign flashes past—this one newer, glossier: **"Four Great Faces. One Great Nation."**

The signs and billboards, RVs and campers, tourists heading for Mount Rushmore sends a familiar anger through their convoy: four white faces carved into the Lakota's sacred *Paha Sapa*, the Six Grandfathers Mountain, often referred to as the heart of everything that is.

Before the dynamite came in 1927, before they sculpted presidents into stone, this had been a holy place where Lakota went for spiritual guidance. The government seized it despite the Fort Laramie Treaty, despite all promises that the Black Hills would belong to the Lakota "as long as the grass grows and the river flows." In 1980, the Supreme Court even agreed, offering the tribes over $100 million in compensation. They refused. As their elders said, "How can you buy something that already belongs to you?"

When the Crazy Horse Memorial appears on the horizon, carved into these same disputed mountains, Black Cloud feels the weight of irony. Four white presidents carved into stolen sacred ground while Crazy Horse's visage—a hero they tried to erase—carving his way out, rises slowly from the mountain nearby, decades of work still unfinished. Like their people's story: always patient, never finished, refusing to be erased.

Several miles behind Black Cloud and Tall Tim, Samuel mutters prayers in Lakota as he restlessly fidgets in the passenger seat, shifting his bottom and twiddling his thumbs.

"I can't get comfortable." Each mile marker is a bead on an invisible necklace. In the rearview, the Black Hills fade like old photographs, sacred land that's seen too many broken promises.

"We should go back."

Pete says, "What? Why?"

"I don't like leaving the mare." He grows quiet when they begin seeing signs for Mount Rushmore.

"I hate that goddamn sign. It's not even a goddamn mountain. Just four white guys carved into our sacred mountain." He rolls down the window and shouts at tourists getting off the exit. "*Paha Sapa*, assholes!"

This sinewy older man leans back in and closes the window. Then, smiling, he looks over at Pete who's staring back at him. He's never seen Samuel let loose like this.

Samuel says, "Damn that felt good."

Pete rolls down his window, "Go back to your own country!" The two share a laugh.

"I'm glad we're going to New York City. You're right. The mare's fine. Step on it. We've got a job to do. Let's show these pricks." His venom helping him momentarily forget about the mare.

After many miles in silence Pete says, "You know, it's madness what we're doing."

"Cloud's right. It's madness that we haven't done this, Pete." He points at the tourists and slaps the dashboard. "That's madness."

Pete agrees and takes it up to eighty miles per hour and honks the horn of the Trail Blazer at tourists like a madman. They double take, looking at him as if they'd done something wrong.

"Woo hoo!" They both shout. Pete slides "Fight the Power" by Public Enemy into the car's CD player. The thumping base comes on with Chuck D's powerful lyrics. Surprised by this, Samuel asks, "You like rap?"

Bullnose Pete nods his head and starts bopping along to the music. Samuel listens and starts doing the same and shouts over it. "This is good," and turns it up.

Windows come down with the power of the song. They bang fists on the dashboard in rhythm.

The mountain where Crazy Horse now emerges from stone holds scope in equivalence to all four presidents combined. His gaze eventually sinks out of sight as they head east towards the high plains. Miles pass along this cold, gray highway. The first hundred miles unwind beneath their wheels like a sacred meditation connecting them to the land.

"I hope Crystal and the Toms are alright." Samuel touches the window with his fingertip as if sketching the contour of the land.

Several miles apart, even Crystal—who claims she doesn't believe in signs—falls quiet in the passenger seat as Tom focuses on the road. The irony is not lost upon her. Miles later they veer off, taking a different route. They have a good time playing tourist and stop at the Corn Palace. The outside of the building is quite literally made of corn.

"Don't birds eat it?" she wonders.

TJ says, "I guess not."

Tom Sr. adds staring up at it, "Just needs some butter."

She looks at him and rolls her eyes at the bad joke but can't help laughing.

"TJ, is he always this funny?"

"Yup."

Tom Sr. looks at his watch, "We better get moving."

Their plan is to stop at the world's largest popcorn ball in Iowa and fossil beds in Nebraska. Tom Sr. takes pictures with his phone and captures Crystal chasing TJ around, throwing corn kernels at each other.

220-pound Ben Blackfeather thunders across the Kansas plains on his Indian motorcycle, a black blur under heavy skies. His long hair whips behind him like dark smoke, his leather jacket glinting with patches that tell more truth than any government-issued uniform ever had.

It was cold—too cold for riding. The wind slices through the fleece lining in his jeans, finding every crease and seam, ones he didn't even know he had. But he doesn't care. The discomfort is earned. It reminds him he is alive, moving, with purpose

It's somehow fitting to be riding an Indian through the American heartland, though he appreciates the irony that his people—the Apache—never rode these northern plains, because they didn't have motorcycles, a metal beast to ride. For if they had, they would have conquered the continent for sure.

Their warriors had ruled the southwestern deserts instead, where

Geronimo and Cochise played cat and mouse with two nations' armies, the Mexican and American using the land itself as a weapon.

Blackfeather's Army training kicks in automatically: stay off main roads, vary your routine, don't be the guy who gets spotted because he had to stop at every Waffle House along the way. Though after fifteen years running military intelligence ops, he knows sometimes the best hiding spot is in plain sight. Nobody looks twice at another biker enjoying America's highways, even if this one happens to be Apache with more combat training than your average Green Beret.

The bike's engine purrs beneath him as he crosses into Kansas on State Road 54. His Army training tells him to stick to secondary roads, avoid obvious routes. His Apache blood tells him to move like shadows, to be the thing others see but can't quite remember seeing. Both instincts have kept him alive this long.

He rides through forgotten towns, winter-stripped fields, churches with one car in the lot and signs that read "Jesus Saves" in chipping paint. He rides up through Tucumcarmi, Texhoma, Santa Rosa—small towns with names from a distant time that are all that's left, along fields stripped bare for the incoming winter.

Truck stops and motel rooms mark his progress toward Manhattan, each night spent studying maps and cleaning equipment while trying not to laugh at the irony. All those years training to protect America from threats, and here he is planning to crash one of its biggest parties. One he was not invited to. All the more reason to crash it.

The skills that made him valuable to the Army come flooding back: how to blend in, how to move unnoticed, how to make people see what they expect to see. His commanding officer used to joke that Ben could blend in with an ocean of sea lions if he needed to, he had the loud yawn for it often waking others several barracks over.

At a Flying J Travel Center, he stops for gas, to warm up, and to text Alex. They'll be meeting in the morning of Operation Sunup at 0800 hours.

Alex is tucked far away from cold winds and prying eyes as he prepares for the biggest hack of his life in the most obvious hiding place he can think of: a cramped sublet apartment in Harlem he's borrowed from his cousin's friend's roommate's sister—or something like that. He lost track after cousin.

Three laptops surround him like a digital medicine wheel, each one running different programs he's spent months perfecting.

He's gotten good at hacking between acting gigs—because yes, he really is an actor and recently did an off-Broadway show playing a detective with an eye twitch. He knows how to crack network security like others crack their knuckles. He's been mapping Macy's broadcast infrastructure. Television networks, it turns out, are like theater productions: everybody's so focused on the show, they forget to watch the side of the stage where characters enter and exit, often without notice.

He runs another diagnostic while practicing his "just another tourist" face in the bathroom mirror. The irony isn't lost on him either; a Nez Perce hacker getting ready to interrupt the biggest parade in America that symbolizes gluttony and overabundance, while so many Native Americans struggle to survive.

His ancestors rode horses across mountains to evade the Army; he's going to ride the digital highway right into their living rooms. A Post-it note by his main screen reads "Remember: hack the feed, not the network." This is his mantra for keeping the operation clean and focused. They're not here to crash systems or steal data. They're here to be seen and heard.

"And so, we shall," he says smelling the food he brought back a while ago, the smell distracting him.

The thought of all those network executives trying to explain what happened to their bosses does make him smile. He's written his code to be elegant, almost poetic. One program is to intercept the broadcast feed, another is to overlay their message, and a third to make it all look like a technical glitch if anyone gets suspicious.

"Like a digital smoke signal," he mutters to himself in the studio apartment with the chipping lead paint walls. Now cracking open the to-go boxes, the smell is irresistible, the hunger overtaking him.

The wall in front of him looks like something from a crime show: maps of network infrastructure, broadcast schedules, contingency plans displayed across the white wall. But instead of red string connecting clues, he's got sticky notes with timestamps and IP addresses. The biggest note, right in the center, reads "8:27 AM: SHOWTIME."

His preparations have been methodical. He's created backdoors disguised as routine system updates and planted dummy files to lead any investigators on wild goose chases. He even set up a false trail suggesting some teenagers in Milwaukee might be planning to hack the broadcast to protest turkey farming.

"Sorry, Milwaukee. You never did anything to me, but we need a scapegoat," he whispers, adding another line of code.

The beauty of it, he thinks, is that they won't actually be breaking anything. Just borrowing the airwaves for a bit.

He does one final system check, then dives into a meal of chicken and waffles, black-eyed peas, and collard greens from Sylvia's famous soul food restaurant. He licks his fingers, trying not to get grease on the keyboard and short circuit the whole operation.

His phone vibrates with a text from Ben, who confirms their meeting spot. The time is coming for him to leave this neighborhood he's grown fond of and pack up his mobile command center to become just another tourist in the big city. Though he's probably the only tourist carrying enough computing equipment to launch a space shuttle.

The landscape blurs past—grain elevators, old windmills, miles of open sky. The world flattens out into shades of gray and brown, dotted with distant barns and fence rails.

Heading east across the high plains, Tall Tim recalls working on a dairy farm one summer in Nebraska when he was young. His face lights up with nostalgia.

"Boy that was hard work. But I slept on hay every night like a baby."

His eyes go distant, watching the landscape roll past as the memory comes into view.

"Course, turned out I was allergic to hay. Spent three months sneezing myself awake, too proud to tell anyone. My nose looked like Bull Nose Pete's by the end of it."

The men laugh, then fall silent again as the truck wheels spin round and round heading down the highway. The space around them closes in as too much space will do and remind you of your past.

Black Cloud drives with one hand on the wheel, the other resting loosely in his lap. The road has a way of stirring memories, and out here, with nothing but space around them, he thinks of Gloria. Everything brings him back to her.

She loved this land—expansive, uncluttered, honest. The way the wind moves through the grass like it had somewhere to be. The birds. The long shadows. The blue sky that never seemed to end.

Black Cloud finds himself replaying Gloria's words again and again. Not just her final words in the trailer or her warnings when he drank too much—but the quiet things she said when she believed he was sleeping. About dreams. About their child. About building something that would last.

He and Gloria struggled financially after she moved in with him on the reservation, but they'd found their own kind of riches, back when love still felt like a resource that could carry them through anything.

They would camp down by the creek, watch the moon rise, and find joy in the simple fact of being together. She'd bring her grandmother's quilt, and he'd pretend to know the constellations, making up increasingly ridiculous stories about "The Great Cosmic Buffalo" and "The Eternal Coffee Pot" until she'd laugh so hard she'd snort and nudge him in the ribs. "You're ridiculous."

They were happiest in those moments—when everything was still ahead of them.

She'd managed to get another job in Sioux City, while he bounced between jobs: mason (terrible at it), carpenter (even worse), painter (decent, until he fell off that one ladder). None of them felt right for a man with a bachelor's degree in history, but they made do. Gloria would pack him lunches with little notes inside, usually history jokes that only he would appreciate: *Why did the archaeologist break up with the historian? Because she didn't dig his dates.*

They were terrible but he loved them.

The first couple years tested them in ways neither expected. Winter nights when the heating gave out, summer days when the car wouldn't start, endless meals of mac and cheese because it was cheap and filling. But Gloria never lost her smile, even when they had to choose between paying the electric bill or buying her new shoes.

"At least we have our stars," she'd say on nights when the power was cut, lighting candles and slow dancing to old country music with him in their kitchen. On these nights the stars seemed even brighter.

"I named one for you: *The Gloria*." They'd look out the window and he'd point. She'd smile up at him, placing her head on his chest as they continued to sway.

Then Gloria got pregnant, and their tightrope got even tighter. Her morning sickness was so bad she had to stop working; it was the doctor's orders after she passed out at her desk twice in one week. At home, she apologized constantly, as if growing their child was somehow letting him down. He'd kiss her forehead and bring her saltines in bed and tell her more of his made-up constellations until she'd smile again.

"I'll find work," he said, even more desperate now for decent employment.

The bills piled up faster and debt collectors started calling. He ventured further off the reservation for work, taking whatever jobs he could find. His car broke down and the repair costs were more than they could scrape together. Then the bank repossessed Gloria's car, leaving him dependent on the bus schedule once again and its driver who seemed to think showing up on time was more of a suggestion than a requirement.

One factory didn't want any real Natives. Others thought he was Mexican or didn't care. The reality of it hit him hard one rainy day at a warehouse on the outskirts of town.

"I ain't Mexican," he said to a warehouse foreman. "I'm full-blooded American Indian."

The stocky bearded man looked him over.

"Well, you look Mexican to me and I ain't interested in hiring no Mexicans. Go back to your own country."

"This is my country," he said, but the metal door had already slammed in his face. A sudden Midwest downpour had broken out over him. The winds picked up and the sky turned black. It was a mile walk back to the bus depot. Thumbing it, no one picked him up.

Soaked and chilled to the bone, he watched trees sway and garbage blow past as trucks and cars drove by, spraying water on him with their tires.

Without any money and a one-way bus ticket home, he felt the lowest he ever had, rejected by the very nation he was supposed to be a part of, reminding him of his father's struggles. With a baby, a wife, and no job, he found a liquor store at an intersection and took to drinking the same way his father had.

That night he slept in the bus station, cold, wet, drunk, and shivering. He sat there watching people come and go. He gathered up old newspapers left behind and a shirt with a kangaroo on it forgotten on the floor by some toddler. He laid down on the wooden bench and placed the newspaper and shirt over him as best he could.

Bitterness consumed him—unable to find gainful employment, unable to pay the bills, and unable to take care of his family.

Upon his return, he would go out all night feeling sorry for himself. That's when Black Cloud's spirit got stuck in the hills under the roots and rocks the way his father's had. He became a cleaner at a casino, a shoe store employee, working two jobs at minimum wage. Stuck.

"Minimum wage means minimum food, minimum clothes, and a minimum life," Black Cloud said one night, reaching for another bottle.

Gloria was nursing their baby, her eyes turning hard as reservation flint.

"We've got love, Cloud. Now put the booze down and take care of your wife and baby. You can't take care of someone else when feeling sorry for yourself." She paused, then fired her last warning shot, "If you don't, I'll go find Stan Whiteman and stay with him. He'll provide. I married a man. Not a child." She knew it would be a blow to him, but she had to say it.

He stared at the bottle, then at her, trying to gauge if it was a bluff. The look in her eyes told him it was not. Slowly, he placed the bottle down on the counter.

"Do you think there's an answer in that?" She nodded to the bottle, then stopped nursing and looked at him. "I have a baby that needs a father."

After that, he cleaned himself up. His father had already been taken by the same darkness and shame.

Later, a cousin of Gloria's helped Black Cloud get a decent job teaching history—their history—at a local Indian school.

While driving, he smiles at the landscape remembering his wife, then frowns at the heartbreak of his father.

He blurts out to the flat land and dairy farms around him, forgetting about the company alongside him in the truck, "Maybe love can save this country as it helped save me. Without it we're all lost."

Tall Tim looks at him strangely, yet nods anyway understanding written in the lines of his face. All these years of friendship and sometimes silence says more than words.

Rolling down the road looking out at the changing landscape, Black Cloud finds himself making peace with whatever's coming. He may get killed but he's finding peace in purpose, peace in light, and peace in living—even if death is waiting on the other side.

SEVENTEEN

Whiteman on the Hunt

He's been watching the rec center every night, cataloging their comings and goings like a man obsessed. A couple days have gone by with no activity after it had been buzzing like a beehive. So when the lights stay dark, he takes note. He pulls away slowly in his black sedan, tires crushing pebbles and soil, mind spinning with possibilities. Everything in him screams that he's missing something. People don't just disappear without a reason. They always have a reason.

Could be nothing. Could be everything. By Wednesday evening, the silence has deepened—no cars in the lot, no shadows moving behind windows, none of the constant motion he's grown used to tracking.

That night he sneaks into the rec center with a flashlight beam cutting through the darkness. Finding the open door to the card room, the light sweeps across the empty space. There's not much in there but a deck of cards on the folding table. He squats after his light spots something laying on the floor. He places rubber gloves on his hands and retrieves tweezers from a sterile kit. There's a slice of paper face down under the card table where Tall Tim had been sitting. He shines the light. It reads like a waiting confession. The message is short. Direct. Chilling.

Let's make this big.

Little Big Horn BIG!

His stomach flips. "Whoa! What? We've got trouble. This is bigger than I thought. I need to call in the national guard," he says aloud at the note and places it into a sealed plastic bag.

He stands. "Their one mistake…I'm coming for you, old friend."

With evidence in hand, he drives over to Black Cloud's place to bust him, interrogate him, but it's empty. No lights. No movement. Just wind and dust. He pounds on the door. Nothing.

Something's happening. He can feel it.

He decides to shake down someone who might talk; Ronny Bones has had trouble with the law and has been in and out of prison. He's the kind of guy who might know something.

Whiteman bangs on the front door with the same urgency he employed at Black Cloud's residence.

The door opens, "Hello Mr. Whiteman. I've been good, I promise."

"I will bust you if you don't tell me everything I need to know about Black Cloud and his cronies."

Ronny looks at him strangely. "The old guys who play cards?"

"Don't be dumb. Where are they going? What are they doing?"

He shrugs. "I heard something about a parade."

"What parade?"

"I don't know. Who cares? It's a fucking parade."

"I will bust you."

"I don't know. Honest. Going to some stupid parade, is that against the law? Because if it is, then throw me in jail." Ronny's casual tone only fuels Whiteman's ire.

"If you're lying to me, I'll bust you so hard you'll never see the light of day again."

The following day he questions Sally, Talks with Trees, outside the Wounded Knee Memorial.

She's organizing the refrigerator magnets on the counter, pretending not to notice him until his shadow falls across her counter.

"Four men came in here last month," he says, not bothering with hello. "The ones with the masks and water guns. What exactly did they say?"

Sally continues organizing her display.

"Hmm, said they were practicing for some show. Probably a school play or something." Her voice carries just enough disinterest to make him suspicious.

"Do you know who the men are?"

"Of course." She moves down the counter behind a display to hide herself from swallowing. "I've known them for forty years."

"Well, who are they?"

"Black Cloud, Tall Tim, and a couple of their friends. Why, agent? Do you think something serious is going on?" She stops what she's doing and places her elbows on the counter, head in her hands with a mocking grin on her face.

"Very interesting. I thought they were involved," he taps the notepad with his pencil.

"Involved with what? Old men being idiots. Do you know those guys, Whiteman? About as sharp as butter," she says to distract him.

"A show, you said." He leans over the counter. "What kind of show involves robbing a gift shop?"

"Beats me," she finally looks up, amusement dancing in her eyes. "But they did have yellow plastic squirt guns. So, it couldn't have been too serious. And they were pretty bad at it. Must've been the least successful robbery in history, because they never took anything."

"Hmm," he groans, pulling out his notepad. "Did they mention anything else about this…show?"

"Just that they were practicing."

"Hmm," he groans again then looks up. "You have done a great service for your nation. We thank you. No more questions." He says in his overbearing tone, as if he represents the nation.

As he turns to leave, she flips him the bird. "Anytime," she says returning to her countertop trinkets.

After Sally's dismissal, he sits in his black sedan reviewing his notepad. There have been three incidents, all with the same pattern: masks, water guns, apologies, returned items. However, nothing was taken here. This was their first attempt and would have returned items if they had taken any. Got bolder after the rez, he surmises.

"Practicing," they all said. Some tourists pull up in a fifth wheel next to him. "But practicing for what?" Starting the car, this notion troubles him. "Ronny Bones mentioned a parade. But what do they have to do with each other? And what about the note? Make it big like Little Big Horn big."

He flips back through weeks of surveillance notes. The rec center meetings picking up frequency. New faces showing up. That smug look on Black Cloud's face the last time they spoke.

"He is definitely hiding something. Why go to the rec center to write down your thoughts? Why not do it at home in private? Because it isn't private." He rubs his chin and five o'clock shadow.

"Something bigger is happening here. These aren't random incidents; they're rehearsals. But for what kind of show needs to practice robberies? What are they going to rob?" Talking aloud he puts on a fake smile for the family filing into Sally's.

He starts mapping the incidents on the dashboard tablet in his car: the gift shop at Wounded Knee, the convenience store in Rapid City, the jewelry store in Sioux Falls. Each one following the same bizarre script: polite thieves with water guns who return everything they take.

"What kind of thieves apologize?" he mutters, tapping his pen against the steering wheel. "What kind of thieves bring stuff back? Unless they're not really thieves at all. But practicing like they said. For what?"

He drives home slowly, mind churning through possibilities. Past incidents of Native protests flash through his memory: the occupation of Alcạtraz and Wounded Knee in the 70s. But this feels different. More organized. More staged, like a show with many characters.

At home, he has the television on. A tradition of delusion served with mashed potatoes and a side of sodium. A Hungry Man dinner sits on a tray pulled up to his chair—the same dinner he eats whenever he feels lucky and about to crack a case. Not that he's cracked many, other than petty cases in broad daylight, but he always eats this comforting meal when he does. The preservatives, gooey gravy, turkey meat, and salt help him chew ideas as he eats.

A commercial for the parade plays between segments of the local news, all bright colors and smiling faces. He settles in to eat and grabs his portly, tabby cat Garfield circling at his feet, eyeing his favorite dinner: turkey, mashed potatoes, and gravy. He named him after the cartoon cat because Whiteman prides himself on his creativity and humor.

Between forkfuls, he gets to thinking what he would do if he wanted to disrupt something big. *Little Big Horn BIG.* He starts thinking like an investigator, or at least how TV shows portray investigators: Columbo or Kojak.

"Nope, I have too much hair," he pats the top of his head. "I know, Sherlock Holmes, the greatest of them all. You can be my Watson." He says to the cat, getting a kick out of his joke and chuckles at his wittiness, believing himself to be an equal to those great investigators.

"Always put yourself in the mind of the criminal," he says to his tubular cat meowing to let him lick the fork. Garfield seems unimpressed with the advice but loves licking the fork.

"I would want to disrupt the biggest most glorious show on earth that celebrates this great nation."

The next commercial shows baton twirlers spinning in perfect formation, a marching band stepping high down Fifth Avenue, and a big musical number with dancers in sparkling costumes. A moment later, he lurches forward, the cat flying off his lap with an indignant yowl. Whiteman almost spits out his dinner knocking over the tray.

"That's it!"

He quickly finds his cell phone on the kitchen counter to call his boss. They'll need to mobilize all units to diffuse the situation before it starts. Yet he is only able to leave a message while Garfield claims the fallen dinner.

"Red alert, sir. Red alert. This is Agent Stanley Whiteman. I have cracked a terrorist ring inside the Sioux Reservation and possibly beyond. It may be bigger than Little Big Horn. I have evidence they are going to attack the Macy's Thanksgiving Day Parade. Please sir, call me back immediately. I know who's involved and how to thwart it. We will need to mobilize all personnel!"

Hanging up, satisfied with his message and breathing hard, he awaits the director's call back. He sits back down to finish his meal, picking it up off the floor. The cat sits on the brown tray licking gravy off the turkey, methodically scarfing down as much food as he can before Whiteman takes it away.

A few minutes later his phone rings on the counter. It's his boss. He clears his throat before answering.

"This is Agent Whiteman. Good evening, Director."

"You have something?"

He grabs his notepad lying next to the phone. "Yes, three burglaries with quotes from proprietors stating that perpetrators all stated they were practicing for a show. And an upstanding member of the Sioux tribe confirmed they were going to attack the Macy's Thanksgiving Day Parade."

"Really? Because there is zero intel on this. Do you know these men we're talking about?"

"Yes, I do."

"You can pick them out in a crowd?"

"Yes. Easily."

"Okay look, the parade's tomorrow. I need you on a red eye flight tonight. Understood?"

Whiteman nods proudly, back straightening. This is his shot to finally get his moment in the sun and the respect he deserves, instead of people snickering behind his back in the office. He gives a thumbs up to Garfield who ignores him while licking the remaining edges of the tray.

The director continues, "I'll reach out to the police chief in New York and bring him up to speed. See if I can even get him on the phone with the holiday. I'm sure all sorts of kooks come out of the woodwork and call about the parade. The bureau isn't designed for this type of situation, and we may not be taken seriously. We also do not have an office there. So, contact local officials when you arrive. I'm sure they will be more than helpful. I'll do what I can on this end. What is this evidence you found?"

He grabs it from the bag. "Well, it's a piece of paper that reads, 'Let's make this big. Little Big Horn BIG.'"

"And this has been confirmed by an upstanding member of the tribe?"

Ronny Bones didn't exactly confirm it and isn't exactly upstanding, but he is a member of the tribe.

"Yes, sir," Whiteman holds firm, his need to get Black Cloud gnawing at him over all these years. It could finally be put to rest with Whiteman on top: the better man.

"Not on my watch," the director proclaims.

"Thank you, sir. We're going to get them."

"Good work, Whiteman."

He opens a drawer and stares at a photograph—Gloria is young, smiling at him. The portion of Black Cloud standing beside her is folded behind.

That night, he books a flight out of Sioux City that will arrive in the morning. He reserves a rental car from LaGuardia Airport. His aunt will watch the cat. This is the big break he's been looking for, to make a name for himself and finally get revenge on Black Cloud: the man who stole the love of his life and, and in his mind, let her die.

EIGHTEEN

The Night Before

It's the Wednesday night before the parade, and they sleep at their respective hideouts scattered across the Eastern Seaboard like pieces of an elaborate puzzle: at campgrounds, in pickup trucks at interstate rest areas, old vans parked along the Hudson River, and in campers with pop ups at KOAs.

All members of Operation Sunup are accounted for, scattered throughout the tri-state area, and all are within a two-hour striking distance of Manhattan. What started as Black Cloud's vision has grown into an intricate web of allies and accomplices. Tribes that once warred with each other now share coffee at midnight diners, pass messages along during gas station stops, and keep watch over each other's safety. Connections and networks have been forged in the past year, friendships growing stronger than old grudges.

Hundreds are involved in ways large and small: from the Mohawk construction workers who've hidden equipment in building sites, to the Cherokee family running a food truck that's been mapping police patterns, to Chickasaw and Seminole braves on foot patrol the night before scouting the locations and parade route.

But only a few dozen will participate in tomorrow's main event. The rest will serve as eyes and ears, getaway drivers, lookouts—a supporting cast in a play centuries in the making.

At a rest stop off I-95, Pete and Sam place shirts on the windows of Pete's green Trailblazer to block out the parking lot lights. Late in the night, Samuel snores in the back, his medicine pouch rests on his chest, the only thing he kept of his father's.

Unable to sleep, the picture of Pete's grandson sways back and forth after releasing it from his hand. Disrupted by the rumbling snores coming from his friend, he mutters, "This guy is out like a light, and I can't sleep a wink. Sleeping and snoring for the both of us." He checks Samuel in the rearview mirror. Pete's nose flairs with all the racket.

"No wonder your wife left you. She put up with this for eighteen years and I've only been with you for a few nights."

On top of the truck, a CB antenna bristles from its roof like a porcupine's quill. He listens quietly for any relevant chatter.

Three sharpshooters from three different tribes—including Denni from the Ojibwa, Scott the Laser from Lummi, and Mack the Attack from Seneca—have tucked their camper into a Connecticut campground, bows hidden under fishing gear. Denni lays on the small bed in the rear while the other two fight for who gets the top bunk three feet away.

She types out a text message to TJ but doesn't send it. Instead, she closes her hand around the phone and shuts her eyes.

Old vans line the Hudson River just outside of New York City, looking abandoned but housing warriors who've traveled a thousand miles for tomorrow. Even a few train cars in a Queens switching yard hold sleeping braves, the clicking rhythm of the tracks covering their presence.

After driving for most of the night, Crystal and the Toms stay at a motel in adjacent rooms, tired from the road.

"I need a shower," she says as they say their exhausted good-nights.

Tall Tim and Black Cloud sleep in the truck at a KOA campground. As teens, they used to camp together under the stars. These same stars have recorded all of human history.

At midnight, Thanksgiving Day arrives and with it the somber Day of Mourning. What began one morning in 1970 to commemorate the landing of the Mayflower, a Wampanoag leader named Frank Wamsutta James was set to speak at a state dinner. The celebration was to perpetuate the oversimplified myth of harmonious Pilgrim-Wampanoag relations centered around that first Thanksgiving feast.

The committee had asked to review his speech to screen its content. Wamsutta had written a scathing indictment of the pilgrims, describing how they desecrated Native American graves, stole food and land, while decimating their population with disease.

His speech was to tear down centuries-old stories that were outright lies and expose the atrocities buried within them. The committee deemed the speech inflammatory and inappropriate, and it was outright rejected. He was given a revised speech maintaining the old tall tales.

He refused to read it. Instead, he stood on the dais not speaking a word. The day was not designed to become a lasting protest. Yet afterwards, his supporters followed him to give his original speech at Cole's Hill, where a statue of Ousamequin, a former Wampanoag leader, stood. This became the first official National Day of Mourning in America.

Yet, halfway across the globe, starting January 26, 1938, a celebration of Australia's "progress" and a National Day of Mourning for Australia's Aborigines takes place.

The story is not new. It is seared into the cells of indigenous people all over the world.

And on this day, Black Cloud and his eccentric band will carry it into the future no further.

At 3:30 a.m. Black Cloud wakes up alert, mind empty for the first time in months as if thoughts have drained out of him. With no anxiety about the coming day, no worries, no thoughts at all, his mind is quiet like a placid lake at sundown: the downloads from the spirit world are complete. But in the nothingness, he lays in the camper next to Tall Tim and begins to feel alone as if the spirits have abandoned him on this vital day.

Restless, needing to get up and move, Black Cloud crawls out while Tim sleeps with a strange smile on his face. Outside it's chilly. The campground is mostly empty this time of year except for a few RVs scattered about.

While building a small fire in the firepit, a chant enters his mind from some distant place and time.

Quietly at first, he hears it like a prayer from a radio growing louder: "Hiya, hiya, hiya, hey, hiya, hiya, hiya, hey, hiya, hiya, hiya, hoya, hiya hoya, hoya, hoya."

He doesn't know what it means and may be getting some of the words wrong, but the intent is there, and it feels good flowing through him. Feels strong in his body. The words hang in the cold air, the fire swaying along with them.

It is an ancient war chant of the Great Sioux Nation and of their unconquerable spirit. His right foot begins to tap then the left.

His feet move up and down in place, as he chants quietly along: "Hiya, hiya, hiya, hey, hiya, hiya, hiya, hey, hiya, hiya, hiya, hoya, hiya hoya, hoya, hoya."

As the words flow up from his gut, he slowly circles the fire, raising his hands up and down in rhythm. Whispering the chant so only the fire may hear him and not bring any unwanted attention.

Moving around more carefree turning and spinning drawn in by the dancing flames and ancient words, he picks up a spear-like stick and dances the warrior's dance.

Cloud is still in his trance when Tall Tim steps out of the truck and stands with arms crossed. He watches at first, mesmerized, and listening.

"What are you singing? You will wake the squirrels with that singing."

Ignored or not heard, "Cloud?" he repeats louder. "Why are you dancing around the fire and singing?"

"Dancing, you fool."

He mocks him in his flat toned voice, "Why? You are not a good dancer."

"Dancing the warriors dance and chanting."

"Oh…can I join?"

Cloud nods while spinning past him. The two friends dance around the fire as warriors.

Afterwards, and out of breath, they sit at the picnic table and drink coffee in silence as cracks of light break the sky's darkness.

Black Cloud's thoughts are now consumed with the parade, logistics, and all the moving pieces. What will happen if it goes wrong? How will they handle unpredictable possibilities, and what will be their fate? So many people are relying on him for this to work. It's prison or worse if it doesn't.

Along with the coffee, he swallows the growing knot in his throat and checks the time on his watch.

Looking up at his lifelong friend, he asks, "Are we really doing this?"

"I suppose, or I'm going back to sleep."

An owl hoots and lands on a nearby branch startling them.

"Oooh they're magical, beautiful birds."

"Okay, that's a sign. We're doing it."

"To crazy old fools," Tim says raising his mug. Cloud does the same. They nod and sip their coffees in peace, resolved. Come what may.

Tom lays in bed wide awake with his hands underneath his head. He's worried about his boy and about what Whiteman said: the threat spinning through his mind, his time in prison, and the repeated locking of his cell door. He shifts positions and presses his head with both hands then looks over at his sleeping son.

"I can't go back," he whispers aloud. "I can't quit on him either. TJ has to know what living a meaningful life is about. A righteous life. What having a man for a father means. Please God. Keep us safe."

His phone lights up on the nightstand between the two beds.

I can't sleep, Crystal texts. *Want to get a coffee at the diner next door? I already checked, they're open.* She adds a smiling face and coffee cup emoji.

"Yes!" he exclaims out loud, then catches himself smiling. He looks over hoping he didn't wake TJ. Letting him sleep longer, Tom slips out into the night to meet Crystal.

She's already outside looking up at the stars. He walks to the end of the parking lot where a long dark field sits before reaching a small house on the other side.

"There are so many stars," she says as he approaches. She takes a moment to look at him. "I've already seen three shooting stars."

"Did you make a wish?"

"Will they come true? I'm tired of things not coming true."

"Well, it can't if you don't make one."

"That's true I suppose." She closes her eyes tightly and clenches her fists.

"You have to feel it in your heart."

She squeezes her fists tighter. "I do."

"Okay, then it must come true."

She opens her eyes and looks at him already holding her gaze. "It had better."

Their eyes linger in the night beneath the glittering universe.

She's bundled up while he's wearing only a T-shirt.

"Don't you get cold?"

He shrugs.

"Well, I can see my breath. See? Hah. Hah." She breathes out to prove it by releasing vapor. "You're making me cold looking at you," she says when a shiver runs through her.

"Come on." Grabbing his hand, she pulls him toward the 24-hour truck stop diner on the other side of the parking lot.

At a booth inside, she blows on her hands as the waitress delivers steaming mugs of hot coffee.

"Cold out there, kids." They smile and half chuckle, enjoying being called kids.

"Thank you, ma'am," Tom says nodding, then grows quiets looking out the window as they enjoy a coffee together.

Crystal takes a sip.

"You're quiet. Sorry if I woke you."

He looks at her and studies her green eyes as if he's looking into her.

"I'm glad to be here with you. I couldn't sleep either." He pauses. "But can I ask you a question?"

"We're just sitting here. Gotta talk about something."

He smiles and takes another sip of the steaming beverage before placing it down.

"Do you believe in second chances?"

"Hmm, I guess so. Tired of carrying this old life around. That's for sure."

He nods. "I was just thinking, what is forgiveness but a second chance?" He pauses again. "I want a second chance, Crystal."

"Hmm, I've never thought of it that way. Well, so do I," she meekly says, then pauses. "I…I was wrong about you, and I'm sorry."

He looks at her then nods. "Thanks. I was wrong about me to," he says with a quick smile on his lips.

They fall silent reflecting on their past choices and what will unfold later today, sipping coffee in the safe space of a new friend. Their fingers brush each other and linger when she hands him the creamer after the waitress fills their second cup. Crystal looks at him with longing then quickly looks away when their eyes meet.

An hour later, cell phone alarms beep in the pre-dawn darkness throughout campgrounds and on the beach alerting warriors to wake in their temporary homes. It's time for the mission to begin. It's time for history to change.

Crystal and Tom look at their phones then up at each other. Quickly, they push out of the booth, leaving a twenty-dollar bill behind as the diner door swings closed.

Across the region, dozens of phones light up with the same message: *It's time. Wakan Tanka kici un: May the Great Spirit Bless you (us).*

While the rest of America will soon preheat ovens and get ready to watch football games, Operation Sunup's warriors wake at 5 a.m. to descend on Macy's, her parade, and the unsuspecting public. From campgrounds to parking lots, rest stops to beaches, they begin moving like shadows toward Manhattan.

Every piece of their plan, every rehearsal, every late-night strategy session has led to this morning. The holiday will never be the same and neither will the nation. Soon, televisions across the country will project the mayhem carrying their message into millions of homes where families gather around turkey, stuffing, and green bean casseroles unaware that their traditional parade is about to get turned upside down.

Morning coffees are had by campfires, some dispensed from rest stop coffee machines serving bad coffee for a buck. Almost everyone is awake before the alarm and message, except for Samuel.

Pete elbows him to wake up.

He stirs, "What? I was dreaming about sweet Marilyn Monroe again."

"Marilyn's going to have to wait. We've got to roll."

Samuel nods and throws the blanket off.

They get out to wash up at the rest stop bathrooms.

Samuel touches the small medicine pouch hanging from his neck and looks up at the sky, then nods to Pete as they walk in. Coffees are in hand on the way out, as they also prepare for the day with caffeine and a silent prayer. Starting the vehicle, Pete pauses before pulling out and kisses his grandson's picture.

All members have something to live and fight for.

At their campground, Denni and the boys finish their coffees and a quick bite of trail mix.

Once tribal enemies, she texts, *Good morning, Thomas. See you soon.*

She looks at the phone waiting for a response, then puts it aside to get ready.

With a handful of trail mix and a coffee in the other hand, she speaks to the guys, "There is no greater cause than this moment. And we won't let them down. Not on my watch, man. Not on my watch. Let's go find TJ and show him and everyone how great we can shoot."

"You like him," Mack the Attack teases.

"Say it again and I'll punch you. Will *you* like that?"

"Well, you still like him," he says quieter.

"Let's focus here, gents."

They put their hands together in solidarity over the fire, feeling the heat rise.

"We will feel that heat today once our mission gets underway. We must have steady hands and sharp eyes like a hawk overlooking a field for mice. We are the hawk today, boys." The other two nod.

She continues, "This will be a day to be remembered. What is life but stepping up when it matters. Think of your lives, our families, the Indian school that so many of our relatives endured and some died at, the murder and theft of our land and culture. What do we live for? Getting by? Hiding? Fuck that! Let's go kick some ass!"

Denni adjusts her green spiky hair under a beanie, her lucky Ramones T-shirt hidden beneath a sensible tourist sweater, which makes her look sweet and demure. That same punk attitude of The Ramones runs through her veins alongside her Native blood.

Remaining pots of coffee are poured on the embers, dousing them. The steam rises up like breath from their ancestors.

A message from TJ is waiting for her when she checks her phone again. *Yup, see you soon,* with a smile emoji and an arrow. She smiles and tucks the phone into her jacket pocket.

"Yup, you like him alright." Mack says while packing up.

She snarls her teeth and squints her eyes.

NINETEEN

Rise and Shine America

All members of Operation Sunup are now in motion. As the sun rises higher, they get moving toward New York City and destiny. Tourists, spectators, and TV personalities are also descending upon the unsuspecting city. The streams of people will provide perfect cover for warriors who've spent months learning to blend in.

In a cramped Harlem apartment, Alex runs his final system checks, three laptops humming like electronic drums.

"Showtime," he whispers, fingers dancing across keyboards, making sure every digital trap door is ready for when they need it.

He exhales slowly watching code run like river currents across his screens. His ancestors rode stallions into battle; today, he rides fiber optics.

Crow scouts position themselves at a subway station, looking like any other morning commuters with tired eyes and coffees in hand, skateboards ready at their feet.

At a bodega near Grand Central Station, two Cheyenne warriors posing as tourists practice their, "Just visiting from Ohio," while ordering egg sandwiches to go.

The lone brave Ben Blackfeather rises with the sun out of the east. He wakes on a New Jersey beach having never been to the ocean before. During the upcoming summer, this beach will be packed, but now it's empty except for two harbor seals resting a hundred yards down after a long swim from Nova Scotia, migrating south. They'll stay for a couple days before moving on. He'll move on before they do.

The day Blackfeather met the four men on the reservation, it was determined that Black Cloud would be his commander in the field. During that brief meeting in the rec center room, he wore a bandana covering much of his face and said, "My friends call me Black."

Tall Tim asked him, "Well, what should we call you?" He glanced around the room at the other men.

He looked them over and thought of past friends who had turned on him, certain events that didn't seem so honorable.

"Just Ben," he said.

Samuel griped, "Well, now we know where we stand with Ben here."

Ben studied him carefully, years of deception making trust a luxury he couldn't afford.

"Sometimes I have found it's better not to stand so close."

On a motorcycle, you can outride them for a short while, but they catch up to you eventually and remind you. Even when movement has ceased, you're alone to wrestle with what you and others have done.

Over the years after leaving the Army, he learned breathing and meditation exercises to quiet his mind and find some peace. The missions he ran, the intelligence he gathered, taught him that nothing is as simple as "us versus them." Both sides in war are not often as clearcut as the commanders would have you believe. Events still flash through his mind, unresolved, like surveillance photos he can't quite bring into focus or forget.

Stripping down to wearing only green boxer shorts on this remote beach, he runs at full speed for a hundred yards to raise his body temperature and knock off the chill. Then he does a hundred jumping jacks. After, he strips the remaining piece of cloth to stand naked with the elements of the earth, sea and sun, in purity, with all that is and all that will ever be.

Running and kicking up the sand, he dives into the frigid waters of the Atlantic for his soul's purification. The cold hits him like a thousand knives, his body instantly revolts against the shock, wanting him to jump out.

Training kicks in: control the gasping, control your breath, master the panic cold water triggers. Letting out a warrior's cry that's half celebration, half defiance, he forces himself to dive deeper into the dark waters. Pressure from the cold increases around him. He pushes through another stroke, then another one down, each movement a prayer through the past and anger, through acceptance and release, seeking hope and faith. Through the pressure, cold and darkness, he presses against it harder not giving in, knowing this battle is not won by compromise. He screams in the water to let it go, to let him go.

After another sixty seconds, his muscles ache and his fingers start to lose feeling. His chest and lungs squeeze from the pressure like an unforgiving vise he entered into unknowingly. This is no place for ego or bravado; the ocean demands respect but can reward it equally as well.

Rising out of the water feeling reborn like a breaching porpoise, "Woo Holy Hoo!" he shouts as his body releases the shocking cold's intensity. With shortness of breath, he emerges from the ocean shaking but grinning, his skin burning with cold as he runs for the towel. The brief immersion has done its work. Sometimes the most powerful ceremonies are the shortest. His military training taught him about survival in bitter conditions, but his Apache heritage taught him about the power of ritual, no matter how brief, can be the most transformative.

He slowly turns to face the sun and lets it warm his body. The rising sun warms him as it warms all of Mother Earth's creatures.

After drying off vigorously and pulling on layers of warm clothes, he settles into meditation on the sand, trying to calm his mind while the cold nips at its edges, far enough from the water's edge to feel the weak November sun.

Fifty feet away, seagulls huddle against the morning chill, eyeing this strange human who just emerged from their unforgiving ocean. The closest house sits a half mile away, smoke curling from its chimney like sacred tobacco rising to the sky.

They say the ocean never stays still as it swirls around the globe bringing nutrients and life. Ben doesn't either. Everything is in motion. The blood of a man circles the body the way the ocean circles the earth. You've got to keep moving, he believes, or you start dying by getting stuck in time and ideas. Stuck in the past. His brief dance with the frigid Atlantic has sharpened his focus for what's coming. A cold plunge was needed to awaken his senses.

Up the wooden staircase, his motorcycle awaits parked in the lot under a tree. Invigorated and alive from his ocean baptism, Ben

Blackfeather fires up his rumbling beast, hops on, and heads north. The beach disappears from his mirrors, but the clarity of purpose remains deep in his soul driving him north into the devil's den. The most intense events bring the clearest vision. This isn't Kabul, yet it is a battle centuries in the making—and one they must win.

It drizzled overnight with clouds that now hang low like wet laundry from a sagging clothesline. But as morning strengthens, the clouds begin to separate, letting the early morning sun warm the streets of Manhattan.

Ben Blackfeather rides his motorcycle over the George Washington Bridge then down along the Hudson River on the West Side Highway. The only song he can think to play is the protest song, "Born to Be Wild." He can't think of a more fitting song for himself or the mission. Where else had the tribes descended from but freedom and wildness? The song blasts on full volume from his motorcycle speakers for any drivers or nearby apartments to hear. He is certainly out there looking for adventure, as the song says. His long black hair flows behind the helmet and waves upon the buffeting wind.

Ben guides his bike through the awakening city, still charged from his ocean ritual and grateful for his heated grips. The sun casts beams between buildings; rainwater burns off the damp streets as steam ascends like a ghost dance—a dance to reunite the spirits of the living and the dead.

Manhattan Island was once native itself, where the Lenape tribe hunted, fished, and camped. For generations, they moved with the seasons across this island of hills and streams, following the rhythms of earth and sky. Famously, they "accepted"—more like persuaded—to leave for $21 worth of beads, though the concept of "selling" land would have seemed as foreign to them as selling the air or the sunrise. Native peoples didn't understand ownership; as far as they were concerned, no one owned the earth. The ground beneath these skyscrapers was merely something to be shared, tended to, and respected.

Ben guides his motorcycle through streets built on someone else's hunting grounds, past buildings worth millions that sit on land that was "bought" with a handful of trinkets. Where deer once grazed, yellow cabs now honk their impatience. Where medicine plants once grew, hot dog vendors stake their territory. Today, those glass beads will be paid back with interest, not in money or blood, but in truth.

Leaving his bike in a parking garage near the Port Authority, he walks over to meet Alex, just outside the massive bus depot on 8th Avenue. The dirt and grime of New York are a far cry from the cleansing New Jersey beach.

TWENTY

The Big Show

The crowd gathers, filling the sidewalk in front of Macy's along 7th Avenue and 34th Street. Several blocks from where Chip Wegney will stand on stage, the floats are lining up. Preparations began last night at the annual balloon inflation, where crowds watched Macy's massive characters come to life under floodlights along Central Park West.

Now, at 7 a.m.—two hours before the official start—two-and-a-half miles of parade route unfolds into managed chaos. Fifty balloon handlers per character take their positions, each trained to handle the massive inflatables that stand up to six stories high. Marching bands from across the country warm up in designated zones, while dancers stretch in front of store windows and down quiet alleys.

The parade itself is a monument to American commercialism. Each float and balloon represent millions in sponsorship deals. Macy's spends upwards of $11.5 million to produce the spectacle but earns it back several times over. Over fifty million viewers will tune in today, making it one of the most-watched events of the year. Corporate America's annual tribute to itself, dressed up as holiday tradition.

The manic morning unfolds as New York City comes to life with car horns, jack hammering due to a sewer main break, buses, people, smells, food vendors, subways, and the eternal whiff of urine. The beehive is buzzing all right.

Operation Sunup is underway. The attack team parks on the outskirts of the city, riding trains, buses, and subways in. Delivery vans and logistics crews have already swept through earlier in the morning, planting gear and materials in designated sites.

Black Cloud and Tall Tim ride the PATH Train in from New Jersey dressed as warrior chiefs with war paint and headdresses. They'll take a different route out if they make it that far.

Moving through Penn Station's vast corridors into the bowels of Manhattan's frenzied rush, they navigate through rivers of people flowing in all directions. Some groups of people are like rocks they bump into and need to move around. Some flow along with them.

Never thinking it could be so big, Tall Tim mutters under his breath, "I'm a little scared."

They walk past a muscular man with a tribal tattoo and bones through nose.

Tall Tim double takes and whispers to Cloud as they pass him, "Um, I don't think that man knows what the symbol means. 'Uh, love is like a varmint.' Should I tell him?"

"No…let's stay focused."

He nods, skipping a step as he stumbles while looking over his shoulder.

"We have to find the subway. Which one again…?"

Tall Tim checks a note from his back pocket.

"The Number One subway. It's red."

"Great. 'To Subway,'" Cloud points to a sign. "Come on."

They enter into another corridor and then head down a flight of stairs where hip-hop music plays from a speaker. Breakdancers spin and twist in practiced rhythm. A small crowd gathers around the four dancers who wear colorful shirts and pants that hang below their bottoms.

After a minute, Cloud, anxious to move, looks at his watch and the two men agree they need to keep moving. Tall Tim leaves a dollar in their collection hat. One of the dancers nods at him as he dives back onto the floor to do the worm.

"They are very good. He dances better than you." Tim smacks his friend on the shoulder and smiles as they walk off.

Cloud agrees as they search for the right subway and wait on the platform.

As it pulls up Tim says, "That's not red."

"Well, the number's red."

"No, the symbol's red. The number's white."

Cloud shrugs.

"It's silver and dirty like all the others. I would prefer a red train," he says as it rumbles to a stop.

"What does it matter? Get on."

"I like red," he says as they watch the gap heeding the words of warning played on the platform speakers above. Hopping on, they merge with the other converging humans. They are shoved in and jostled about; people lean and breathe on each other in the packed early morning car.

As the bell dings alerting passengers to the closing doors, the subway begins moving. The conductor speaks over the PA. Struggling to understand, they lean their heads to hear.

"I can't understand her," Tall Tim reveals, grabbing onto a clammy metal pole.

"I don't think anyone can." Cloud can't help it but leans onto a woman reading as the train begins moving.

"How will we know when to get off?"

Cloud looks out the car windows. "Look, the stops are written on the tile walls." he points through the car window. "And on the map next to car door."

Relieved, Tall Tim's shoulders relax. "It's just one stop on the map. So, when the doors open, we get out." He nods proudly figuring it out.

Cloud nods his stoic look that matches the serious visage of the traditional war chief.

The train rolls, bounces and bobs around a bend. Their headdresses almost brush the top of the subway car as they lean onto strangers, no one seeming to mind. Just part of living in the city.

Tall Tim gawks and can't stop his head from swiveling.

"I'm exhausted just looking at all these people," he says. "So many sets of eyes, and all so different. Different hairstyles. Maybe I should do something cool with my hair. Dye it or spike it maybe."

"Probably," Cloud says, also overwhelmed by the spectacle of New York. Every sense taking in so much.

A few subway riders look at them: two American Indians dressed like warrior chiefs with paint and headdresses. Tired eyes stare briefly from vacant expressions, looking up from books, eyes over newspapers, or heads bobbing slightly beneath headphones tuning out the audible world. New Yorkers have seen it all, and, well, it is Thanksgiving after all. Even if it wasn't, these two chiefs could be part of a play, a troupe, or well, just a couple of Native American chiefs vising New York City like everyone else. Nothing unusual.

The plan is to first ride up to Times Square playing the part of wide-eyed tourist—a calculated diversion that would both expose any potential surveillance and offer them a chance to disappear into the crowds if needed. If a tail is spotted, the event would have to be scrapped.

Afterall, they did just travel all the way here. No reason to go up to Times Square if on their way to Macy's and her parade. Nope, they are just tourists in New York City, with a plan.

As they clear the subway entrance and exit into the daylight, they nod to the Crow scout on the sidewalk next to the entrance. He is waiting for their arrival. The tide of humanity sweeps them into Times Square as they step into the noise, lights, massive TV displays, chaos, and people on 42nd Street.

The scout makes sure they aren't followed and waits until they are a block away. *Clear*, he texts, then flips his skateboard into his hand and drops it onto the sidewalk in front, skating away and jumping off the next curb.

Christmas music plays from somewhere, everywhere it seems. Decorations are up in most stores and on lamp posts, teasing Black Friday deals. Intoxicated by New York, Tall Tim smiles at Santa in the windows and sings along with Rudolph.

"I love Rudolph. But who doesn't, right?" he says to anyone within earshot. Keeping close, he tries not to gawk at everything like the tourist he's supposed to be pretending to be.

As they walk into Times Square, the sensory assault is almost overwhelming: sausage, onions and peppers, hot dogs, car fumes, cigarettes, coffee. Every step takes them deeper into the canyon of buildings and the alluring fragrance of NY. The Square itself hits them like a fever dream, with massive screens flashing advertisements in every direction, the noise, the crush of bodies, the sheer vertical scale of it all making their reservation seem like another world.

Like so many tourists on this festive day heading over to the parade, they wear costumes. But for them, their disguises are to hide their identities, not to indulge in frivolity like so many. Tucked in their belts are plastic gray tomahawks.

A few people give them thumbs up.

One guy walking with his buddy almost bumps into them, and says, "Hey, it's the Village People."

Tall Tim looks at the man and says, "Yes, we are from a village." Then nods at Black Cloud, who rolls his eyes, having understood the reference to the musical group.

Strolling deeper into the heart of Times Square, they stare at the flashing lights and giant television screens; billboards the size of buildings. With their jaws dropped, they spin around in overwhelmed surprise. Black Cloud notices how many police are stationed here, their faces tense with parade-day vigilance and an everyday edge.

"Um, this is very different than home," Tall Tim stammers. "The largest television there is fifty inches." He keeps turning in circles, nearly stepping on a guy sitting on a blanket selling CDs of his music. "Whoa, sorry."

Black Cloud nods at the grandeur, but his mind is already mapping escape routes, counting uniforms, noting which buildings match their intelligence reports.

They open the map and begin strolling south along 7th Avenue.

Tall Tim says, "This way, but I'm starving."

Black Cloud shoots him a look. "Are you serious? We just had breakfast. At a time like this you're thinking about food?"

"Come on, Cloud. The smell is irresistible," he says. The smell of hot honey-roasted peanuts lures him over to a street vendor. But first he must dart and weave around the sea of pedestrians, nearly colliding with a Japanese family taking selfies.

Black Cloud notices the cops standing on the street corners and on their beat, walking the pavement. Tom Sr. had warned them about the NYC police force being the size of some country's armies.

"Be quick about it," Black Cloud barks, looking at them and then his wristwatch.

One cop stares at Black Cloud as he passes him. Cloud half smiles, but the cop doesn't and just keeps on walking. He waits for Tall Tim while traffic and people edge past.

Tall Tim sidles back over, shoving his face into the little wax bag. He takes one out and pops it into his mouth like candy.

"Oh, so delicious and warm," he says in between bites, speaking and munching.

"Great, let's go. We have a job to do."

"Come on, try one."

"No time. Let's go already."

"Oh, be quiet. There's always time," he says and shoves one into Black Cloud's mouth. He chews and nods as they continue walking south toward Macy's.

The closer they get, the denser the crowd becomes: parade-goers mixing with commuters, tourists pausing for photos, and vendors setting up their carts. Security presence increases.

The crowd grows thicker with each block. Parents hoist children onto shoulders, tourists jockey for better viewing positions, and vendors do brisk business in everything from pretzels to parade programs.

Up ahead, they can see the floats being positioned, bright colors visible through the gaps between buildings. The police presence intensifies—uniformed officers on every corner, plainclothes detectives trying to look inconspicuous, while security teams check credentials at barricades.

Tim and Cloud look at each other nervously knowing that an hour earlier, outfits and supplies for the sharpshooters and the attack team were placed in locations by delivery teams in vans. These delivery teams then left the city. This happened all over from the Lower East Side to Midtown to Chinatown and Chelsea.

Samuel and Bull Nose Pete came in together on the east side riding a commuter bus after leaving their car at a Park and Ride outside of the city. As they make their way toward their positions, they move south along Lexington Avenue parallel to Tim and Cloud—who are only a few avenues over—with a careful nonchalance they've practiced for months.

Tom and Ben Blackfeather separately planned out the attack phase with intel for the ground troops, braves, and sharpshooters. Ben and Tom work individually through Black Cloud while both remaining anonymous to the other.

Tom and Crystal walk with TJ until they're a block away on 35th Street. Laughing with a newfound ease together, they keep finding reasons to brush against each other and smile, looking in a storefront window or pointing at a building. It's still new, this thing between them, steadying their nerves made more intense by the morning's danger and clamor they've entered; they need to rely on each other.

Tom Sr. says to his son, "Be careful. Do your job and leave. We'll be waiting for you at the rendezvous point. You have your map and location? Your group is in place?"

TJ nods, pauses, then says confidently, "All twelve of us, we're the best there is." He knows how good his team can shoot. He raises an eyebrow and smiles, shaking his head, seeing his father stand closer to Crystal than necessary. Her usual toughness softens when she looks at him.

His father nods. Crystal rubs TJ's arm—the gesture carrying more warmth than her bar days would have allowed.

The attack group will be embedded within the crowd. The sharpshooters will be just outside of it along the perimeter in a crescent shape formation.

This is where Crystal and Tom Sr. leave to be tourists. If asked, they *are* a couple.

Denni with her green spikey hair, stands a dozen feet away. She doesn't ask too many questions, the less she knows the better; she only knows the man as Tom's dad and not part of the operation. She thinks he's just a tourist with his girlfriend dropping him off.

Before they part, Tom Sr. says to him, "They'll be plenty of time to watch it on the news later. Just do your job and get out of there."

Crystal gives TJ a kiss on the cheek.

"Okay."

Denni shouts, "Let's go Thomas!"

Tom Sr. looks at his watch. "Remember where to meet us—and be careful."

TJ nods, looking at a note from his pocket on where to meet them and how to get there.

Denni steps closer and slaps him on the back, smiling and says, "I just love parades. Don't you?"

TJ smiles and nods, walking off with her. From a secret location nearby, they will pick up backpacks with outfits and foldable crossbows inside.

Crystal and Tom Sr. leave them in front of a building with scaffolding up half its brick face.

Their hands find each other as they disappear into the crowd, just another couple enjoying the parade.

From his cramped Harlem apartment, Alex does one final equipment check, his fingers traveling over each component like a musician before a concert. Three laptops, backup drives, the custom code he's spent months perfecting, are all packed carefully into what looks like an ordinary duffel bag. The computer that will help broadcast their message to millions sits innocently between his MacBook and a copy of *Acting for Professionals*.

An identical computer will be awaiting him in a storage place down the road. He will store this bag and pick up a smaller one in order to leave no physical trail. Doing his best to negate any tracking software and erase any web footprints, he inserts a flash drive and uploads the codes then deletes them after double checking they are secure on the portable drive. Shutting the computers down the way a painter would close up his paints case, he packs up his few belongings then looks around at the studio apartment.

Walking over to the window, he peers down at the waking city. Somewhere down there, thousands of people are already lining up for a parade that's about to come off with a bang! Being Nez Perce and gay has taught him plenty about wearing masks, about playing roles. Today he'll play his biggest part yet as he speaks through the window to the many as if on a stage.

"Academy Award worthy, and one not to be forgotten: Alex Fortune. Yay!"

He reluctantly locks up the apartment after having grown fond of it and the neighborhood. Dropping off his duffel bag at the storage place near the 125th Harlem train station, he spots the black backpack waiting inside the locker. Inside is the computer he will need to pull this off without a trace.

He boards a bus heading south on Madison Avenue. Like any actor worth his salt, he uses the commute to get into character and psyche himself up.

"I'm an amazing actor and can't wait to perform today for my greatest role ever," he repeats it again, just loud enough for nearby passengers to hear. His nerves are real, but so is his excitement being a part of something meaningful—just a struggling actor heading to his big break.

A lady sitting diagonally across catches his enthusiasm, raises her eyebrows with the excitement that tourists reserve for aspiring performers.

She leans over to her balding husband and whispers, "He's an actor..." Her husband barely nods, more interested in the construction site passing by his window, while the bus engine groans on through Manhattan's morning traffic.

Alex uses the slow journey downtown to run through his mental checklist one more time. The flash drive sits in a zippered pocket. He checks the bag on the floor for the piece of equipment he has chosen carefully, nothing that would raise suspicion if searched. The real power is in the code itself, lines of programming that look innocent enough until combined in just the right way.

Satisfied, he watches the city scroll past his window: early morning delivery trucks, tired night shift workers heading home, excited kids already wearing parade gear. None of them know they're about to be part of history. None of them know *their own* history. They are about to. A few people dressed as pilgrims walk down the sidewalk heading into a subway entrance.

Ben and Alex meet and set up a couple blocks away at a coffee shop; it's one of those generic places that cater to locals only, no flare for incoming tourists. Even though the city is vast, there are pockets of neighborhoods all over it.

They sit on barstools along a window counter that looks out onto the busy street, appearing to any observer like old friends catching up before the parade.

Alex says under his breath so only Ben can hear him, "With the right equipment and codes, you can hack into anything."

"I'm glad you're on our side." Ben hands him a steaming cup of black coffee, then sips from his own macchiato with whipped cream. For someone who just swam in the Atlantic, he's looking remarkably composed. A cold plunge in the ocean will do that.

After inserting the flash drive, the computer boots up in the clamor of the restaurant. Alex says under his breath, "I am a homosexual actor and Native American. Hello, New York City. You've heard of Navajo Code Breakers? Well, you are about to meet a gay Nez Perce computer hacker."

"That's a lot to put on a business card," Ben says, slapping him on the back as Alex brings up the server to begin typing. He hits some keys and functions typing in additional codes that will disrupt the system once the transponder is in place for the open feed.

Alex's fingers move across the keyboard with practiced precision, each keystroke part of a dance he's rehearsed for months. Lines of code scroll across his screen, looking like gibberish to anyone glancing over his shoulder but containing the power to hijack one of the biggest broadcasts of the year. Next to him, Ben sips his macchiato and plays his part: just a friend waiting for the parade to start.

"Testing connection," Alex mutters, more to himself than Ben. The coffee shop's Wi-Fi isn't ideal, but that's part of the plan. Once

Black Cloud's team places the transponder, they'll have all the bandwidth they need.

Alex looks up at Ben and nods finally taking a sip from his black coffee.

Ben texts an encrypted message to Black Cloud, *It's go time.*

TWENTY-ONE

And So It Begins

9:00 a.m.

Uptown along Central Park West, the parade begins. Handlers grip balloon ropes as giant characters begin their slow lumbering dance above the streets of Manhattan. The first marching band strikes up an exploding rhythm. Sounds from the horns and drums fill the air as their brass instruments gleam in the morning light. Performers in elaborate costumes do last-minute stretches while float drivers rev their engines. Years of choreographed traditions are about to collide with centuries of suppressed history.

The first floats and balloons should arrive in front of Macy's at approximately 9:30. At street level, the crowd presses against barricades, parents already lifting complaining children onto shoulders for better views. The air is dense with so many onlookers pressing in. Tangy perfumes and cologne spread from underneath winter jackets and scarves. Lines of hot pretzel and hot dog vendors are ready to serve the masses.

NYPD officers patrol their assigned zones, some mounted on horses, others walk the crowd perimeter with practiced indifference, often blowing on their hands to stay warm. Above them, snipers take their positions on pre-selected rooftops, watching the parade route through rifle scopes and eyeing any suspicious movement.

Operation Sunup's members embed themselves within this carnival-like atmosphere. Their ancient feuds dissolved in service to something greater.

Now they work together placing equipment in pre-arranged spots. Arapaho scouts, whose ancestors would have died before trusting a Pawnee, now share hand signals with their former enemies. Cheyenne and Crow, Nez Perce and Blackfeet—ancient boundaries and old squabbles dissolved by a common purpose. Even the Iroquois Confederacy sent warriors, their traditional role as peacekeepers between nations is now serving the greater good.

"If the winds of time cannot take our differences away, nothing can," they had reminded each other during months of preparation. The true enemy isn't white or red, but a closed heart that perpetuates injustice and suffering.

They shook hands from the plains to the sea. "We will be enemies no more."

All of them carry the same prayer: that today will mark the end of being invisible as they demand equal dignity upon this national stage. The suffering of the innocent must end.

When Black Cloud and Tall Tim arrive in front of Macy's, the crowd is already ten people deep, stretching down 34th Street as far as the eye can see. It's a perfect spot for them to blend in and wait for the clandestine attack to unfold. Several spectators are also dressed like American Indians or Pilgrims, so it's easier for them to blend in then fade away like a morning's rain after the sun comes out and warms the earth. If they make it that far.

The sidewalks pulse with holiday energy; children are wrapped in winter coats and perched on parents' shoulders, tourists clutch phones and parade programs. Black Cloud and Tall Tim draw the occasional curious glance, but in New York's fevered chaos, they go unnoticed.

The Herald Square streets feel like canyons of steel and glass: buildings pressing in from all sides. Posh department store windows gleam with Christmas displays, while corporate logos above blaze against the morning sky. NYPD officers stand at their posts, bomb-sniffing dogs weave through the growing crowd. In the distance, the first sounds of marching bands drift down, the sound echoing off the buildings like gunfire.

The buildings are taller than anything they had ever seen before. Taller even than the South Dakota sky. Leaning backwards, they can hardly see the building tops.

Black Cloud looks around and says, "I prefer the rez." Tall Tim studies the urban maze of the map they'll need to navigate if things go wrong. The nearest exit routes are already crowded with parade-goers and television trucks.

Tall Tim agrees looking up at him, "Sure, but this place is amazing."

After wedging into the crowd a few more steps, Tall Tim says, "The air don't taste right though. In fact, one shouldn't be able to taste the air. Crunchy. Nothing sweet about it except for those honey roasted peanuts."

Black Cloud barely hears him, caught between scanning the

crowd for their team and rehearsing escape plans in his head. Every few seconds, another police officer walks past, their radios crackling with parade logistics. Sweat beads under his headdress; they could get trapped in this foreign land.

Black Cloud feels like Little Wonder looking up and almost falls backwards turning and staring up at the Empire State Building looming over them.

He thinks about his sister, niece, and nephew back home who are likely ready to sing and dance with the parade's start. He apologizes to them over the wind, hoping they will learn to understand and forgive him. Especially if the operation falls apart and they get caught and sent to prison—or worse: get shot and killed. He couldn't forgive himself if that happened. His soul would get trapped here.

He shakes the negative thoughts away and focuses on the plan at hand and asks for guidance, "Please mama, ancestors, guide us. Don't let us fail."

A boy standing next to them looks up and says, "How," and raises an open hand facing out. His mother quickly pulls his hand down, muttering embarrassed apologies.

Tall Tim bends slightly and raises his hand, "How what? I don't know, you tell me." Then laughs to himself, the humor helping to settle his nerves.

The boy looks at him with confusion like that isn't how the conversation is supposed to go. His mother hurries him deeper into the crowd.

Tall Tim glances at Black Cloud then shrugs. Blending in with the onlookers, Black Cloud stands next to a woman on her tippy toes trying to get a better angle and see the platform where Chip Wegney will be speaking from and performing. She spots Black Cloud dressed in regal attire, sunglasses, and war paint. He stands six feet tall, almost seven with the headdress.

"Look at that magnificent Indian with feathers and war paint," she says to a friend.

Her friend smiles up at him.

"Chief, can we take your picture?"

He loves being called this and does his best deep proud voice, shakes his head, and says, "No pictures. Steals souls." Then he looks solemnly away with arms crossed.

"Oh, sorry. We didn't mean any offense." The women cower into one another while looking up at his towering presence.

Black Cloud responds in his regular voice looking at them and laughs, "Nah, I'm just kidding. Of course you can." He winks, and smiles, and the women laugh too. He isn't used to such warm smiles from white women. Usually, he receives a distrustful glance at stores in Rapid City and Sioux Falls.

"We're taking pictures with a real life Indian! Oops, I mean Native American," the woman announces, drawing a few glances from nearby spectators.

A broad-shouldered Italian man from Long Island with black hair and a mustache stands with his young kids and gives him a thumbs up.

With a New York accent he says, "Lookin' good, Chief."

Black Cloud shrugs, then looks sternly and solemnly crossing his arms for one picture with the women, then smiling broadly for the next. He loves the attention and tries the same joke where Tim's failed, "How," he raises his palm and laughs. "How what?" he says and shrugs laughing, "How come no one ever asked for my picture before?"

The two women laugh along with him. Production lights surrounding the stage brighten and with the final sound check, speakers crackle alive.

"One, two. One, two."

Black Cloud sees Tall Tim motioning subtly; it's time to move. With a final regal nod to his impromptu fan club, he steps deeper into the crowd, letting the flow of bodies hide him from view. The real show is about to begin.

Black Cloud refocuses on the parade. The plan is to let it get underway by a half hour. This way they can scope out the police positions and alter their plans, if need be, as Tom Sr. and Ben had suggested. He checks his phone; it's 9:02 a.m.

Chip is thin and handsome with short sandy hair and baby blue eyes. He wears a long black leather jacket and welcomes the crowd and viewers at home as he struts across the stage, waving his hand. Music begins playing as he thrusts his hips from left to right. The song playing is his last big hit "Dance Your Boots Off." Wearing black leather boots and with a handkerchief in his jacket breast pocket, he sings and dances his way across the stage spinning and gyrating, ending with his signature up-on-his-toes move.

After product placements and commercial breaks, a dozen or so of the Operation Sunup team disperse throughout the crowd. The various warriors are in position. The twelve sharpshooters, including TJ and Denni, blend in with maintenance workers and window washers on surrounding buildings. Tom Sr.'s careful planning means each one has a clear line of sight, their equipment hidden in work gear and instrument cases. Crystal and several others mix with the tourists, ready to create strategic distractions, like getting into a fight, if need be.

Samuel and Bull Nose Pete stand near opposite corners of Herald Square, each responsible for coordinating their section of the operation. Runners disguised as program sellers maintain communication between groups.

Black Cloud surveys it all from his position, knowing each person's role as warriors filter through the growing crowd, taking their positions for what's bound to shock the world.

He begins sweating as worry sets in. Looking at his phone again: it's 9:18. His heart rate quickens, and his breathing shortens as the reality of what they're about to do settles in. It is as real as his sister had said, not some show at all. Real people. Real cops. Real consequences if things go wrong.

Through the crowd, he spots more officers arriving, some with dogs, others speaking into shoulder radios. He shoves his heart back down into his chest and clears his head as best he can, remembering his mother's words about becoming a warrior.

"You will do something special, Black Cloud."

Special or get killed, he thinks as the time approaches. The staccato and very loud rhythm of the marching band stomps past, the crowd getting more riled up.

Enthusiastically, Chip croons, "Okay folks, that was amazing. Thank you, Denver Academy. Our first float is now coming your way. So, get ready for the fun." From a block away they can hear more music playing as the marching band fades.

Introducing the first act, Chip spins across the stage, his black leather jacket accenting his moves. The crowd presses forward and children squeal with excitement.

"It's a song from one of your favorite new Broadway musicals: Larry the Dancing Mouse!" He waves his hand and a giant mouse pops onto the stage with him. They begin dancing a choreographed routine that has the crowd cheering. The mouse, with exaggerated movements, jumps onto his own float as it rolls into view, bidding Chip farewell with an oversized mouse hand wave. Chips waves back in return.

Dancers in white skirts wear mouse ears and painted whiskers spin and twirl around Larry, their plastic smiles never wavering as they lip-sync to the pre-recorded track.

The kids on the sidewalk applaud wildly and shout in glee while a thousand phones record the spectacle.

Black Cloud watches it all, thinking how this single float probably cost more than his reservation's annual education budget. All the more reason to attack this spectacle of hypocrisy. His breathing slows knowing this is long overdue.

TWENTY-TWO

Whiteman is Coming

"Good morning, sir," Whiteman says, calling his boss. "I'm stuck on the ground sitting in traffic. Are they ready for us?"

"Stan, I wasn't able to speak with anyone. They must have a million kooks crawling out of the woodwork on this day and someone calling from the BIA must sound just as crazy. You're going to have to take the lead on this."

Stan straightens up in his rental car, the seatbelt straining against his puffed-out chest. This is it. Take the lead. The words ring like divine permission. Finally. The glory, the authority—*it's mine.*

His chance to be the hero. No more mockery from junior agents. No more being passed over for promotions or sneered at by slick recruits with psychology degrees and perfect teeth. And of course, it's his chance to finally put Black Cloud in his place.

"Roger that."

"Stay in touch. I'll fly in this afternoon. And Stan, this better be worth it and not some wild goose chase."

"I assure you, sir, it's not. I'll call you once they're apprehended." They hang up.

He smacks the steering wheel surrounded by cars, music, and exhaust. His enthusiasm quickly turns to frustration.

"Come on, get out of the way!" He slams the steering wheel again and honks the horn desperate to get into the city and catch his man. Other horns join the chorus as traffic inches across the Queensboro Bridge along the east side of Manhattan. His rental car, the cheapest option available at LaGuardia, wheezes in protest at all the stop-and-start motion.

He looks at his watch then calls Black Cloud. It rings and rings and he's forced to leave a message.

"Whatever you're planning, Cloud. Don't do it! Turn back!" He smacks the steering wheel again and hangs up.

"Damn it. Get out of my way you godless heathens!" He shouts with the window partly down.

A tow truck driver sitting in front flips him the bird.

"We're sitting here in traffic when we should be driving!"

From somewhere nearby he hears, "No shit, Sherlock."

The bridge groans under the weight of it all. People begin honking as the wall-to-wall traffic is now at a standstill trying to get across the bridge and into the city. Another mile to go.

The parade is underway.

TWENTY-THREE

A Stolen Show

Black Cloud looks down at his phone, and mutters, "Oh shit. It's Whiteman." Seeing his name come across the screen hits him like a blow to the ribs. That voice from the past, full of blame, grief, and unfinished business, is now pressing at the edges of this moment. He scans the restless crowd for those beady blue eyes. Is he here? Watching?

Black Cloud swallows hard; his anxiety heightens knowing his old nemesis must be near having not spoken on the phone with him since Gloria died. Cloud knows he's been snooping around and is now scared he found something.

Tall Tim stands next to him but doesn't hear him as he claps along with the music like any other tourist, a smile plastered on his narrow face. But Black Cloud sees how his friend's hands shake like an old man's before each clap.

Black Cloud swallows against his dry throat, needing water, feeling sweat collect under his headdress despite the November chill. All their months of planning come down to these next few moments and the decisions they will make—or not.

Another float glides past, a blur of color and music that Black Cloud barely registers. The baton twirlers spin their silver staffs in perfect unison, followed by a marching band from the blue blood state of Kansas; their crimson and blue uniforms gleam as they high-step down 7th Avenue.

He mutters again with eyes closed, "Please mama, ancestors, guide us. We cannot fail."

Minutes crawl by, each second feeling like an hour. Sweat trickles down Black Cloud's back as he watches the police officers stationed along the route, their hands resting casually upon their holstered weapons.

"Look, daddy, a hawk," a child yells from nearby as one lands on a telephone line just above their heads.

"Huh?" The father looks up while holding his young son's hand. "In New York City? That's so weird. I guess he wanted to see the parade too."

Black Cloud and Tall Tim look at the hawk and then each other. Tall Tim nods at him in encouragement, seemingly knowing his friend's mind.

Recommitted, Black Cloud shakes off the negative thoughts when Tall Tim leans over.

"We have a job to do, Cloud." Tim stares at him unblinking with a seriousness he seldom exhibits.

Cloud nods then glances at his watch: 9:30. At this exact moment, nearly 150 years ago—and eight years prior to Little Big Horn—Custer's 7th Cavalry massacred a Cheyenne village on reservation soil after the commander of Fort Cobb guaranteed their safety. They even flew a white flag of capitulation.

The attack came early in the morning. Black Kettle, known as the peace chief who tried working with the U.S. government, was killed alongside his people. Over one hundred men, women, and children were murdered. The village was then set ablaze.

These stories and others like them are etched in all the warriors' blood as they stand in their somber positions gathered around the platform.

History is always with them.

In 1876, Little Big Horn was a victory for the Sioux, Cheyenne, and Arapaho. But it was the last major victory before the backs of the American Indian were broken by western expansion and an overwhelming army they could not defeat.

Black Cloud remembers his sister's words, "If you're going to do this in the early morning, have the sun at your back." He glances over and sees the sun sparkling between buildings.

He leans over to Tim and says, "We fight now, Timmy. For centuries of oppression, we fight now. For our children, even if we don't make it back. And damn it, we fight for some peace."

"Oh, I love peace," Tim says with his great big smile, crooked teeth and all. This relaxes Cloud and makes him chuckle.

He raises both hands up high to adjust his headdress: the signal they've all rehearsed.

Across the parade route, warriors disguised as tourists, vendors, and maintenance workers take notice and are set in motion.

One scout sees it from his position near a pretzel cart and touches his baseball cap in acknowledgment. Up on the scaffolding, TJ notices his father's subtle nod. Even Crystal, playing tourist with her phone raised to record the parade, shifts her stance ever so slightly and nods.

There's a pause in the activity between floats as the marching band moves along 7th Avenue. All is as it should be. The parade's corporate backers should be happy with their advertising bonanza unknowing that today's parade will not be as advertised.

Black Cloud quickly ponders, *7th Avenue, 7th Cavalry, interesting coincidence*. Encouraged, he now turns to the parade in anticipation.

Down the block, chaos erupts when a Snoopy balloon breaks loose from a cable. The massive black and white beagle lurches sideways in the morning air, twisting its cables, its handlers scrambling to regain control as the crowd gasps. Banging into Macy's storefront just south of the stage, it bounces off the facade where Christmas wreaths and twinkling lights frame windows of million-dollar apartments. Chip Wegney ducks instinctively.

As the handlers battle with the slowly deflating Snoopy, and with the production team distracted, several braves are set to dance out of the crowd toward their target: Disney's sanitized version of Native American history. The Pocahontas float: a pastel fantasy of what white America depicts Native life looked like.

Mechanical woodland creatures peek from behind plastic trees while speakers blast "Colors of the Wind." It's one of Lilyanna's favorite songs from the movie; she used to walk around the house singing it without fully understanding the alienation felt in the lyrics, but knowing the beauty of the earth and berries, rocks and trees. Wanting to be like Pocahontas, but a princess of the prairie.

Atop the float, a half dozen actors in historically inaccurate costumes pose beside a Styrofoam recreation of Plymouth Rock. Wooden pilgrim mannequins stand stiffly around a fake harvest table on the small cabin porch. The actress playing Pocahontas, her costume more Hollywood than history, waves from her perch near a wooden wheelbarrow filled with artificial corn and pumpkins.

The first wave of warriors duck beneath wooden horses and dance out of the crowd, their movements deliberate and practiced as if part of the exhibit. They slide left then right. A dozen braves, six on each side, hop onto the float with fluid grace then fan out into perfect formation. The costumed Disney characters aboard freeze in place, looking at each other with growing confusion, their rehearsed smiles faltering.

The braves continue dancing as the float rolls into the camera's eye and pauses in front of Macy's. The braves stop in perfect unison, march in place, their faces painted with traditional war paint. From quills on their backs, they pull flint tipped arrows, the movement so practiced it looks like part of the dance. The crowd, thinking this is part of the show, claps along appreciatively.

The braves take aim at the wooden pilgrim mannequins. The Disney characters, knowing this isn't part of the scheduled performance, begin backing away. Arrows are released in precise arcs, striking the mannequins in the chest with piercing thuds. Turning and lowering to one knee, sharpened tomahawks are thrown, spinning through the air, whizzing past Pocahontas and her family. Wedging into the wooden shack and splintering the wood, the shack tumbles and crashes to the street below, breaking apart upon impact.

"Whoop Whoop. Hi ya, hi ya, hi ya, hi ya, hi ya," the braves chant in unison, dancing in a circle, their voices rising above the parade music. They move with a warrior's crispness, each step calculated, each motion telling its own story of practiced resistance.

Then, as coordinated as their arrival, they jump from the float and march in line as if it is all part of the show. They drop smoke bombs and disappear back into the crowd to wild applause.

As the song comes to an end and the wrecked Pocahontas float passes by, one tourist is overheard saying near Black Cloud, "Oooh, this is like a reenactment of circling the wagons. What a great idea. I love old westerns."

Another person says, "We've been coming here for years, and Macy's has never done anything like this. I feel like I'm part of it."

The next person over nods and says, "It's interactive."

The pilgrims wave weakly from what's left of their perch, fear having replaced their plastic smiles.

Moving quickly through the crowd to escape, the braves strip off their outer layers with practiced efficiency, latex gloves coming off last. Everything goes into pre-selected garbage cans—some near hot dog stands, others by subway entrances, none used twice. War paint disappears under quick swipes of hand sanitizer. Within minutes, the dozen warriors vanish like fog, replaced by casual tourists checking their phones, buying pretzels, and studying parade programs searching for the next amazing spectacle.

Each warrior implements their practiced escape plan. Under their disguises, they wear ordinary tourist clothes: jeans and sweatshirts, Rangers caps and Giants hoodies. One by one, they duck behind vendor carts and into doorways, emerging moments later as different people entirely.

They spread out to leave the city, leaving it all behind without looking back. Each take their pre-planned route. Some head for subway stations, others for waiting buses. A few merge with the crowd flowing toward Penn Station. In their ordinary clothes, they become invisible—just more faces in New York's endless stream of humanity.

During this uncertainty, the second wave of attack begins. A lone arrow flies true, striking the already wavering Snoopy balloon with surgical precision.

Chip Wegney covers his head and sidles over asking the producer standing off camera, anxiety creasing his Hollywood-perfect face, "Was that an arrow? What's going on here?"

The producer quickly reads through the script while shaking his head. As the producer checks, more arrows stream like confetti from all sides, striking the approaching balloons and sticking into floats lined up along the street. Chip and his producer dive for cover.

The first few balloon strikes seem to do nothing; these massive balloons are built to withstand winter winds and rainstorms. But as more arrows find their marks, the first signs of trouble appear. Small whistles of escaping helium grow into sustained hisses.

The giant green dinosaur balloon, struck in multiple chambers, begins an eerily ungraceful transformation. First its tail starts to droop, then its neck begins to sink, creating a bizarre undulating motion as each compartment slowly loses pressure. The handlers below, trained for wind gusts but not arrow attacks, struggle to compensate as their seventy-foot charge starts to list dangerously to one side.

The dinosaur flaps about, losing air, its short stubby arms are helpless banging into the production lights and cameras, then bumping into buildings, and eventually gets wrapped around a telephone pole and electrical lines.

The crowd's response shifts like waves through the packed streets. Those closest to the action gasp and point upward, phones raised to capture what they think is a balloon gone wrong. Parents lift children higher on their shoulders for a better view. But as the dinosaur continues its ungainly descent, the mood changes. A mix of concern and excitement ripples through the spectators.

"Oh no, it's falling!" a child shouts with delight. "It's farting daddy, just like you." The child looks up innocently and covers his mouth to giggle.

The handlers' growing panic infects the crowd as they begin shouting at each other to pull harder. People begin backing away from the sagging behemoth, creating pockets of chaos in the tightly packed masses. Some push forward for a better video, while others try to retreat, but there's nowhere to go. The crowd has become a shifting, anxious organism, trapped between curiosity and fear.

An officer's radio crackles with urgent requests for backup. Through gaps in the crowd, Black Cloud watches as first responders begin to realize this is no accident. Their hands move to their weapons, eyes scanning lower rooftops as more arrows continue to fly.

Over their radios, panicked reports overlap: "Balloon going down on 34th!" "Multiple arrows, unknown origin!" "Need backup at Herald Square!"

"Did you say arrows?"

"Yes, arrows!" the radio confirms.

"Like bow and arrows?"

"I don't know. I'm a beat cop. I've seen a lot, but I ain't never seen arrows shooting balloons at no damn parade before. So, yes, bows and arrows!"

"Affirmative."

Behind the dinosaur's slow-motion collapse, Toy Story's Rex balloon takes multiple hits. Its once-proud form starts to buckle, first at the neck, then the tail. The handlers strain against their ropes as the massive form begins to drift sideways pulling them as they fight this aerial beast. From side to side like a crazy mosquito, it fizzles out of air and goes dragging along the ground.

Beyond that, Mufasa's majestic shape begins its own transformation, as arrows find their marks in precise succession. Like a lion on the Serengeti, attacked at the neck and hindquarters by trophy hunters. Three mighty balloons, each worth hundreds of thousands of dollars, slowly surrender to gravity and assault.

Chip and his producer scramble for cover beneath the announcer's platform.

"Cut to commercial!" the producer shouts into his headset, but it's too late; this is all going out live. Chip peeks out just in time to see another volley of arrows arc through the morning air, their trajectories too precise to be random.

Mufasa zigzags like a rabid animal before draping over the float behind it and its dancers. People quickly run to help them. Sounds from marching bands up the block still play unaware of the consuming frenzy.

In the mayhem, some of these sagging balloons sink onto parked cars, triggering a cacophony of car alarms that adds to the growing chaos. Sections of the Rex balloon drape across traffic lights while its still-inflated head bobs against a building's third story. Handlers scrambling to maintain control of ropes that now work against them. The partially deflated balloons become unwieldy sails in the gusting November winds.

Smoke bombs attached to the next wave of arrows land and detonate, creating a thick cloud that begins to fill the street level space. Chaos spreads in the streets as people choke on the carbon dioxide.

Unfolding crossbows emerge from knapsacks positioned around the crowd perimeter. The next wave of sharpshooters, still disguised as maintenance workers and window washers, line up a hundred yards out around the parade perimeter hidden in their construction zone and scaffolding.

They draw their bows as thickening smoke fills the air while the lower portion of buildings disappear into an expanding white cloud. Their next targets aren't balloons at all.

With practiced precision a multitude of arrows are released like missiles through the air and fly just above the rising cloud, striking brick buildings before the smoke fills the sky.

These shots carry a different purpose: releasing massive banners that unfurl down the sides of buildings—installed days earlier in secret—bearing truths of the past and wounds of the present.

From rooftops, from scaffolding, they drop like truths long denied: black and white faces of ancestors, broken treaties, suicide rates, starvation, massacres. Ten-story truths smothered in helium, smoke, and confetti.

The television monitors turn gray as the cloud spreads into the television sets for millions of viewers at home. Eye watering screams and choking erupts from within the cloud.

Cops and spectators don't know what to make of it. Is it a prank or accident? New York City had been through worse, yet there is no intel or terrorist chatter. No guns have been shot and no one harmed. Caught flat-footed, cops begin mobilizing. *Red Alert.* Doing their best to access the manic crowd looking for those with bows and arrows, and whoever is behind this.

The crowd attempts to disperse while choking on the smoke. But there's too many people and no one can go anywhere. They're wedged together like cattle. All of them quickly realizing this is more than just some Macy's parade day stunt. This is an attack!

Run!

The cops shift into position around the parade taking up their walkie-talkies. Their lines buzzing with information. Yet it's too chaotic to see the aggressors with all the smoke around. And no guns have been shot to trigger their instincts and follow the sound or direction. No one is standing off against them. Not yet anyhow.

One twenty-foot-tall balloon gets loose and floats up into the sky. It's one of the small purple dinosaurs from the upcoming fourth movie in the *Dino Times* series. It flies into the sky over Manhattan like an ugly prehistoric bird.

The sharpshooters have completed their mission exactly as

planned. TJ signals for the others to fall back as they begin their orchestrated disappearance, folding up their bows and dispersing into pre-arranged exit routes. Each piece of equipment is methodically sanitized—latex gloves and bows are wiped down with alcohol before being discarded, abandoned in different locations just as they'd planned.

Mack hesitates at the garbage can on 36th Street, his hand lingering on the best crossbow he's ever owned. The weapon represents three months' salary from his job at the reservation gas station. Instead of trashing it, he pulls out his smart phone and finds a Shipping Depot nearby. Even on Thanksgiving, this location stays open until noon; capitalism never sleeps in Manhattan, especially during the holiday shopping season. He walks in and ships it to himself.

The clerk, unaware of the parade chaos outside (and the roll this bow played in it) says, "With ground shipping, it'll be there next Friday."

"Great. Happy Thanksgiving," he says and walks out feeling lighter, pulling a baseball cap on and removing his fake mustache.

Many are not dressed as Native to maintain surprise. Some wear orange road worker outfits, others look like construction workers with paint splattered across their clothes. A few pose as garbage men in green jumpsuits. One guy has a hardhat on and wears a climbing harness like he's there to service telephone poles.

They all don baseball caps—Mets and Yankees, Knicks and Nets—purchased individually upon arrival to avoid any pattern. And the guy painted as the Statue of Liberty simply slathers more green sparkly paint on his face after discarding his equipment, then walks over to stand a block from the Empire State Building, where he poses, frozen in place. People are amazed and study him, wondering if he's real. Some even take pictures with him.

The mayhem continues as panic spreads through the crowd like a growing storm. People scream while the cops are trying to figure out what's happening and control the crowd of thousands. Parents clutch their children; tourists stumble over each other trying to record and retreat at the same time.

The NYPD's practiced crowd control begins to falter; their usual parade protocol is useless against this combination of chaos and choking smoke, with no suspect to pursue. Some officers help elderly spectators away from the worst of the smoke while others shout contradictory orders into radios that have begun to crackle with strange interference.

Meanwhile in his position near Herald Square, Alex's fingers fly across the keyboard.

"Showtime," he whispers, initiating the sequences he's spent months perfecting. First, the police radio frequencies begin to fill with static. Then the cellular networks light up his screen as his code spreads like digital wildfire.

He watches the parade's broadcast feed, waiting for Black Cloud's signal. One more keystroke and he'll own every screen within twenty blocks. He shifts to a nearby table and turns his computer so his back is against the wall and nosy patrons can't look over his shoulder.

From his vantage point above the chaos on the second floor of a nearby building, Ben Blackfeather coordinates it all through a series of encrypted texts, hand signals, and short radio bursts. His military training shows in how he positions his people—each one placed to maximize impact while maintaining multiple escape routes and cover.

His eyes flick from scaffold to sidewalk, noting each warrior still hidden in plain sight, waiting for the signal. His Apache ancestors would appreciate this kind of tactical precision. *It's time.*

Black Cloud and Tall Tim shift with the slow-moving mass of humanity. Standing several people apart, they glimpse at each other through the chaos. Around them the warriors in disguise maintain their positions.

Black Cloud nods. The time is now. They are the last wave of attack and wait for the chaos of the crowd to spread. As the crowd goes wild choking and running past the PA and electrical system, Tall Tim and Black Cloud join them.

Ben's voice comes through their earpieces: "Production truck is at your two o'clock, minimal security. PA system clear. Cell tower teams in position. You've got about two minutes."

"Splitting up," Black Cloud murmurs. He nods to Tall Tim, who peels off toward the PA system while Black Cloud edges toward the broadcast truck with its satellite uplink pointing skyward.

"First device planted," Tall Tim's voice crackles through their earpieces as he sets the Bluetooth repeaters near the PA system, and continues moving with the mass of people, splitting away from Black Cloud.

Covering his mouth with a handkerchief to block out the smoke, Black Cloud reaches the production truck, slipping between vehicles in the chaos with people all around. He attaches their second device to the truck's main power supply.

"Second target locked." The device should override the system for Alex to pipe into the speakers, piggybacking the network's feed.

"Beginning sequence," Alex announces, his code spreading through New York's digital nervous system. "PA system compromised. Television feed overridden. Cell tower boost initiating."

His screen lights up in sequence as each system falls under his control. His eyes reflect the screen lights inside the busy diner.

"We own every screen within the city. Audio and visual feeds are yours when ready. All channels synced," Alex confirms. "Going live in three…two…" He taps the final key and simultaneously across New York City and TV's across America, the revolution begins.

Every smartphone in the crowd, though still usable, suddenly lights up with the same feed. Store window televisions, digital billboards, even the Jumbotrons in Times Square a few blocks up, switch to their broadcast. The police radios fall silent except for the eerie crackling. Through the PA system, a low drumbeat starts: the heartbeat of a nation, ancient and powerful.

Through gaps in the thinning smoke, Black Cloud looks around and sees Herald Square fill with their message.

Billboards and banners in all directions hang from every building in the square. Statistics about broken treaties and tribal poverty rates appear in bold letters stories high. Black and white photographs of ancestors stretch between buildings, their eyes gazing down upon the modern city below.

In store windows, on phones held high to record the chaos, and on every TV tuned to the parade, they now control the narrative. History may be written by the victor, but the present will be written by them.

The drumbeat grows stronger. People look around. The nation is seeing this.

"Broadcasting recording," Alex says into their earpieces. "Full spectrum penetration. Every device within range is receiving. National feed successfully intercepted." His voice carries the quiet pride of someone who has just pulled off the impossible.

From his surveillance position, Ben watches the confused crowd turn their attention as screens light up around them and the stark banners are revealed. The smoke is thinning.

TWENTY-FOUR

White Feather and the Kids

Back at home, Lilyanna and Little Wonder watch wide-eyed as braves suddenly appear on the Pocahontas float. They lean forward on the couch, cereal bowls forgotten in their laps, as braves draw their bows. Arrows arc through the morning air, striking wooden pilgrims and sending them tumbling. The cabin splinters, the harvest table crashes down, and Disney's sanitized version of their history comes apart piece by piece on national television.

"Did you see that?" Lilyanna squeals with delight, not fully understanding the significance, but feeling the power of the moment. "They're like real warriors, Mama!"

With pride, White Feather rubs her daughters back and says, "They *are* real warriors, honey."

Through the window of their TV, they watch arrows stream across Manhattan's skyline. The giant dinosaur balloon takes the first hit, and the children gasp as its massive form begins to tilt.

"Oh no! The head is falling!" Little Wonder points as the Rex balloon starts its slow surrender to gravity. Section by section, the mighty balloons begin to droop and sink. Mufasa's proud form buckles, handlers struggling with their ropes below.

"Aww!" The kids say in unison when smoke fills the screen, the picture turning gray and fuzzy.

"It's just a technical malfunction," White Feather says quickly, her voice tight with worry. She knows her brother too well to believe this is the end. Not wanting them to watch whatever comes next, she tries to sound firm. "Go outside now."

They argue back, unwilling to miss what's happening, somehow sensing this is more than just a parade gone wrong. White Feather worries and prays.

"Do as you're told," she says sharply, but the children remain glued to the couch, their eyes fixed on the static-filled screen, searching for the next brave, their people on the screen. They aren't going anywhere.

"Something's happening, Mama," Lilyanna adds, more perceptive than her mother sometimes gives her credit for. She points at the screen where forms are seen through the smoky static.

Before White Feather can insist again, every electronic device in their small trailer springs to life: the TV, her phone on the kitchen counter, even Little Wonder's game tablet. A familiar drumbeat begins to pulse through their speakers. Startled, they look at each other, then the devices.

The Indian drums grow louder but they still can't see. Little Wonder gets up and looks at the TV from all angles.

"Be patient sweety. It'll come back on. And I bet there will be a real treat for you when it does."

His big eyes grow like a cloudless sun.

"Okay, Mom."

He sits back down placing his hands on his lap to wait patiently. The drums grow louder still.

Watching through the smoke, they see an occasional costume scattering about. Smoke shifts into pockets as it rises along the buildings. When the chaos subsides, from the edge of the couch she shouts, "Look!" and points proudly at the television set with so many Native Americans among the glamour of New York City.

Lilyanna's face lights up with pride and she hugs herself.

Little Wonder adds, "This is amazing!" as his jaw drops with wonder.

When the screen clears to show present-day Manhattan, smoke rising and drifting between buildings, their people emerge from the crowd.

Using a fake profile from an encrypted server, Alex had posted on every social media site he could think of for the 50,000 Native Americans that live in New York City, to come. And come they did.

Those who had been hiding in plain sight now stand proudly with feathers and outfits of turquoise, greens, and reds, catching the morning light.

"Mama, look!" Lilyanna points at the TV. "We're there. People like us. They're everywhere." She bounces on the couch, clutching the pillow in her lap.

White Feather's eyes fill with tears as she recognizes the vision their mother and brother had seen last year. The one she had doubted.

The darkness on the TV screen gives way to images of their ancestors, murdered laying prostate and frozen on cold hard ground, old photographs, paintings of warriors and tribal villages, proud faces that stare back through time.

The drums grow louder, the beat matching the rhythm of their own hearts. White Feather pulls her children close as the pictures show their people's history in flashes.

Posters, murals, and banners have unfurled from buildings

with leaders on them from many different tribes. The banners share broken treaties, infant mortality rates, unemployment, and a list of other injustices.

The Indian drums subside when White Feather hears a booming voice coming through her television set. She knows it's Black Cloud who's speaking through some sort of voice altering device.

TWENTY-FIVE

The Speech

A dozen blocks up, Times Square's massive screens flicker and go dark for a moment. Cell phones stop working mid-call, the feed temporarily interrupting them. Every digital billboard, every television in every store window, every device capable of displaying an image synchronizes to their signal. The low drumbeat pulses through every speaker in range. The city is alive with native drums.

The crowd that had been panicking moments ago grows still, faces turning upward to the screens, to the banners, to the emerging warriors.

Police officers lower their weapons, their own radios now carrying only the low drumbeat. Even the traffic nearby stops, drivers getting out of their cars as phones and tablets spring to life with the same images and sounds.

A mighty voice begins to speak, altered but clear, carrying a bold message across this suddenly silent city.

"Good morning. Many Native people do not celebrate Thanksgiving. Instead, we refer to this day as the Day of Mourning.

A smaller select group may also refer to this day jokingly as Thanks-for-Taking because so much has been taken from us, and sometimes all you can do is laugh. Yet I have recently learned that laughter only masks the pain."

People settle down to listen and stop running. The rhythm of the city falls still. Conversations halt. Manhattan is holding its breath.

As the voice speaks, images of rampant poverty are displayed depicting many reservations which look like third world nations. The screens show modern reservation conditions contrasted with the wealthy cities, including the glitter and glamour of New York.

"Please know that we are not here to harm you, only to be seen and heard. And to possibly heal some. To open a dialogue: a national dialogue."

Historic photos dissolve into faces of Native children today, their eyes full of hope despite the statistics that scroll beneath their images: high infant mortality rates, poverty levels, unemployment numbers that tell a story of systematic neglect.

"I stand here today for the ancestors of our past, for the children of our future, and for the present in which we find ourselves." People look around trying to find the man this voice is connected to, but can't find him anywhere. The drumbeat grows stronger as the smoke continues to clear.

In Times Square faces are turned upward toward the massive screens; tourists, office workers working overtime stand at windows, police officers, parade performers, are all transfixed by the images flowing across every display. Parents pull children closer as they recognize the weight of what they're seeing. Some people wipe tears from their eyes; others stand in shocked silence.

Ben Blackfeather coordinates from his position above, watching his warriors stand taller. But there's something else in his eyes now:

pride, purpose, and the weight of generations.

Crystal and Tom Sr. stand among the crowd, their hands finding each other again. She notices how some of the police officers, especially those of color, have lowered their weapons, their own eyes drawn to the screens. Denni finds TJ one block over and slides her arm into his.

Pete looks over at his friend beside him. For one moment, Samuel claps his hands, smiles, and does a little dance stomping his feet, seldom letting out or knowing joy.

"In the early days before this great country was founded, we battled, and we were at odds. Yes, we had our differences as anyone would. Those battles are long over now. Yet this nation still inflicts cruelties upon us because of what happened back then. It is not with weapons and armies now, but apathy, suppression, and indifference.

"You called us savages, murdered us, and attempted to indoctrinate us into Christianity to save our souls, but it was not our souls that needed saving. Do you know the story? Do they teach it to you in schools?"

Images flash across every screen from Herald Square to Times Square. The fast-moving city is still as everyone pauses to watch and listen.

"Do you know what they did to our children when they forced them into your Indian schools?"

The screens show black and white photos of Native children forcibly loaded onto trucks and trains, stripped away from their parents, as young as three years old.

"They were taken from their mothers' arms and shipped to boarding schools where they cut their hair, beat them for speaking their own language, told them their culture was savage, stripped them of cultural identity, and often forced them into labor hundreds of miles away for ten to twelve hours a day. Some were raped and molested. Many died and were tossed into unmarked graves. This abuse lasted for one hundred and fifty years. Now, whose souls were you saving? I will ask, whose souls were you crushing? Parents who refused to let their children go were arrested."

The voice pauses, letting the facts sink in. In the crowd, parents pull their children closer. Some older viewers look away, unable to face these truths and look at the recently found unmarked graves. Others stand transfixed, seeing this history for the first time.

A Latino mother clutches her children closer, tears streaming down her face. A Black police officer removes his riot helmet, his eyes fixed on the screens.

"They sterilized our women. The same for many Black and Latino women, without consent, telling them they were getting routine checkups. Into the 1970s, they were still trying to eliminate us, not with guns but with medicine twisted into weapons."

Historical documents appear on screen, government records showing the systematic sterilization program.

"When they couldn't kill us or sterilize us, they tried to scatter us, stealing our lands for a money grab under the ruse of helping. Ninety million additional acres were legally stolen by laws and promises. We were promised jobs and homes in cities, then you abandoned our people to poverty and isolation, suicide. Many stand before you."

Around the crowd perimeter hundreds raise one fist above their heads in silent protest.

The screens show images of the Indian Relocation Act, Native families standing lost on urban streets, beggars.

People who had been enemies moments ago begin to look at each other differently. An elderly white woman wearing jewelry and a fur coat reaches for the hand of a young Chinese girl standing beside her. The girl looks up at her mother. The mother nods that it's okay. The girl smiles up and takes the woman's hand.

Ben notices the change from his position, seeing how the police officers—especially those of color—standing at ease, their own histories reflecting back at them from the screens.

"This story isn't ours alone." The images shift to show Japanese internment camps, Black Americans being attacked with fire hoses, Latino children in border cages.

"They tried to break all people of color. Enslaved some, imprisoned others, separated families, stole children. But they failed. We are still here. All of us."

In the crowd, an elderly Black man removes his WWII Veteran's cap and places his hand over his heart. A lone tear runs down his cheek. He mutters the words "Lord have mercy," and shakes his head.

"The darkness of the past lives in us all," the voice continues as the images shift to show moments of unity: historical photographs of Native Americans sheltering runaway slaves, Black Panthers standing with AIM protesters, and people of all colors marching during the Civil Rights movement.

"But so does the light. We did not come here to harm you. Year after year we watch your celebration on this day, and many of you have no idea the pain it causes us. It's not taught in schools. Not mentioned in your newspapers."

The screens show modern classrooms, history books with pages missing or stories rewritten. Then the images shift to show diverse faces in the crowd: African Americans nodding in recognition, Latino parents explaining to their children, Asian Americans recording on their phones not as spectators now, but as witnesses to a shared truth.

Black Cloud and Tall Tim watch as something remarkable begins to happen. The marching bands, still in their positions along the parade route, begin to quietly pick up the Native drumbeat. The high school band from Kansas, their uniforms still crisp, their instruments shining in the morning light, starts first. Then others join in, brass and drums merging with the ancient rhythms.

"How many treaties have been broken? How many deceptions lured our leaders in only to murder them? I have the list here in my hands. You can read it upon the buildings with the murals and statistics. There are hundreds of them. Each one leading to the theft of our land and death of our people."

The unfurled banners flutter in the November wind, each one listing broken promises. The screens show treaty after treaty, signature after signature, followed by the systematic violation of each one.

"Promises were made. Promises were broken. Hundreds of them. Treaties are laws, agreements. What is a nation without laws? You, the government, have betrayed the very core of this land. There is rot in your fat bellies as so many of us starve. The foundation of this Nation was built upon the bones of our ancestors you deceived and murdered along with the people you enslaved to help build it—then lynched with your white law and centuries of hatred, prejudice, and injustice."

People's heads swivel, still looking for the source of the voice that seems to come from everywhere all at once. Chip Wegney steps back onto the stage transfixed, tears streaming down his face as he watches history unfold before him.

The booming voice continues, "To quote Dr. Martin Luther King, Jr., 'Darkness cannot drive out darkness, only light can do that. Hate cannot drive out hate, only love can do that.'

"Why do some of you hate a group that you enslaved? Is it that you hate yourselves and your heritage for doing it? Our ancestors are your history too. They whisper upon the wind—your pain and ours— intertwined through history just as slavery is interwoven. And a brutal history it is. Yet so many have not healed. This Nation has not healed from slavery or the genocide of its First Peoples.

"No one heals by hiding from this truth or by suppressing another's. No one heals by hiding from the past the way many of you try to, by whitewashing your sins and history from your children's minds and history books. Yet you cannot wash away something that is scarred upon this Nation's consciousness and heart, scarred upon its soil."

From his position at the coffee shop, Alex's fingers dance across his keyboard, monitoring every feed.

"Signal holding strong," he murmurs into his mic. "Every device still receiving. National broadcast feeds compromised and stable."

His screens show millions of phones lighting up across the country as the message spreads beyond Manhattan.

Ben's voice crackles in his earpiece, "Police channels?"

"They're hearing every word," Alex confirms, a smile playing at his lips. "And their body cams are capturing everything. This is going straight to their archives."

"Good."

Across town, Bull Nose Pete stands among the crowd, his Snoopy mask long since discarded. He watches people's faces transform from fear to understanding. For once, his nose isn't flaring with anxiety; instead, he stands tall, proud to be seen at last.

"Would you look at that," he says to Samuel as another marching band picks up the drumbeat. "They're listening and hearing us."

With a tear in his eye, amazed by the spectacle, Samuel nods to his friend.

Black Cloud continues, "Many accuse us of laziness. It is the same smear tactic used to diminish African Americans and Native Americans alike.

"Hundreds of years ago, on this very day, you were kept alive by the Wampanoag people who fed you. Without their help, you would have surely starved to death during the harsh winter months. But then you turned your back on them. You murdered us and called us savages. But who is the savage that deceives and murders? Who is the savage that enslaves?"

In the crowd, a Black police officer shakes his head and wipes away a tear. His grandparents had been beaten in the streets like dogs. Crystal squeezes Tom Sr.'s hand as they watch barriers—both physical and symbolic—begin to fall.

"Our reservations struggle with high infant mortality. Meaning our kids die twice as much at birth as yours do. Our unemployment rate is several times higher, and yet we also have the lowest average lifespan, dying several years younger than you do. Our kids drop out of high school almost two and half times as often as yours do. And only seven out of a hundred will get a college degree."

The numbers roll across the screens like gravestones, etched with centuries of neglect.

The statistics appear on every screen, stark numbers telling their brutal story. The crowd watches as images show the reality of reservation life: crumbling schools, inadequate healthcare facilities, homes without running water.

"We never knew poverty or alcoholism before the reservation system. Your backs are turned as you continue to wage wars and inflict casualties. When one starts a race a hundred feet behind everyone else, it is a rigged race. During COVID, one reservation received body bags instead of masks."

Alex notices people pulling out their phones, not to record now, but to fact-check these statistics. His screens show internet searches spiking across the city as people discover for themselves that every word is true.

"You underfund education and healthcare, then blame those of us who stumble, blame us for being unemployable, blame us for being lazy when you are fat from what you have taken. We want work. We want clean water. We are stuck on some of the poorest land in the country where there is little industry. Many African Americans are stuck on reservations as well."

"What? I ain't on no reservation!" one heavy set black woman shouts out. "No sir!"

The speaking pauses as the screens show side-by-side images of urban ghettos next to reservations, showing parallel struggles and statistics.

A barrel-chested black man with a powerful voice shouts out, "That man is speaking truth!"

"There is even one in New York City. But it is found in tall buildings made of brick and concrete. Harlem is just uptown, and it is a pattern found throughout many big cities where crime rates soar and incarcerations affect one in four black men. High unemployment rate, high incarceration, poor education system, drugs, violence, and poverty. Sound familiar?"

The black woman shouts again, "Oh yeah, I knew that."

Many Black people in the crowd now nod their heads and speak out in agreement. A group of Latino teenagers stops filming with their phones and start really watching, seeing their own story reflected in these words.

Some African American police officers exchange glances acknowledging each other with a nod.

"In the cities, ghettos are reservations. Same result. Same suppression. Same smear tactics and underfunding."

Throughout the crowd, people begin reaching across divides—hands clasping, stories being shared in whispers. The marching bands and Native drums share a common rhythm that pulses through the streets like a conduit.

"We are not relics or antiques, artifacts living in some museum of the past for tourists to poke and prod. We are the flesh and blood of this earth—of this Nation—as you are."

The screens fill with images of modern Native life, of children playing and families celebrating, mixed with similar scenes from all communities of color. In the crowd, phones lower as people stop recording and start connecting with those around them.

"Can we put our differences aside and move together into the future as one? Not by homogenizing diversity but by honoring it? We want the same for our families. The best for our children. But what can we give to our children as their future? Casinos? The present crumbles under the sins of this Nation's past when our children must look to a parade for hope, unrepresented."

On stage, someone from the show runs across to pull the electrical feed.

Chip Wegney raises his hand in protest and shouts as he lunges toward the assistant, "No! Stop! I want to hear this. This is great television." He whispers to his producer, "Fighting to be heard. That's what this country is all about. That's what music and creativity are all about." The producer nods and shoots him a thumbs up with his headset still on, giving the camera the green light to keep rolling.

On the Pine Ridge Reservation, people who had been bitter enemies over tribal politics stand shoulder to shoulder, united in this moment. The same is happening on the Rosebud Reservation where other bands of Sioux gather.

On reservations across the country, people gather around any screen they can find.

In the Cherokee Nation, a woman runs into where her elderly father is sleeping and shouts, "Quick, Dad, turn on the parade!"

He startles out of his nap in his favorite brown chair and barks at her for the disturbance, "What the hell for?"

She scrambles over to the television and stands beaming with pride, "This is what for."

His eyes grow wide at the unfolding chaos and Natives standing in solidarity. "Hot damn!" he bolts upright. "Call in the kids."

"They're already watching, Dad."

He looks up at her with tears in his eyes.

In Oklahoma, families stand together in front of a tribal center's TV. In New Mexico, they watch in community centers. In Idaho, they peer into trailers and tribal offices, watching their truth finally being told. Children sit at elders' feet as stories they've heard in whispers are now broadcast to millions.

From reservations to urban housing projects, in barrios and Chinatowns, people who had felt invisible for generations watch as their shared struggles are finally acknowledged. On the Pine Ridge Reservation, Morning Sparrow's constant chatter has fallen silent as she watches with her daughter in her arms.

"Thank you, *Wakan Tanka*. The powerful force of nature and life you are. Thank you."

Back at the parade, Black Cloud continues, "The past does not have to define our future. All of us are immigrants on this glorious planet, just visitors for however long. Is the difference in our skin enough to kill? To hate? It may have been once. Perhaps some still hold onto this bitterness, but why? It is time to move forward. It is time to love each other, and to love this planet which we all call home. After all, we are part of the human family."

Some women are crying in the audience along with the two women who took Black Cloud's picture earlier. Some men hold their children high on their shoulders, knowing they're witnessing history. Chip wipes away a tear.

A pause lingers, allowing the words to sink in as people look beyond the color of their neighbors' skin, searching not for differences but for the commonalities that unite them.

"We will no longer be swept away into the past by the Gatlin Gun that once mowed us down like bloodied blades of grass. We will no longer walk this Trail of Tears. For I have cried too much. We are here for respect. Ours."

There's a pause in the speech as the drums beat on. Black Cloud and Tall Tim exchange looks in the crowd. This is the moment, the pivot point between hiding and being seen. Everything they've planned, every practice raid, every sleepless night, has led to this choice.

The woman who had first taken Cloud's picture offers, "Oh Mr. Wegney, this man is a real life Indian. Oops, I mean Native American. You should have him on stage."

Chip Wegney looks at the woman then to Black Cloud standing near her.

"Well, why not? Come on up, sir."

Black Cloud gulps and glances at Tim who shakes his head, no. This was not the plan, but life has a way of altering one's plans. Black Cloud weighs his options of declining with all eyes upon him or walking up and throwing caution to the wind. This was not the way he planned on them being seen or himself for that matter.

"It's time," Black Cloud says softly nodding his head, pondering this pivotal decision, but it's putting them at further risk if he does.

Instead of retreating as planned, he straightens his spin, and adjusts his headdress. Around him, the crowd has transformed from hostile to understanding, police officers stand with lowered weapons, and Chip Wegney waits on stage with an extended hand.

"You sure about this?" After Cloud takes a few short steps, Tall Tim asks, but smiling, he already knows the answer.

Black Cloud steps forward. The crowd parts as they recognize him as the friendly chief from their earlier photos, not realizing he's the man behind the voice as they witness history unfold. His traditional dress, once just a tourist's costume for their snapshots, now carries the weight of generations.

He walks toward the stage where Chip stands holding a microphone. Even through the makeup and disguise, his presence commands attention; each step is deliberate and grounded in purpose.

Chip understands that something extraordinary is happening and pulls Black Cloud onto the stage, offering both the microphone and his support.

At home, White Feather leans forward, recognition hitting her like a thunderbolt. Through the makeup and false features, she sees her brother plain as day. No one else might notice the familiar tilt of his head or the way he squares his shoulders before doing something bold, but she knows.

"Look!" Lilyanna points at the screen. "That's Uncle Cloudy!"

Little Wonder presses his face closer to the TV. "He's not hiding anymore, Mama."

"No, he is not." White Feather clutches her children closer, tears streaming down her face as she watches her brother emerge from shadow into light. On their small screen, they see him climb the steps to stand beside Chip Wegney. The cameras catching everything: the way Chip offers him the microphone, the respect in the gesture, the moment when history shifts.

In the coffee shop, Alex's fingers freeze over his keyboard. Through the camera feed, he sees Black Cloud mounting the stage. This wasn't part of the plan; they were supposed to stay hidden, let the recording finish, and fade back into the city.

"What are you doing, Cloud?" he mutters, watching Chip hand over the microphone. Making a split-second decision, Alex's fingers fly across the keys, cutting the pre-recorded message mid-sentence.

The silence hits Herald Square like a physical thing affecting all in its presence like a sudden shift in weather. Every screen, every speaker goes quiet as Alex types in new commands.

The broadcast screens freeze mid-statistic. Every speaker goes silent. People tense—some expecting violence, others awe.

"Switching to live audio feed, all channels."

For a moment, all of New York holds its breath.

Ben bangs on the window of the room he's standing in overlooking this as it unfolds. He says while pressing the earpiece, "I don't like this, Cloud. Clandestine, remember? Clandestine!" Ben paces the room glancing out the window.

All across the Indian Nation, people lean forward as they recognize what's happening. A warrior, one of them, is about to speak; not from a hiding place, but standing in the full light of day.

Then Black Cloud's real voice—strong, clear, unaltered—fills the square, "You can hear me now, not through a recording, but heart to heart. I stand before you as flesh and blood."

"Wait, you're the guy?" Chip's face is in shock and eyes are wide with inquiry.

"I'm just a man sent to New York City like so many others," he says to Chip. His voice carries, no longer filtered through technology but raw with truth.

"Good morning," he addresses the crowd. "It nice to see you all, really see you." He pauses and looks slowly at them sweeping his eyes over the crowd. "Our message is one of love. And yet, if we are to die here today, let it be standing in the light, not hiding in the shadows." He pauses again, looking out at the sea of faces to see so many nodding. "I see something different in your eyes now. I see understanding. I see the chance for change."

The crowd shifts, police officers glancing at each other uncertainly stepping closer toward the stage. Overhead, the hawk circles, its cry piercing the morning air. Black Cloud pauses and smiles looking up in reassurance. People look up, then back at Black Cloud, feeling the weight of the moment.

"We didn't come here to fight," he continues, his voice strong. "We came to be seen. And now I see you seeing us— not as the past, or as mascots, but as human beings standing before you. And we see you too." He looks them over, all the different faces and colors in the crowd.

The drumming from natives and marching bands gets louder. The music becomes a bridge between worlds—neither fully modern nor fully traditional, but something new and born from both.

A slow applause begins growing within the crowd, clapping along with the rhythm of the drums. Black Cloud's voice rises above the unified rhythms, carried on every screen and speaker across the city.

"If history is ignored it will repeat itself. Instead of you against us, let us heal and unite. What matters more than the content of one's character and healing of one's own past? It is the only way forward out of the darkness. This is what I have come here to say."

He pauses, feeling the weight of every eye upon him. The drumming continues beneath his words, a foundation of truth. The police close in from the crowd's edges.

Chip notices this. "Sir, that was powerful. But… you might want to say your farewell now." He nods to the approaching officers. "Exit this way." He points to exit the stage into their production tent.

Cloud sees the police closing in and panic twinges—until Chip's hand gestures again, calmly. He quickly waves goodbye and jumps off the rear of the stage, slipping behind the production curtain—the closed off production area of tents, make up, lighting, and trucks.

He rips off the headdress, squirts sanitizer in his palms and rubs the war paint away. Jacket comes off. Face clean. Another man. *One among many.*

He ducks around a lighting rig and quickly emerges in another section of the massing crowd having not seen him.

Once back into the crowd, ducking and blending back in he says, "Activate feed," to Alex over the earpiece. The drums come back on, and the altered voice speaks as he slips away protected by the mass of people.

The ominous and challenging words speak as he escapes through the crowd where people lose sight of him without his disguise.

Alex says, "Thank God. Reactivating feed." He quickly strikes the commands, sips from the black coffee, and sighs, leaning back against the diner wall.

Ben shouts, "Get out of there, Cloud!"

The address continues as planned as Cloud escapes the watchful eyes of the police: "If we are to die here today, and you will not let us go in peace for breaking your laws, meet us in Sheep Meadow of your Central Park. If you must destroy us as we retreat, we will be there. We have only come to say this and show that we are not antiques, but living flesh and blood, children of this nation. Hiyayaya. Hiyayaya. Hiyayaya." The voice fades and Indian drums play.

The drums grow stronger as shouts erupt from the crowd, "Let them go! Let them go!"

Chip chants as well and begins waving his hand walking along the stage, "Let them go! Let them go!"

An older couple, Bob and Pat from New Hampshire agree, "Let them go! Let them go!" Pat claps her hands together.

As the final smoke fades up over building tops, the drums fall quiet.

Through the silence, Black Cloud's voice carries one final ominous warning: "We know your police, who often act as a military force and do the bidding of your leaders, will not let us go in peace. If you must, meet us in Sheep Meadow for one last stand. But know this: we come in peace and are here to protect these innocent people. You, the government, are not innocent. You are the criminals. For centuries you have kept us in chains. No more. Now we take our stand."

The drums begin again: *Bum bum bum bam. Bum bum bum bam. Bum bum bum bam.*

The crowd stands stunned and silent, understanding they're witnessing something historic and potentially tragic. Silence spreads among the spectators who look at each other knowing that this pending battle will most likely end in slaughter.

Near Chip Wegney, two cops exchange worried looks.

"This makes us look bad, bro," one says to the other.

"We have advanced weaponry," his partner responds. "What do they have, sticks and stones? Maybe a tomahawk or two. This isn't even gonna be funny."

Boos erupt from the crowd. "Let them go! Let them go!"

"We can't, folks," the one officer says, shaking his head. Then he and his partner hurry to their patrol car.

In the coffee shop, Alex's screen suddenly lights up with warnings.

"No, no, no," he mutters, fingers flying across the keyboard. "They're breaking through our signal."

Ben's voice crackles in his earpiece, "Police channels are reverting to command control. Get out. Now!"

Across Manhattan, police radios come alive with official orders: "All units converge on Sheep Meadow. This is not a peaceful assembly. Repeat: This is not a peaceful assembly. Move in and begin arrests. Take 'em down."

Officers exchange uncertain glances, torn between the humanity they've just witnessed and the commands crackling through their radios. Some begin to move, conditioned to follow orders. Others hesitate, looking at the faces in the crowd—faces that no longer seem like adversaries.

"Immediate response required," the radio demands. "Any officers failing to respond will face disciplinary action."

A Black officer drops his radio on the sidewalk. A Latino sergeant stares at her radio, then turns down the volume. But others are already moving toward their vehicles, lights flashing to life across Herald Square.

"This is your final warning," the commander blares. "Move in now!"

Police units respond slowly, caught off guard and unsure how to handle this unfolding situation. A battalion forms down at city hall while SWAT teams roll uptown to secure the area. Armored cars and helicopters launch in attack formation. This is an attack on their city, and it must be defended at all costs.

Officers try clearing the area, but the crowd stands firm.

"The show's over folks."

But for those watching—the families with children on shoulders, the officers with their own histories, the tourists who came for a parade and found themselves part of history—something has shifted. Even as the police begin to mobilize, the crowd's energy transforms from spectators to participants in something larger than themselves.

Through it all, even after the feed had ended, the marching band continues their steady *rat tat tat* beat. On every screen, the statistics and faces remain, impossible to ignore. What started as an attack on a parade has become something else: a moment of truth, a choice, a possible transformation. Right from wrong.

But it was only the beginning.

TWENTY-SIX

Whiteman On the Move

His car crawls across the Queensboro Bridge. The morning sun reflects off the skyscrapers ahead, mocking his slow progress. His rental car's cheap radio sputters to life, cutting through his frustrated drumming on the steering wheel, when he hears trouble on the radio.

"Breaking News from 1010 WINS, New York's all-news station. We're getting reports of major disruptions at the Macy's Thanksgiving Day Parade. Multiple parade balloons appear to have been damaged, and there are unconfirmed reports of smoke in Herald Square. We go live to Jenny Chu at the scene. Jenny?"

Luckily for Whiteman, AM radio is a different frequency and unaffected by Alex's signal override.

"Tom, I'm here at 34th Street where chaos has erupted. Several of the signature parade balloons have been punctured by what witnesses say were arrows. There's some kind of message being broadcast across all screens, though we're unable to determine the source. Police are advising people to stay clear of the area. Stay tuned for more of this late breaking story. Now back to you in the studio."

He calls Black Cloud again. His fingers shake as he dials Black Cloud's number again. No answer. Straight to voicemail. He slams the steering wheel.

"Whatever you're doing, stop!"

He then starts hearing the Native drumming over his phone and the screen goes gray with smoke.

The cool November air seeps through his window as his mind races to the worst scenarios. Is this another 9/11? But this time, he's watching it unfold. He tightly grabs the steering wheel in frustration and shakes it, glancing at his phone.

"Screw it!" he says and jams the car into park, shutting it off. Jumping out, he abandons it on the bridge. The November air slaps his face as he starts running, flashing his badge at drivers standing outside of their idling cars. Traffic is at a dead stop.

"Coming through. Official bureau business!"

A family leans against their minivan, kids already whining about missing the parade. A woman in a business suit paces while arguing on her phone. Others stand in clusters, peering ahead to see what's blocking traffic.

"FBI?" a Hispanic woman shouts.

"Wrong bureau," he says while running, dodging between cars.

She scowls, "Wrong bureau?" she asks with her New York accent. "What other bureau is there?"

"Indian Affairs!" Stan Whiteman shouts back at her.

"Indian affairs?" A cabbie standing by his yellow taxi waves dismissively. "Well, move your fucking car, Indian Affairs. It's blocking everyone back there."

"Sorry, can't."

The honks erupt like a symphony of frustration, blame, and anger that follows him down the bridge as word spreads about the abandoned car.

He's huffing and panting as he runs across the bridge onto 59th Street, then turns south. His tie sways from side to side like a metronome. Running with the phone in his sweaty hand, the GPS is set for Macy's.

He's in good shape for his age, but not good enough for this. Now sweating through his dress shirt in the cool air, he throws his blue sport coat to the ground and keeps going. It hits the sidewalk as he picks up speed, getting closer, into the forties and past the United Nations building. He turns right on 42nd Street. Now approaching 1st Ave then 2nd as he heads across the city, zigzagging diagonally south toward the parade.

After several more exhausting minutes of running, he sees the smoke rising over Herald Square and a partially deflated dinosaur balloon drifts between buildings.

"Oh my God, what have they done?" The sight slows him in his tracks. "I'm too late."

The parade crowd disperses slowly toward him.

"Is everyone alight? Is everyone alright?" he turns, asking while pushing against the flow of bodies. No one answers, too busy discussing what they witnessed among themselves. He heads into this dense mass toward Macy's a couple blocks over.

The streets are thick with people. One man slips off to urinate in an alleyway.

Whiteman jogs in, breathing hard, when he sees this suspicious guy with a headdress lurking in an alley, glancing back every so often.

On high alert, Whiteman walks up from behind and grabs the man's shoulder to spin him around. "Alright Black Cloud, you're coming with me."

As the man turns, Whiteman is surprised and stares in, processing what he's seeing. Furrowing his brow, anger rippling across his face as he's now putting it all together, "Tim?" he inquires.

Zipping up his pants, Tim responds with shock, "White. Whiteman?" He looks around, trying to find an escape.

Whiteman twists his expression and grimaces, staring in with his cold, beady eyes. "You're a part of this, aren't you?"

Panicked, Tim looks left then right, wanting to escape but realizes he's trapped in the alley, surrounded by the buildings on each side and Whiteman in front of him. Looking out at the sea of people just a few feet away, cornered, he has nowhere to run.

"You're coming with me," Whiteman says reaching out to grab him, but Tall Tim blocks and grabs his hand, applying a wrist lock, then sweeps out Whiteman's leg; he goes down hard onto the pavement.

With Whiteman down, Tim looks at his own hands in surprise. It worked!

Raging and glaring, Whiteman shakes his head and gets up slowly, "You're going to pay for that." He tightens his fist and pulls back to punch, but his fist is caught from behind. He turns and a group of people have peeled off from the street and surround him, men and women: brown, black, white, and red. He zeroes in on the large Native man who came because of Alex's post.

With teeth clenched and a ragged beard, the guy who caught his fist releases it and says to the people around him, "This white guy is trying to beat up this poor old Native American." He then faces Whiteman. "Hate much? No more." He drives a hammer of a fist into Whiteman's face, contorting it.

Dazed, head knocked to the side, Whiteman tries shaking it off. He recovers enough to say, "No, I'm with…" he grabs his wallet and badge, but it goes flying as he gets jumped by the angry mob who want better from society.

"Don't like indigenous people?" A woman with long curly hair says while kneeing him in the groin. Tim watches in horror and flees during the melee.

TWENTY-SEVEN

A Confluence of People

Sheep Meadow stretches across the lower west side of Central Park like a vast green canvas, equivalent in size to a dozen football fields. Originally home to actual sheep until 1934, it remains one of the largest open spaces in Manhattan, surrounded by the forest-like edges of Central Park and towering buildings.

On this cold November morning, the well-manicured grass sparkles with frost under a cloudless sky. From the air, it appears empty at first glance, but closer inspection reveals figures positioned throughout and clustered in open defiance: some moving, some still as statues in the morning light awaiting the ensuing battle.

Three police choppers fly up 5th Avenue in attack formation, their rotors slicing through the morning air just a few hundred feet above the buildings. They bank left at Central Park along 60th Street.

In the lead chopper, Captain Harris leans forward, squinting through the sun's morning glare.

"Command, this is Air One. Approaching target from the east."

"Roger that, Air One. Contain and neutralize any hostile action."

They fly over horse-drawn carriages awaiting tourists, necklace bead makers, and portrait painters as they fly low over the ice-skating rink. Past the tree line, the large field opens up before them.

"Got eyes on hostiles in Sheep Meadow," the lead pilot Harris reports.

"Multiple subjects with bows, several on horseback. One guy's pumping his arm up and down with what appears to be a rifle. They must think this is Geronimo's last stand."

Lieutenant Mitchell's voice cuts through the radio from the second chopper, "Something's not right about this, Sir."

"I repeat. There are confirmed hostiles in Sheep Meadow," Harris snaps back. "I count twenty, maybe more. Several mounted, pumping their arms almost daring us to attack."

From the third helicopter, Sergeant Rodriguez watches the scene unfold below.

"Sir, requesting verification before engagement. I've got what look like women and children in my scope."

"They're decoys, Rodriguez. Has to be in broad daylight with so many people around. They want us to attack them."

"More like sacrificial lambs."

"These people attacked our parade. Command wants this finished now. They think we won't shoot because of women and children present."

"Just like Wounded Knee," Mitchell's voice carries an edge. "I'm not participating in a massacre. They attacked the parade, yes," Mitchell replies carefully, "but so far, no civilian casualties. We should verify targets before doing anything drastic."

"Not your call, Lieutenant," Harris responds, his jaw tightening. "We have orders," his hand tightens on the chopper's stick while his finger caresses the gun trigger.

Below them, the morning frost casts a pale sheen across Sheep Meadow. Through his scope, Mitchell studies the figures, their stillness unsettling him.

"Something's wrong, Sir. Look at how they're positioned. Too perfect, too still..."

"Got a dozen subjects with what appears to be rifles," Rodriguez cuts in. "Southern edge of the meadow."

"That's it. Going in for a closer look. Be ready to engage," Harris announces, dropping the chopper's nose.

"Wait," Mitchell's voice rises. "Remember the radio chatter? They said to meet at Sheep Meadow. They wanted us here. Think about it, Sir."

"And for all the world to see," acknowledging the news choppers flying above. Rodriguez hovers holding the right flank. His grandfather had told him stories about government men who acted first, realizing the truth too late.

"Captain, Lieutenant Mitchell might have a point."

Harris scoffs, already calculating his attack run. "Either way, it ain't gonna end well for them."

"Look at the pattern down there," Mitchell continues, his chopper holding steady. "Those figures are positioned too strategically. Like they're inviting us to attack them."

Harris's laugh comes sharp across the radio, "Exactly, because they're stupid. The same reason they lost two hundred years ago."

"Or because we are," Rodriguez interrupts, surprising himself for speaking up against his superior. Through his windshield, he watches a hawk circle around the meadow below, seemingly unbothered by their presence above.

"Look at that stupid bird," Harris steadies his gunsight on it. "Command wants this finished. Deploy crowd control tactics."

Harris reminds them. "These people disrupted our city, made us look weak, unprepared."

"We were, Sir," Mitchell counters. "Did anyone even listen to what they were saying at the parade?"

Before Harris can respond, bright flashes erupt from the meadow. The crack of what sounds like gunfire and explosions echo across the park.

"Taking fire! Taking fire!" Harris shouts, the leader chopper's nose dives away, and the other two follow, peeling away to stay in formation.

Rodriguez notices his chopper hasn't been hit.

"Captain, wait," Rodriguez starts.

"Too late for waiting." On edge Harris snarls, staying high and just past the tree line out of sight. "We're going to end this now. Coming into our city like this and firing on us unprovoked," Harris growls, his chopper hovering and descending toward the tree line.

Mitchell's voice rises with urgency, "With all due respect, Captain, those weren't muzzle flashes. Did you see the pattern, the timing? It's too perfect."

"I did not, Lieutenant. I was too busy getting us out of there. I didn't want to find out how perfect their positioning was as we got blown out of the sky."

There's chaos and confusion about the decision as news choppers fly above them.

"We've got to get this right, Sir," Lieutenant Mitchell says looking up through the windshield. "The world's eyes are on us. Something's not right. Why would they announce their position like this?"

"Fine," he says flipping on the choppers speakers that squeal at first. He moves the chopper into harm's way, just past the tree line into the field, exposing them. Several braves are far down below within shooting range.

He turns up the speakers to full volume, "This is the police. We have you surrounded." Ground units approach from the south and east sides as he says this.

"Lay down your arms. You will not be harmed."

While he's speaking, another series of bright explosions illuminate the frost-covered grass as loud thunderous booms echo off the nearby buildings. Machine gun fire fills the air with violent exploding bursts.

The park trees sway with the chopper rotors, but Rodriguez notices something strange.

"Sir, no impact signatures on the ground. Whatever's firing at us isn't hitting…"

Harris cuts him off, "Well, there's your answer Mitchell."

He continues now on the frequency with HQ. "Bright explosions down below, Commander. We're taking on enemy fire. Awaiting orders."

"Take evasive action."

The choppers peel off as explosions erupt beneath them.

"Repeat. We're taking on enemy fire, Sir," Harris shouts over the com. "Commander, they lured us in to attack us here. They lied." To avoid any further attacks the choppers circle higher and back away, awaiting orders. The news choppers match their rising distance.

Harris says, "A just miss. I don't know how much more we can sustain without returning fire or getting blown to bits."

Their commanding officer demands accurate intel, "How many are there?"

"About twenty. Headdresses. War paint. The whole nine. One

dude's in a loin cloth holding up a gun, almost daring us to come down there and blow him away. Several are on horses."

"How the hell did they get there without us noticing?"

"People must've thought they were part of the holiday celebration or something."

News choppers circle a few hundred feet higher staying out of the way but are filming the whole exchange. There are also news reports of a giant dinosaur floating over the city.

Back at the station, the commander is watching this unfold on the local news station.

"We can't have them embarrassing us like this. We'll be a laughingstock and terrorist organizations will be encouraged. Why don't you welcome them to New York, Captain. Show them how we do it here. But deploy non-lethal munitions. The mayor's already on my ass."

"Roger that."

"No, wait!" Mitchell implores, but Harris' lead chopper has already dropped his nose and is moving fast up the field. The choppers descend near the far end of the field just past the tree line so they can take a more accurate pass and stay covered until then.

They come in low over the softball fields just to the north. The trees blow and sway from the chopper blades. As they approach, their guns blaze with heavy rubber bullets and tear gas canisters.

"Sir, it's a set up…No!" Mitchell shouts.

"Engaging targets," Harris cuts him off, his guns already blazing.

The meadow erupts in chaos as rubber bullets tear into the morning frost ripping up the earth as tear gas unleashes a toxic cloud. Blood sprays from headdresses while bloodied bodies are knocked to the ground. Appendages are ripped in two. There's carnage everywhere. Blood on the grass. Tufts of the well-groomed field fly into the air from the barrage. The morning air fills with the sound of destruction and the smell of gunpowder.

"Targets confirmed," Harris reports with grim satisfaction, pulling up.

"Coming around again to get a closer look," Rodriguez announces, his heart heavy as he brings his chopper lower for another pass, seeing no one flee. They are only fifty feet off the ground now and fast approaching up the field; he slows to hover closer to the carnage. The air is filled with blowing smoke and the fiery wreckage below. There is no movement. No return fire.

The TV news choppers above relay video footage of the police choppers unleashing their payload of bullets. Except for the whirring of hovering chopper blades, an eerie silence fills the field as onlookers begin walking over to take witness.

As the smoke and tear gas clear, and the bloodied scene is revealed, Rodriguez shouts, "Sir! Sir!" His voice cracks over the radio. "We've been had. They're just wooden cutouts, cardboard, paper mâché. Even the damn horses. Plus, we have eyes on several loudspeakers. Damn."

Remaining ears, noses, and heads go flying off as they're struck by the wind of the chopper. Red water spurts from small tanks below the horse's ribs and from inside the wooden people.

"What? Repeat, Sergeant," the commanding officer demands.

"We've been had, Sir."

"Ghost army," Mitchell says quietly. "Shit."

"What's that?" Harris's voice has lost its edge.

"I'll explain it back at the base, Sir." Mitchell responds, his tone heavy with understanding. "Someone knows their history."

Rodriguez hovers closer, the morning light revealing the elaborate deception.

"They even put blood—I mean food dye—all over. Wow, so damn real." Another spurt of red liquid catches the sun as it sprays up from a fallen horse. The blood mixing with the soil and staining the grass.

"Christ!" the commander says. "Bring it home."

The captain nods, visible in his cockpit, previous bravado deflated.

"Why would they do all this? Why go to such extremes?" he asks while passing over FAO Schwartz and million-dollar apartments.

The hawk that Harris noticed earlier circles once more, then lands on a wooden warrior's outstretched arm.

Over their radios, their commander growls through the open channel, "Where the hell are the actual suspects?"

"Unknown, sir. They're not in the field."

"Well, they must be on foot. All units, they must be on foot. Keep an eye out for all Native Americans on foot. All Points Bulletin. I repeat. All Points Bulletin. I want them and I want them now."

"How will we know who's Native American in this crowd?" a beat cop asks over the channel.

"Best guess. Stop everyone."

"We got burned profiling before, Sir."

"I Don't Care. Do it!"

After pacing, White Feather sits on the edge of the couch, Little Wonder and Lilyanna pressed against her sides. On their small TV screen, the live news chopper's feed gives them a bird's-eye view of Sheep Meadow: the vast green space stretching out like a canvas below, morning frost making the grass sparkle.

"Look how big it is, Mama! The field and city are so beautiful," Lilyanna whispers, smiling to herself.

"What are those, Mama?" Little Wonder points at three dark shapes moving fast across the screen.

As the news camera zooms in, White Feather's breath catches recognizing police helicopters approaching in formation.

"Those are…" she starts, but her words cut off as the shots ring out.

White Feather lunges forward, hands covering her children's eyes as bullets tear into the figures below.

She screams out in helpless frustration, stomping her feet, "No!"

She watches the police helicopters fire, the carnage and red liquid spraying across the frost-covered grass; the mechanical pumps dying with a few remaining spirts.

"Mama, let me see!" Lilyanna protests, grabbing at her mother's hand, but White Feather holds firm.

"They're shooting at us! They're shooting at us!" Little Wonder has managed to peek around her fingers. "But what about Unca Cwoud?" He cries looking up at his mother with worry in his big black eyes.

Relief floods through her as the camera zooms in on a splintered wooden warrior laying on its side.

"Look, they're not real people." She relaxes some.

The news helicopter circles higher; the cameraman makes sure to capture every angle of the destruction. His lens lingers on each fallen figure, each splash of red against the green earth, telling the story without words; his finger on the trigger of the camera snapping shots instead of deploying bullets.

Moments later, all three of them cry as the news camera zooms in on the wooden carnage and red dye-stained field. The bullets and danger are real. The torn-up field is real. Yet the true natives had blended back into the city.

As she looks away in relief, the newscaster states that one person has been apprehended.

"I repeat, one man has been apprehended. Stay tuned for more details as the story unfolds." The camera view opens up on the streets near Macy's. A camera man rushes with bouncing lens to the scene where the man has been taken into custody. A tall man with dark hair is being placed inside a police car.

He's wearing a full headdress of red, black, blue, and green.

The police chief states at a brief press conference, "He was carrying a sharpened tomahawk. It's a good thing we caught him, folks, or there might be some real injuries. When we know more, you'll know more." He then walks off in a huff without taking questions.

White Feather tries moving around the television to see who it is.

"No. No. No."

"What's the matter, Mama?" Lilyanna asks with fear and confusion. Little Wonder stands closely beside her.

In the living room, they stand watching the television. She pulls both of her children tight.

"I think your uncle's in trouble."

The remaining crowd at Macy's stands transfixed as the news broadcast shows the police helicopters opening fire on Sheep Meadow. Parents cover their children's eyes. Some turn away. Others can't look away.

"They're shooting them down like animals!" a woman pleads. "Stop it! Please."

"It's madness," a man from India surmises. "This is not the America I came to."

Then a collective gasp as the smoke clears, revealing the truth of splintered wood, paper mâché, the stage effects meant to mirror historical violence. The lesson isn't lost on a watching Nation.

Chip Wegney angrily grabs the microphone from the stage floor.

"This is what happened then," he points to the banners hanging from buildings. "This is what's happening now." He points to the monitors showing the event play out in Sheep Meadow. "When will we learn? And when will we stop being such dicks?"

At a loss for words, he drops the mic and jumps down from the stage to begin walking with protesters.

Near Chip, a Black grandfather with short gray hair and his twenty-year-old grandson attend the parade for the first time. He says to his grandson next to him, "See how quick they were to shoot? Didn't even try to negotiate. Some things never change." He shakes his head in disappointment.

"But some things do, Grandpa," his grandson responds, pointing to the screens now showing people streaming toward Sheep Meadow from all directions. "Plus, you could hide the truth in the past. You can't hide the present, Grandpa."

Nathaniel, his grandson, raises his smart phone. "Everyone's got one. Now we can all record history, together."

"You're smarter than you look." The old man smiles and pats him on the back looking proudly at him. "History in the making. Let's join in—reminds me of Dr. King's marches," he says as they blend in with the forming moving mass. It's like a river of humanity that wants better things from the world around them, knowing that better things are possible.

A woman says to her husband, "It's not entirely their fault. They didn't know it was paper mâché and wood, I guess." Confused, she shrugs as they walk off.

Even though the police attempt to disperse the crowd, many bewildered spectators linger along the parade route, drawn to the giant banners and statistics still visible on buildings.

Small groups form beneath them, reading aloud the numbers that can no longer be ignored. Some weep openly. Others shake their heads in anger, taking photos with their phones, sharing what they've learned and posting messages on social media.

The news report showcasing what just happened at Sheep Meadow plays on every screen, and the crowd's reaction shifts from shock to understanding. They see now that Samuel's ghost army and Bull Nose Pete's mechanicals served its purpose: it made visible the pattern of violence that's haunted their Nation for centuries.

Sheep Meadow was Samuel's brilliant idea: wooden characters, much like the floats in the parade. From afar, they were hard to distinguish. There were bottle rockets, mechanical arms for the braves on horseback, and tanks of red dyed water connected to ejector pumps.

Pete created the explosives, timed diversions, and mechanics of it all. Money had been pooled from all the tribes involved to make it happen. It had taken months to create that display, all of it destroyed in seconds—just as planned.

Samuel and Bull Nose Pete worked late into the night, crafting each figure by hand with the help of several volunteers. Placing in the mechanical pumps for the fake blood, the carefully positioned speakers, the staging that made wooden figures come alive in the morning light.

When Samuel first told Bull Nose Pete about the ghost army, Bull Nose Pete looked at him strangely and said, "That sounds scary.

Do you conjure the dead or something? Like a ghost dance?"

"No, you idiot. It was a tactic deployed by the U.S. Army during World War II to make the Germans think there was an advancing unit at a front when it was all just inflatable tanks, wooden structures, plastics, and tarps."

"Oh," Bull Nose Pete had responded. "Well, still sounds scary," his nostrils flared as he thought about it while standing outside of Samuel's barn.

The news helicopter circles high above Midtown, its cameraman capturing a city in transformation. Streams of humanity flow through the streets below; one river moves up Broadway from Herald Square, others converge on Sheep Meadow from all directions. Smaller tributaries of people stream and trickle through, cascading down apartment staircases and out of restaurants to meet history as it unfolds at their door. The city is alive—a living, breathing organism.

A movement of people flow through Manhattan's concrete canyons. People who had been watching the news step out of their apartments to be a part of it. Patrons and workers step out of restaurants. Owners flip signs to "Closed." The few office workers doing overtime look out their windows, then close their computers and grab their jackets, leaving the work behind for another day.

The parade route, once rigid with corporate floats and giant balloons, now pulses with something organic and unplanned, a life breathing on its own. Marching bands that practiced standard parade tunes now merge into the park and syncopate with the Native drums. The Kansas City band, their brass and percussion finding harmony with ancient rhythms. Others join, creating a new sound that echoes between buildings—the heartbeat of a pulsating city.

Many parade spectators join the growing procession. The police, initially formed into blockades, begin stepping aside, letting them in. A few remove their riot gear and fall in with the crowd to walk beside them.

This impromptu event is a reminder to all participants and spectators about the importance of togetherness and sharing, what Thanksgiving is all about. It is not based in religion like many holidays but unity: the sacred vow that America means to so many.

At Sheep Meadow, something extraordinary is taking shape. Where wooden figures once stood, real people now join hands. The wooden figures burning from the attack and explosions have become a bonfire where people witness and gather.

Many hold hands. Some weep at the overwhelming emotions of unity and togetherness, what could have been a terrible tragedy and what could have become a burial ground.

The Round Dance, an ancient ceremony of unity and healing begins. For centuries, tribes have used this dance to bring people together: the circle representing life's continuity, the joined hands showing strength in connection. There is no hierarchy in a Round Dance, no beginning or end, just the infinite power of moving as one.

It starts with a small group of Native Americans who emerge from the crowd. They begin the simple side-stepping motion that's been passed down through generations. A drum circle forms outside the group, like the cell ring around a nucleus, their steady drumbeat carrying both sorrow for what was lost and hope for what might be.

"Join us," they call to those watching. "The circle is open to all."

A Hispanic woman steps forward first, taking the offered hand. A white family from the suburbs joins next.

Soon, the original circle expands as more people step in, learning the steps, becoming part of something larger than themselves. The first of the peace marchers reach the meadow's edge as the Round Dance grows. The drums from both groups find each other, synchronizing into one heartbeat with over fifty drummers, many showing up with bongos from nearby buildings. Circles within circles form across the frost-covered grassland as thousands of hands join in a living symbol of unity.

Past Columbus Circle, along Central Park South, streams of people flow into every entrance of the park. The synchronized drums echo off buildings, calling more to join in like a beacon to all.

From above, the circles ripple outward like growth rings of an ancient tree. Native Americans teach the steps to newcomers: businessmen still in suits, tourists with shopping bags, children riding on parents' shoulders. The police helicopters still hover, but now they're witnesses to something their bullets couldn't stop.

Approaching the park's edge, Chip Wegney walks with hotel maids, doormen, cabbies, and parade performers.

Nearby, one police officer hears over the radio, "Johnson, what are you doing?" She looks up to the police chopper above.

"Our motto is to serve and protect. Serve is the first word. I'm serving, Sir, and I'm protecting. I swore an oath to this city and this nation, and I am upholding it."

"Understood. Keep up the good work and keep your wits about you."

"Will do, Lieutenant."

As the marchers coming in from Fifth Avenue crest the hill toward Sheep Meadow, they pause. Below them, hundreds of people move in concentric circles, the Round Dance growing larger with each passing minute filling out the space of Sheep Meadow.

Soon, the two movements merge from east and west; the march flows naturally into the expanding circles until thousands move together across the meadow where wooden warriors once stood.

Even as the peace march and Round Dance merge into something beautiful, forces move in to stop it and maintain the status quo. In the Macy's executive suite overlooking the parade route, phones ring off the hook.

"This is a PR nightmare," the VP of Marketing barks into his phone. "Someone has to be held accountable. Find whoever's behind this and shut it down. This is costing us millions. Tell Chip to shut the fuck up. We don't pay him to aid a rebellion and make us look bad."

His young assistant stands next to his boss's desk, "Sir, maybe we could spin this in our favor?"

"I'm listening…"

"Well first, our viewership is up 140 percent over last year's, and well, if we show that we care…"

"140 percent! Wow! Those numbers are off the charts," the VP interrupts him.

His assistant points out the floor-to-ceiling windows of his boss's office. "You see all those people out there. Show them Macy's cares…Those are Macy's customers."

The executive nods his understanding and approves. He looks at the sea of people below, and on the screens in his office forming circles and marching with drums.

"Alright," he says. "Let's pivot."

"Sir?"

"Tell the press Macy's stands for inclusion, healing, and… what's that dance called again?"

"Round Dance."

"Right. The Round Dance. Slap it on a banner. We support it. Print shirts. Get Chip on Fallon. Make sure he cries. Let's capitalize on this. Thanksgiving is back, baby."

TWENTY-EIGHT

Fading Back

Across the city, police commanders try to regain control of their units.

"All officers return to your positions. This is an unauthorized gathering. I repeat, this is unauthorized. Anyone participating will face disciplinary action."

Sheep Meadow is a public space and a historical place for peaceful protests. As individuals first, some officers remove their earpieces and step into the crowd. Others turn down their radios. But the SWAT teams are mobilizing and unmarked cars filled with federal agents thread through side streets driving fast.

"We've got facial recognition running on every camera feed," a commander announces.

"Priority is the man who took the stage. Find him."

Alex, from his position at the coffee shop, watches warning signs flash across his screens.

"They're trying to shut us down," he tells Ben through his earpiece. "Corporate security is fighting to reclaim their systems."

"Time for our people to disappear," Ben responds. "Send the signal."

Throughout Manhattan, phones buzz with a simple encrypted message: *The seeds of change are planted. Time to scatter in the wind.*

In the meantime, Black Cloud walks among the transformed crowd of the Meadow, his inconspicuous look without disguise keeps him safe with so many other Natives and Hispanic people about.

Around him, something unprecedented unfolds: marching bands play with Native drums, children teach their parents the steps they'd just learned to the Round Dance, police officers remove riot gear to walk alongside those they'd been ordered to arrest.

Through gaps in the crowd, he spots more people streaming in from park paths. Someone hands him a bottle of water. A grandmother takes his arm for support as they walk. No one recognizes him as the man who started it all, but he knows he can't stay. He looks at his watch knowing he needs to meet Tall Tim and get out of there, seeing the police approaching from all sides.

While looking around and side stepping in the Round Dance, laughing and smiling with strangers, this isn't the ending he'd planned; it's better.

The authorities will be looking for someone to blame, to punish for their embarrassment. His capture would give them the excuse to end this moment of unity and lock it down with potentially more violence. The SWAT teams are advancing on the park and will create a noose as they begin profiling participants. He needs to slip away fast and clandestine-like before that happens. Before this beautiful event has the chance to turn into something ugly.

As he breaks from the dance and steps away, he sees several clusters of police emerge from both sides of the field. He's learned from his own experience—you might be able to negotiate with one cop, but not a dozen. He lowers his head and begins walking away.

As he exits Sheep Meadow, Chip Wegney passes nearby arms

locked walking with a hundred others. For a moment, their eyes meet. Something in Chip's expression suggests recognition, but the entertainer simply nods and keeps walking, choosing to protect the magic of what's happening. He was one of the only people to have seen him without his disguise on.

Black Cloud sees the hawk on a nearby tree and feels his mother's presence.

"It's time," he whispers to no one in particular. His phone buzzes. Alex's message is clear: *The seeds of change are planted...*

Then, like his ancestors who could disappear into forests and hillsides without a trace, he lets the crowd's movement guide him toward his escape route. Behind him, the drums continue their steady beats as thousands move together in circles.

Cops are clustering at points within the park. Police vans are pulling up and doors slam as they hop out of the back with tactical riot gear, bullet proof vests, helmets, and police batons, having not experienced the event, only their orders.

He doesn't know where Tall Tim is but looks at his watch and remembers the meetup point nearby. He texts Tim, *We gottta go.*

A police helicopter sweeps overhead along the park perimeter. Black Cloud keeps his head down, just another face in the crowd, but heading west out of the park and away from the parade and people. The transformation he'd dreamed of is happening without him now, perhaps that's how it should be. No single person can own a movement this large.

He leaves the drums and dancing behind. His part is finished. The people will write the rest of this story themselves.

He texts Tim again as he steps out of the park onto Central Park West. After a few blocks he turns left onto 72nd Street to meet him.

But Tall Tim is MIA.

Where are you? Did you not get the message? It's time to scatter. Text me back. Cloud waits to see if the message is read but it goes unread. His third one sent.

He shakes his head and moves toward the agreed meeting spot.

Samuel now stands with Crystal, Tom Sr., and TJ where the foot path begins over the Brooklyn Bridge. Pockets of morning fog roll off the East River. They've already stripped off their items and washed their hands with hand sanitizer. They are now wearing regular clothes: jeans, overalls for Samuel, baseball caps, a blue hair bow for Crystal.

Samuel hugs Crystal. She steps back looking them all over.

"Thank you, guys, for everything. This was *a-mazing*." Overwhelmed with joy, her youthful innocence has been restored for the moment. With a broad smile, she hugs all three men and turns to leave.

"I'll see you back home." She then pauses and looks at Samuel, "Did you ever think it would turn into this?" Crystal pauses and leans against the bridge railing not yet ready to leave them or the moment behind. "All those people joining in…" Her hazel eyes sparkle in the morning light off the river.

"Never," Samuel admits, his usual gruffness softened by wonder, and the feeling of a surrogate daughter smiling at him. He shrugs, "We thought maybe we'd make the news, make them think a little. But this…" He shakes his head, watching young people coming off the bridge jogging into Manhattan talking about it. "Never."

"Dad," TJ looks at his phone and points to the screen. "Look at those circles getting bigger. It's crazy."

They all lean in to watch as the Round Dance expands across Sheep Meadow, the peace march flowing around its edges like tributaries joining a broader river.

"Your ghost army worked, Sam," Tom Sr. says quietly with astonishment and a smile on his intelligent face. "Even better than what we hoped for."

"Thanks, but Pete's work brought it to life." Worried, he looks down at his phone hoping for a text from Bull Nose Pete, but nothing. "I better get going to meet him at the rendezvous point in case there's a problem."

After another moment, they continue with their goodbyes. Crystal hugs all three men again, her usual hardness has given way to joy. She turns to leave, but Tom Sr. calls after her.

"Uh, that's it? See ya?" He gently elbows TJ, who knows his father's heart.

"Crystal," TJ asks, glancing at his father's hopeful expression, "Um, would you like to come with us? We're heading up the New England coast for a few days."

Tom Sr. nods at her, smiling. "Yeah, will you come?"

She looks at Samuel for guidance like one would a father, with vulnerability in her eyes. The woman who once couldn't trust anyone to watch her back now stands at a different kind of crossroads.

The old warrior nods his approval.

She had planned on taking a train up to White Plains, a city just north of Manhattan, to visit a friend.

"Hmm," she says looking them over and meeting Tom Sr.'s eyes and pauses after being caught in them. After recovering she swallows and asks, "Could we swing by my friend's house first?"

"Anything you want," Tom Sr. says. "We'd just love to have you with us."

"Love to have me?"

They both nod.

TJ repeats, "Yeah, Crystal, we'd love to have you."

"Well, how can I refuse two handsome fellows?" She stares at Tom Sr., then over at TJ.

Samuel hugs her again then releases her like a father giving away his daughter. This wayward group has become a family forged in fire and shared purpose.

Samuel says his goodbyes to the three of them. He considers not returning to the reservation and finding a new life, but the pull of the ties-that-bind are too strong to ignore. Plus, he misses the mare.

"Come see me when you're back. I have space for all of you, if you need. All of you," he says looking them over one last time.

"But where's Pete?" Crystal looks around then down at her phone, shaking her head.

Samuel frowns. "I don't know. But he ain't good with maps. I need to get to the rendezvous point to find out."

He leaves them and says in parting, "Don't forget my offer." He then pauses realizing something. "It's never too late to have a family."

They nod at the offer and the three begin the trek over the bridge. They had parked in Brooklyn and are simply tourists now taking pictures, laughing, and eating cotton candy. Crystal and Tom Sr. let their guards down for the first time in years. Tom Sr. buys her a balloon, which makes her smile. TJ takes pictures of them with the Manhattan skyline at their backs. Halfway across, seeing other couples doing the same, Tom Sr. kisses her. She holds onto him tightly, as tight as forever.

In Chinatown, Samuel is actually smiling as he walks the few blocks to where he and Bull Nose Pete are supposed to meet. For the first time in years, his face feels strange without its usual scowl. The streets buzz with life: vendors sell trinkets at tables along the sidewalk, cooked chickens hang in windows, fish on ice ready for sale, merchants calling out prices, while cars jam the roadways. The sidewalks bulge with people. He pauses at the intersection of Spring and Canal Streets—the busiest place in the world. They are to meet here to take the Chinatown bus out of New York.

His father's medicine pouch rests against his chest as he takes in the scene. Drums still echo in his mind while he thinks about the horses back home, especially the old bay mare who's been with him for twenty-three years. Realizing she's the only thing he's ever really known how to love.

A few blocks away, police sirens wail. No Bull Nose Pete yet. He checks his watch again, running through contingency plans in his mind. Would he leave without him?

He glances at the many strange faces, not unlike his. No, he would not. He would find his friend.

"Come on Pete. Wherever you are."

He touches the medicine pouch again. His father had been a closed off man, and he learned that too. The horses will be waiting, if he can get there, but maybe it's time he learns to love something more and not be closed off to possibility.

Bull Nose Pete had gotten a little turned around after the grid of Manhattan ended at Houston. Now the streets are on weird angles and have names instead of numbers. He can count numbers.

He can't count names.

A few blocks away he takes off the costume and stuffs it into a garbage can, takes a few steps with his makeup still on, then stops to remove the bandana from his head when he sees two cops walking fast toward him.

His smile turns to alarm as the bandana drops to the sidewalk in front of him. He freezes. The garbage can with the headdress and tomahawk sit only a few feet away. If they peek in, he'll be caught.

The bandana sits at his feet frozen in time. The cops approach studying him while one slaps a police baton into his hand. Staring at the approaching officers, Bull Nose Pete notices the paint still on his hands reminding him of what his face must look like. They step closer and could almost grab him when he sticks his hands up as if there is a wall between them. A wall he is trapped behind. There's also a ceiling pushing down on him as if he's trapped by that too. He then sticks his hands out to the side as if there are walls on all four sides closing in on him. With all his might he pushes out, but they keep closing in.

He acts scared with a sad face and begins looking up and to the sides as if trapped inside a box. He rubs his chin in confusion: what to do. Suddenly, he flashes a smile like he just had a bright idea and raises his pointer finger as if a light bulb went off. He makes a circle with a finger on his right hand as if he is creating a doorknob and cuts out the doorway as if with a knife. He turns the knob, opens the door, and steps through into the beautiful sunny day.

Smiling broadly now, he extends his arms out as if breathing fresh air. The warm sunshine has found him. He pounds his chest. Taking a deep breath, he draws air into his chest and pulls it toward him with his hands. A smile bursts upon his face as he wipes an imaginary tear away and throws it to the ground. He takes another step forward. Looking back at the box he shakes his head and waves goodbye to it. He stands straight up with arms wide open as sunrays rest upon his face. He bows to the officers and a couple pedestrians who had stopped to watch his performance.

The cop with the baton says, "Not bad. I don't usually like mimes. But not bad at all." He steps closer and drops fifty cents into the bandana. He and his partner move off as scrambled information about Sheep Meadow and the attack chatters over their walkie-talkies.

"All nearby units respond." The cops take off running.

Bull Nose Pete places glasses on his face, picks up the bandana and tosses the fifty cents up and down in the air. With the bandana he wipes off the remaining paint then throws it into the next trash bin.

At the diner, Alex grows quiet while packing to leave. Introspective, he says to Ben, "I think I'm going to stay."

"Like at the diner?" Ben looks around at the busy place.

"No, here. In New York. It just feels right for me." Alex stands looking at Ben.

Ben nods and says, "Oh, okay. Well, then I think you probably should."

Alex nods and they hug.

Ben continues, "Just know you've got a red brother if you ever need one."

The idea was for the two of them to take a train out, then Ben would come back in a couple days to retrieve his motorcycle.

While Alex folds up his laptop to place it into the case, he looks out the window and onto the busy New York City street that has calmed after the melee.

"Yeah, this is where I belong," he says.

"Mate, if you ever need me, just reach out. I'll come find you." Ben Blackfeather hands him a card that simply reads *Feather* with an email address—no phone number.

"I will," Alex smiles.

"Me, I'm going riding for a while. I've always wanted to see Maine," Ben says.

Alex agrees. "You should."

"Can I give you a lift?"

"Nah, I think I'll walk around a bit and get my bearings. You know, figure out my next step."

Ben nods, excited to ride his motorcycle up into New England and figure out his own next chapter. Instead of heading west, he'll head north to Acadia National Park—the ocean calling to him once more. He'll buy some warmer clothes along the way.

Alex's part in this is finished.

"Being Nez Perce and gay has taught me plenty about wearing masks," he says, after closing his laptop for the last time. "Think it's time I tried living without one."

Ben nods pondering his statement, understanding something similar in himself. "Like I said, you've got family now if you need one," Ben's voice carries the weight of someone who knows about masks and hiding. "Though something tells me you're going to find your own kind of tribe here."

"Academy Award worthy performance today, wasn't it?" Alex grins.

"One not to be forgotten," Ben agrees. He stands, adjusting his leather jacket. "The road's calling, brother. Time for me to slip out of here."

They embrace one final time: the Apache warrior and the Nez Perce hacker who helped change history. Ben heads for his motorcycle while Alex steps out into his new city, both of them carrying a story that's only just begun.

At home, White Feather clutches her children closer as they watch history unfold on their TV screen.

"Look!" Lilyanna points at thousands of people joining hands across the meadow. "They're all dancing together." She hugs herself then gets up and spins.

Little Wonder leans his face closer to the screen, "Is that a ghost dance, Mama?"

White Feather wipes tears from her eyes. "No honey. This is different. It's called a Round Dance, and it's for everyone."

He smiles up at her with wonder.

She thinks of her brother out there somewhere, hidden in the crowd he helped create. She thinks of their mother's prophecy, that he would do something special. She remembers their father's dreams of his children belonging to a larger American story.

"Will Unca Cwoud come home now?" Little Wonder asks.

White Feather pulls him close, her heart full of pride and worry. "Soon, baby."

"Will you be nice to him?" Lilyanna frowns while asking.

She tears up and nods vigorously. "Yes, sweetie. I will. I promise. You kids go play now."

After they leave the room, she stands and bites her nails, needing to find out about the man who got caught. She flips from channel to channel trying to find out what's happening. The network switches to breaking news. The news anchor appears both flustered and energized.

"In a developing story, police have arrested Daniel Branston, the man suspected of organizing today's events. Branston, known locally for appearing at protests in various costumes, claims he was 'channeling alien energy through his headdress' at the time of his arrest."

White Feather lets out a breath she didn't know she was holding.

The police chief appears at a hastily arranged press conference, adjusting his tie before stepping up to the podium.

"We have some more information for you. The suspect's name is Daniel Branston. He has been in and out of mental hospitals, has two felonies, and is known for violent outbursts and conspiracy theories. We believe we have our man."

Footage plays of Branston's arrest, showing him running through Herald Square shouting, "Yup, I planned it all! Me and my pals. Geronimooooo!" As officers tackle him to the ground, he continues his crazed performance, "We are an uprising against this authoritarian regime!"

From the back of the police car, his voice carries across the crowd, "They are my braves. I am their leader, and they will come for me. We will rise again!"

White Feather shakes her head, relief and amusement mix with lingering worry. But she keeps watching, knowing somewhere out there her brother is trying to make his way back home. She breathes a sigh of relief and clicks off the TV. She finds the kids in their rooms: Little Wonder playing with his action figures, Lilyanna brushing her long black hair.

"Come on," she says softly. "We need to go next door."

"But Mama…" they start to protest.

"Now." Something in her voice makes them set down what they're doing and take her hand.

In her mother's bedroom, she sits on the bed and cries. She is alone with her children and her grief—no brother, husband, parents—and yet she feels a sense of elation and relief.

Through tears she mutters quietly, "He did it," and grabs her children, hugging them tightly.

She can feel her mother's presence, the old woman's knowing smile. She had seen it coming, had known Black Cloud would do something special. The empty trailer still holds traces of sage smoke, and she imagines her mother watching from somewhere beyond, up in the Black Hills proud of both her children—one for having the courage to act, one for having the strength to understand.

"Why are you crying, Mama?" Little Wonder asks, touching her wet cheek.

"Because sometimes," she says, pulling them closer, "you cry when your heart is too full to hold everything inside."

"I cry like that too," Little Wonder says hugging her.

On his leisurely stroll uptown, Tall Tim buys a soft, squishy Statue of Liberty, a small Yankees flag he waves on occasion, and a snow globe of Manhattan. He shakes it and stares at it joyfully. He places it back into the shopping bag he got bopping into the stores for tourists. The stuff is for his wife and grandkids.

Tall Tim comes upon a sea of food vendors and lined up horse carriages on 60th at the bottom of Central Park near Columbus Circle. After what they've just accomplished, his urge to celebrate manifests in the only way he knows how: eating everything in sight, which means hot dogs, pretzels, and knishes. He stops to admire the horses, even petting a few and speaking to them in soft tones.

After wolfing down another pretzel, he gets more honey roasted nuts and walks with his head in the bag as cops run past him toward the park. Eating and walking, with the bag of knickknacks on his arm, he stops at the last vendor as he places glasses on his face, ignoring the commotion.

"Hot dog, please."

"What do you want on it, pal?"

He places his thumbs into the belt hooks of his overalls and thinks. He is an old man again, with thin gray and black hair mostly to the side. Some of the hairs are a little unkempt. The headdress and paint have already been discarded.

He feels better than he has in a long time.

"Oh, um, mustard."

"Relish?" the vendor asks.

With eyes widening like a child, Tim says, "Oh yes, lots of relish."

He takes a big bite, watching another group of officers hurry past. For once, he doesn't feel feeble or useless. Today, he helped change history, even if no one will ever know his name. In his own way, he feels like a hero.

Cop cars pass as Black Cloud waits for Tall Tim at the corner of 72nd Street and Central Park West. He studies a building a hundred feet in from the park. This was their meeting place. He keeps glancing out to Central Park West, but no Tim. He checks the time again then sees a cop car with lights blaring down the street along the park.

"Come on, Timmy," he says under his breath, getting a little nervous. Shifting his attention to the building once more, he had purposely set the rendezvous point here.

He studies the building and waits, trying to stay calm. But with each passing police car, his worry increases, and breath shortens, feeling they are close to being caught.

The famous medieval building with gray chiseled stone columns, European marble archway, and tall pointed wrought iron gate holds his gaze as he avoids eye-contact with other onlookers.

He looks west toward the sun and home after another cop car blazes past.

Come on Tim, he thinks, when he sees this thin gangly old man come around the corner eating a hot dog and carrying a bag. Black Cloud breaks into a laugh and shakes his head with joy.

As Tall Tim get closers, Black Cloud says, "I should have known." He smiles, embracing his old friend.

"I love it here," Tall Tim says.

Black Cloud nods. "I want to show you something." They both step in front of the building. Both are old men again, not warriors or chiefs.

After pausing a moment, Tall Tim says, "Nice building." And looks over his shoulder. A few mounted police gallop along the park boundary, the clip-clop of the horses echoing.

"Come on, we need to get out of here," Tall Tim says, his mouth full of his last bite of hot dog. He wipes the relish off his face then looks at the napkin.

"It's okay." Black Cloud raises a hand as if to say, *one more second*, and steps off the curb a few feet into the road where it happened. "It's fitting that he was killed in front of a building called The Da-kot-a."

"Who?"

"John Lennon." Black Cloud pauses pensively, the moment affecting him deeply. "He was a good man."

Tall Tim nods swallowing the last bite. "Good music, too."

"All you need is love, John," Black Cloud says, raising a peace sign with his two fingers. Then he takes a Yankees cap from his back pocket and places it on his head.

They walk west to pick up the next uptown subway. Tall Tim glances back at The Dakota one last time, then at his friend.

"You know what's funny, Cloud?"

"What's that?"

"You see this place on TV and it doesn't look real. Like it's just some movie you're watching. Until you come here and it's all real. What happened to him," he motions to the building where John Lennon lived and got shot in front of, "what we just did here and what's still going on in the park. I mean, his song, 'Imagine'—Betty always loved that song. But it's real. It isn't abstract. We could have a better world."

He says this with a sparkle in his eyes, then scavenges for his last bag of honey roasted peanuts from his bag.

Black Cloud is struck by the effusive nature of his friend, never hearing so many words strung together all at once and with such wisdom.

They approach the dark stairs to the subway.

"All these years playing cards, drinking beer, complaining about everything…who'd have thought we'd end up making history?"

Black Cloud adjusts his Yankees cap, smiling. "Just a matter of doing. Bellyaching never got anyone anywhere…You were always braver than you knew, and smarter than you let on." Cloud laughs at his friend.

"Not brave," Tall Tim says smiling, patting his stomach. An unspoken understanding is shared between them. "Just hungry." He smiles as they descend the stairs.

The team of Operation Sunup fades from the city. No one was wounded except for a float, a few balloons, and a village of wooden dummies.

And perhaps, Black Cloud thinks as they descend into the subway, some old wounds have finally started to heal.

"You know what else?" Tall Tim asks as they swipe their metro cards at the turnstile.

"What's that?"

"I miss the rez, Betty, my grandkids," he says as the squealing subway rumbles in for a stop.

After stepping on and the doors close, the subway rattles off, disappearing into the next tunnel. Two old friends heading home, leaving behind a city forever changed.

Indelible marks were left upon the lives of a watching nation.

TWENTY-NINE

Whiteman's Demise

Stan looks down at himself, taking inventory of his disgrace. His suit pants are soaked through with alley water and garbage juice seeps into places he doesn't want to think about. His shoes, once polished to a government-grade shine, are caked with grime and feces. He rubs his swollen jaw, feeling blood from his split lip transfer to his fingers.

He lost his badge in the scuffle. Somewhere between the dumpster and where he now sits, thirty years of federal service lies buried under coffee grounds, seeping garbage bags and yesterday's newspapers. His legs look like he's had an accident—which, in a way, he has. A very expensive, possibly career-ending accident.

Looking around at the filthy alley—at the dumpster twenty feet away, the rusting fire escapes above, the towering brick walls that seem to mock his predicament—he realizes he's become exactly what he'd accused Black Cloud of being: wrong.

Sitting in the puddle, his phone rings.

"Stan, it's Director Hodges. Meet me at Grand Central Station in two hours."

He lost his bags and all his belongings to save a day that didn't need saving. But he didn't know that. He also didn't know that the tow truck driver sitting in front of him on the bridge had towed his rental car away.

When he arrives at Grand Central Station, Director Hodges is standing at Junior's Bakery sipping a coffee and eating a black and white cookie. As Stan walks up, Director Hodges almost spits out his coffee.

"Jesus Christ. What the hell happened to you?"

About to open his mouth, Director Hodges cuts him off, "Never mind, I don't want to know." Black eye, swollen cheek, grime on his pants, and gunk on his shoes.

"What is that brown stuff on your shoes?" He leans in, "Ugh. You smell like wet cat shit." He gags a little and raises his hand. "Step back. Step back."

Whiteman backs off a few feet. "I haven't had a chance to get cleaned up."

Director Hodges shakes his head, annoyed he's missing Thanksgiving with his family to deal with this mess.

He loves black and white cookies and nods to the display case. He takes another bite of the one he has and stands next to a small table with a wax bag sitting on it.

"I told the missus I'd bring her back one. Look Stan, I'll be brief," he says between bites of his cookie and sips of his coffee, "I'm heading back this afternoon so I can salvage a hint of Thanksgiving with my family."

"But Sir…"

"Don't, but sir me. Look at you. You're a mess. And they caught the guy. Case closed."

He takes another bite and chews, enjoying the frosted cookie and good coffee.

"Boss, I have proof someone else did it."

"Where is this so-called paper?"

"Well…" he pulls it from his rear pocket. The paper is folded and saturated from the mud, feces, and water. "I took it out of the bag."

Hodges looks it over and raises an eyebrow at Stan. "Ran tests on it?"

"It was clean. But I swear it said, *Big Like Little Big Horn Big*, and I know who's behind it."

"Behind what? What the fuck does that even mean, Stan?"

Stan sheepishly shrugs.

"This is worthless. Wet, saturated, falling apart, piss-stained, inadmissible garbage. Eww, disgusting too. It smells like you do. You want me to hand this to a judge?" He grimaces and shoves it back at Stan then wipes his hand. "Plus, they caught the guy who admitted to it. There's no case. What do you have against these folks anyway?"

"You've got to listen to me…"

"No Stan, you listen to me. You were always a snively little shit, and I never liked you. We all know you cheated on the entrance exam. Look, I don't know what's going on here, but I'm restationing you to an outpost near Albuquerque, New Mexico where you can't annoy anyone or get into any more trouble." He pauses, "And my goodness, clean yourself up." He holds his nose while picking up the bag of black and white cookies and walks away.

Whiteman stands with a black eye, stinking of garbage. He crumples up his piss-stained evidence and throws it into the nearest trash can. He steps up to the counter and orders a cookie and a coffee. He grabs some wet, smelly cash from his soaked wallet and hands it to the female cashier, who frowns.

Through the station's massive windows, he can see people

streaming west toward Central Park. Drums echo off the granite walls from televisions on the wall broadcasting the whole thing. Even here, history is unfolding—the very thing he was supposed to be watching out for. But he'd been too obsessed with personal revenge to see the bigger picture, having never tried to understand it.

"Your coffee, sir," the cashier says, holding the cup as far from herself as possible.

Whiteman takes it, finding a quiet corner where he can nurse his wounds and drink his coffee. Thirty years of pursuing the wrong kind of justice, and all he has to show for it is a one-way ticket to New Mexico.

On the monitors, he can see more people heading toward the park. The drums are getting louder—not sounds of war, but of unity. On a nearby TV, footage shows the Round Dance growing larger, people of all backgrounds joining hands.

He shakes his head and spits blood into a napkin then slams the table with his hand. He thinks about Gloria, about that summer in the Bureau office, about how much he loved her, and everything since that he's twisted into bitterness over the years looking for reasons to take Black Cloud down. It was never Black Cloud but her rejection that coursed through his veins like a virus.

Outside, a group of Native Americans passes by, heading toward the gathering. They're not sneaking or hiding; they walk proud, welcomed by others on the street.

Everything he thought he was protecting against, everything he thought he stood for, seems hollow now.

He takes a sip of coffee and winces, both from his split lip and the bitter taste in his mouth. Looking down at his ruined suit, his garbage-stained shoes, he finally understands that he was stuck in old hatreds.

He stands, tossing his half-finished coffee in the trash. Through the TV monitors, he can see the city transforming, not into the chaos he'd feared, but into something he can't quite understand. The drums continue their steady rhythm echoing across the mosaic tiles of the Grand Central Terminal.

A young Native American woman passes by. She glances at him and smiles innocently without judgment, the same way Gloria did, but for everyone she encountered.

Even with his bruised face, his ruined suit, for a moment their eyes meet. There's no hatred, no fear, just a kind of pity that cuts deeper than any revenge could. A pity that sees someone less fortunate and earnestly cares for their well-being.

"Señor?" A Hispanic janitor approaches with a bucket and a mop. "You're dripping…something."

Whiteman looks down at the trail of alley water he's leaving on the terminal's polished floor.

"Sorry," he mutters. "Rough day. I'll be going now."

"That's okay. There's a bathroom around the corner. You might want to buy some new clothes and clean yourself up. We've all had bad nights, huh?

"Can I give you some words of advice?" he says in broken English. "Whatever happened, you don't want to take it with you." He drops the mop head onto the putrid smelling liquid.

Whiteman nods then limps toward the exit, the bag of cookies forgotten on the counter behind him. Tomorrow he'll be on a flight home to pack up, then he'll board a train to Albuquerque, where he'll process paperwork in a dusty office until retirement. But today, he's just another man who chose the wrong side of history.

On the platform the train pulls up. Behind him, the drums grow louder, and time moves on without him as the train doors close.

THIRTY

Back Home on the Rez

Miles pass in comfortable silence as their truck heads west. Black Cloud drives while Tall Tim dozes in the passenger seat, occasionally waking to unwrap another sandwich from their gas station stash.

"You know what I was thinking?" Tall Tim says, brushing crumbs from his shirt.

"That you're still hungry?"

"No. Well, yes. But I was thinking about all those people joining hands in the park. Never seen anything like that before," he says biting into a ham and cheese sandwich.

Black Cloud nods, remembering the circles growing larger, the drums finding each other. "No one else has either. Shoot. I still can't believe you beat up Whiteman." Cloud shakes his head and slaps the dashboard in amazement.

"Yeah, he swung, and I blocked. Then I razzle dazzled and danced around him like Muhammad Ali. I floated like a butterfly and stung like a bee." He shifts in the seat with his hands up reliving it, and then some.

"You're a hero, buddy."

Tim gulps and says, "But I sure hope he does not come snooping around again. That would be bad."

"Ah, the hell with him." They nod and fall back into silence with the humming hymn of the road and open spaces.

They pass through small towns where TVs in diner windows still show footage from New York. At a rest stop in Ohio, they overhear a young girl and boy argue about how to do the Round Dance, trying to copy the steps. In Illinois, a waitress serves them pie "on the house" without knowing who they are.

"Mighty fine parade this year," she says, refilling their coffee cups.

Tall Tim nearly chokes on his pie, while Black Cloud smiles. "Sure was."

The Midwest miles roll past as they continue west, each state line bringing them closer to the reservation and home. Their discussions drift between memories of what they accomplished and what they're going back to—and missing their families.

"Didn't think those old legs of yours could walk that far," Black Cloud says, referring to Tall Tim wandering through Manhattan.

"Didn't think your plan would actually work," Tim responds, opening a bag of chips. "I'm still not sure how it did."

They fall quiet, watching the landscape change from eastern forests to the open plains. The news still crackles over the radio about the "Thanksgiving Day Transformation" as some are calling it. They listen without commenting, occasionally exchanging glances.

Near the Nebraska border, Tall Tim speaks again. "Do you think things will really change?"

Black Cloud considers this as farmland stretches to the horizon.

"Some things already have. The rest…" he shrugs, "that's up

to everyone else. But the Lord knows we need it to. We still need a miracle to come to the people. That's a fact."

Tim nods, placing his sandwich back down then looks out at the Nebraska horizon. "Yeah," is all he says.

As they near the reservation, familiar landmarks appear: the water tower, the trading post, the glittering churches scattered about. The Black Hills rise in the distance, eternal guardians of their homeland.

They drive past the rec center, and Tall Time exclaims, "Look who's back," pointing to a golden finch perched on a fence post. Black Cloud slows the truck, taking in the hard-baked landscape, feeling more connected to it now than ever before.

"Betty's probably worried sick," Tall Tim says, gathering his things from the floor of the truck.

"You didn't call her?"

"Figured some things are better explained in person." He pauses, "Though I'm not exactly sure how to explain this or much else for that matter."

He grabs the bag of gifts from the floor and briefly looks at the snow globe with the Manhattan skyline.

As he and Tall Tim pull into the driveway, Cloud's mother's wails no longer drift from her trailer—somehow the silence feels right. Birds playing in the bushes have replaced it.

White Feather rushes outside with the kids and gives him a big hug before he can even fully step out of the truck.

"Oh, I missed you guys." He hugs them tightly, tighter than expected. As tight as the fear that held him just a few days earlier, love and courage releasing him from it.

As they break from the hug, Little Wonder asks, "Did you bring us anything Unca Cwoudy?" He looks up in awe at his big proud smiling uncle who's looking back down at him.

"Yeah, Unca Cwoudy," Lilyanna mimics.

"Oh, we missed you, Cloud." His sister touches her hand to her chest. "I was so worried."

"Why were you worried, Mama?" Lilyanna inquires.

Black Cloud looks at them both and gets down on one knee and hugs the two kids again so tightly.

Little Wonder's muffled voice says, "I can't breathe, Unca Cwoud."

"It's hot in here," says Lilyanna.

"Oh sorry, sorry." He gets up and wipes a tear from his face and steps over to the truck to grab a bag. "I have a Yankees cap and a Mets cap for both of you. And a Statue of Liberty for you, Sis. Because I can always count on you in my darkest nights. Corny, I know, but true."

She takes it in hand and feels the weight of it bouncing it slightly up and down then looks at him. "We thought you were in trouble."

"Honestly, I thought so too a couple of times."

Tall Tim stands nearby watching when White Feather says to him, "I'm even glad to see you, Tim."

He smiles and nods. "Quite an adventure, Cloud. Well, I'll be shoving off now to my family. Besides, Betty's the only woman I need. I got the girl long ago." He turns to walk down the driveway.

Cloud shouts after him, "Tim!" who turns back. "I'll never forget this…and thanks for being my best friend."

"Friendship ain't always easy, but it's worth it." Tim nods and smiles.

After a big dinner, Black Cloud and his sister watch the news.

The kids are off in their rooms.

She drags him by the hand to the couch and turns on the television.

"Come, I want to show you something. You probably haven't seen this because you've been on the road. This is from over the last few days." She hits play on the recording she made and sits.

On the streets of Manhattan, many people are interviewed. A trucker from Staten Island says, "It was incredible. I saw the whole dang thing. I gotta tell ya, I never cared about the parade before, but my daughter begged me to come. I'll never miss it again."

A homemaker from Vermont says, "Great. Amazing. Scary too. We didn't know what was happening."

A student from Fordham University confessed, "What Thanksgiving is all about. Minus the smoke bombs and arrows."

A well-dressed spokeswoman for Macy's said, "It was unfortunate the parade was disrupted with certain floats and balloons affected. But it was a unique year, and we look forward to a more inclusive show next year."

With the microphone in his face, a nearby police officer brushes it aside, "No comment." And waves at the cameraman to keep moving.

The last interview is with Chip Wegney, who steps out of NBC studios.

"It changed my life. Whoever they are changed the course of America."

"Wait, hang on a sec." White Feather fast-forwards the recording to another interview from yesterday.

"Wegney started a fundraiser with celebrities." In a large room with Brad Pitt, Sean Penn, George Clooney, and other celebrities taking phone calls.

The camera zooms back to Chip Wegney on the street who says, "It's urgent. We can't brush aside these atrocities any longer if we are the Nation we claim to be. We've already raised over a million dollars. And there's more to do. The website to donate and phone numbers are listed below."

Black Cloud shakes his head in shock and stares at his sister.

"It's a miracle, Sis." Through tears of laughter he says, "Word does travel fast on the prairie. Or the World Wide Web. Wow."

Almost in a whisper, she says, "You did it. You made them see." She rubs his back briefly then gets up to check on the kids in the other room.

With eyes widening he says to no one in particular, "So we did. Hot damn. So we did." He leans back against the couch, closes his eyes and thanks the ancestors and the friends he made along the way.

His phone rings next to him sitting on the couch armrest. He expects it to be Tall Tim or someone from rez. He fumbles for it.

"Hello."

"Hi Dad. It's me. Crazy what happened, huh? It's all over the news. Well, I've been meaning to call you."

He bolts upright and smiles as tears come to his eyes hearing his daughter. "Samantha Blue…it's so good to hear your voice, honey." He leans back against the couch and closes his eyes, imagining her at the beach with blue skies above and sand under her feet.

"I miss you, Daddy."

His heart swells at the words. After Gloria died and Samantha left for California seeking her own path, he'd wondered if the distance would grow too wide to cross. But here she is, reaching across it.

"The Round Dance," she continues, her voice carrying a hint of awe, "they're still doing it in cities out here. People learning the steps, sharing stories. It's gone viral. Dad…did you…?"

"Just watched it on TV like everyone else," he says, but he can hear her smile through the phone.

"Sure you did." A pause. "Mom would have loved it."

"She would have," he agrees softly, remembering Gloria's laugh, her way of dancing while cooking Sunday breakfast. "Remember how she used to say everyone should dance more?"

"And sing more," Samantha adds. "And love more." She pauses. "I've been thinking about coming home. Just for a visit at first, maybe around Christmas?"

His heart skips. "The reservation's pretty dull this time of year. Not like your California beach parties."

She chuckles. "Dad, nothing about the reservation is dull anymore. You're all over social media, you know. Even if they don't know it was you."

Caught, he straightens up and sits forward. "What do you mean, me?"

"Come on, Dad. I know your voice. Remember, when you were on the stage, that was you talking. No recording. No voice tech. I mean only you would think of something so perfectly crazy to overthrow the Macy's Thanksgiving Day Parade. I mean who does that?" Her laugh sounds just like her mother's. "I know that was you on the stage with Chip Wegney. I'm proud of you for doing something, instead of complaining like everyone else."

"You were always too smart for your own good," he says, pride mixing with emotion.

"Well, I had good teachers. You and Mom," she pauses, the sound of the ocean rolling in the background. "You taught me to stand up for what matters."

"Your mother did that. I mostly just caused trouble."

"Sometimes trouble needs causing," she says wiggling her toes in the sand. "The Pacific's still blue here, Dad. Still matches my middle name. But maybe it's time I came home for more than just a visit."

His hand tightens on the phone. "You know where to find me."

"Yeah," she says softly, and smiles. "Under the same stars."

After they hang up, Black Cloud sits in the quiet of his sister's living room, feeling the weight of everything: the loss of his mother, the success of their mission, his daughter's possible return.

Outside, a hawk circles against the evening sky.

THIRTY-ONE

Changing Times

The true perpetrators are never found and Daniel Branston is back at Bellevue Hospital, happily explaining to his doctors how he led an army of alien-channeling Native Americans to transform the Macy's Thanksgiving Day Parade.

"You should have seen it," he tells anyone who'll listen, his headdress confiscated but his enthusiasm undimmed. "The mother ship sent me messages through my dental fillings. That's why I had to act." They nod looking at him then jot notes down in his file.

Meanwhile, across the continent, the real warriors blend back into their communities. A postal worker in Arizona sorts mail with steady hands that once fired arrows at parade balloons. A tires salesman who rode a skateboard across the plains to deliver intel keeps an eye out for injustice. A hairstylist uses colorful hair dyes to match the colors of a warrior.

Crystal and the Toms drive up the New England coast as planned. After stopping at her friend's house in White Plains, they spend several days exploring Maine's rocky shores. Something shifts between Crystal and Tom Sr. during those quiet moments by the ocean—her usual guardedness softening, his past regrets fading like tide marks upon the rocks.

After they return to Pine Ridge, Crystal begins to teach young women self-defense on Sunday mornings. Her scar doesn't seem as prominent now, softened perhaps by the way she smiles more. Tom Sr. often stops by with "plumbing emergencies" that somehow always coincide with her breaks. TJ rolls his eyes at his father's transparent excuses but helps him pick out his best shirts.

Samuel builds them a loft over the barn, "If you ever want to stay…" he says hoping they will.

She looks at Tom Sr. who looks back and nods. "We do Samuel. We all do." She takes Tom's hand into hers.

Enthusiastically TJ asks, "Can you teach me how to ride? I'd love to train for mounted shooting competitions." TJ eventually calls him *Tunkaila*, grandfather.

Samuel beams with pride, some of the old bitterness healing. "I'd be happy to. Only if you help me muck the stalls."

"Deal."

Up in Maine, Ben Blackfeather has found his place near the ocean. The cold waters that once cleansed him now draw others seeking healing. He leads veteran support groups, teaching them to find peace in the waves through cold water therapy.

Alex thrives in New York, his acting career takes off after a critic noted his "remarkable authenticity" in a play about cultural identity. His email account receives congratulatory cryptic messages signed only with a feather.

Bull Nose Pete's newfound mime skills have made him something of a local celebrity. Children beg him to do "the invisible box trick," never knowing it once saved him from arrest.

The world didn't change overnight. But it tilted, just a little.

A few weeks after they all return to the rez, Black Cloud is outside the rec center with Tall Tim. The first trucks appear on the horizon, the dusty soil kicking up against the morning sky. They come in waves: contractors' pickups loaded with lumber and tools, medical vans equipped with modern equipment, flatbeds carrying classroom supplies and computers. Teachers step down from buses, doctors emerge from SUVs, industrial developers study blueprints against their truck hoods. The morning air fills with the sound of doors slamming, voices calling out instructions as they pop out of truck cabs and jump down, hard hats being passed around to those in need.

Tall Tim lowers his cup, blinking as the scene unfolds.

Black Cloud and Tall Tim stand frozen, watching their quiet reservation transform into a construction staging zone. Workers unload boxes of medical supplies next to crates of books. A group of engineers unfold architectural plans on a pickup's tailgate while electricians string temporary power lines together and run generators. It's like watching decades of neglect undone in a single morning.

"What's going on?" Tall Tim whispers, his voice carrying both hope and disbelief. "It's your miracle, Cloud," he says with mouth agape.

Sally, Talks with Trees, is on the development board and walks past them waving at the arriving crew.

"They're here to help," she says over her shoulder.

"Help with what?" Tall Tim looks at Black Cloud who shrugs.

A project manager wearing a yellow hard hat asks, "Where do you want it, Sally?"

She raises a finger for the man to hold on a moment. She turns and steps closer to Black Cloud and Tall Tim giving them both a kiss on the cheek. Tim blushes.

"I know you two idiots are somehow behind all this." She pauses, then winks and whispers, "You can rob me anytime." She walks off pointing. "Right over there, Bob."

Black Cloud notices several of the contractors he knows in the area meet and shake hands with these men while Sally stands nearby nodding and going over blueprint plans.

These aren't just off the rez companies looking to help, but also local workers who've waited years for a chance to build something meaningful on their own land. Men who grew up here, who understand what the reservation needs because they've lived it.

He watches them gather around the plans, pointing and discussing, their work-worn hands tracing out future buildings. Some he recognizes from high school, others from construction jobs he'd worked years ago. Now they stand as equals with the developers and engineers, their knowledge of the land and community finally being valued.

Sally oversees it all, her usual sharp tongue softened by purpose. The woman who once watched them play at being warriors now orchestrates real change, translating between the old ways and the new, making sure nothing important gets lost in the details.

Journalists from across the nation begin to focus their reports on the systemic poverty, industrial corruption, and abusive land deals plaguing reservations. Reporters chase down politicians, demanding answers.

"Why have these Americans been treated so poorly? Why did you vote for this bill, Senator? Weren't you on the board of that company?"

Many politicians shy away, diving into cars. "No comment."

Money begins flowing into reservations from all over the world to help with children's health and education, jobs, and industry. The rec center is finally finished with enrichment programs, including dance and music classes.

The band Pearl Jam sends musical instruments with a note from front man Eddie Vedder that reads, *There is power in music. Music speaks it all. Rock on. —Eddie.*

The rec center is now the biggest building in town—three stories high—and pulses with new life. In the evening, their windows glow with activity. Where there was once an empty building meant for greater things, music now plays day and night. From dance studios to art rooms and music lessons, children who once had nowhere to go after school now learn traditional dances along with computer skills.

A new hospital center for veterans hums with modern equipment while traditional healers work alongside doctors, combining old wisdom with new medicine.

Down the road, new businesses open their doors. Industrial parks break ground where empty lots once collected trash. But it's more than just buildings; it's the pride in people's steps, the way they hold their heads higher, the laughter of children who no longer have to leave the reservation to chase their dreams.

Looking out to the Black Hills one morning, Black Cloud can feel that his father's spirit is no longer trapped there among the rocks and pine trees. His own spirit is free too, no longer weighed down by anger and helplessness. The land feels different—not just a place of past wounds, but of future possibilities.

He reaches into his denim jacket for a tissue and finds his mother's and wife's hair in the breast pocket. He smiles faintly, kisses them both, and places them back inside. Startled, he looks up hearing his birth name whispered upon the wind.

Abraham, he hears softly.

Liberator.

THIRTY-TWO

Next Thanksgiving

Standing on the Macy's platform in New York City, the President of the United States makes an historic speech.

He grips the podium, looking out over a crowd that's different from previous years; it's more diverse, unified, and aware. The nearby streets are bulging, and additional roads needed to close due to the expanding crowd. Many wear Native American attire, headdresses, colorful beads, and war paint to stand in solidarity.

The parade route is already lined with people who've camped out overnight, many wearing feathers in their hair, not as costumes but as a symbol of understanding.

Several Macy's execs stand in the wings and nod in satisfaction.

The President begins: "As I stand in front of Macy's, an American institution, we must acknowledge the atrocities of the past. In truth, our ancestors' treatment of the Native American people was nothing less than a genocide, and acknowledging this is the only way for this nation to heal. Suppression is never the way forward. Native American history will now be taught in every school in this country.

This will be the law, for knowing our history is the only way to make sure it does not repeat itself. It is never just one side that must heal after a great battle, but both sides."

A few banners hang behind him. From the podium he looks at them then turns to the camera.

"As the great Apache leader Cochise once said, 'You must speak straight so that your words may go as sunlight into our hearts.' And that is what I intend to do here today, against the advice of many advisors. It may cost me the next election, but hubris and ignorance must not prevent progress. There are more quotes we could have up here. But this demonstrates the insightful and prophetic nature of these people.

"I was moved last Thanksgiving as the parade events unfolded. These people were demanding that we pay attention to them, much as we ourselves would want someone to pay attention to us, our wounds, our needs, our hurts, cares, and concerns. Far too often the Native people of this land have been forgotten by society's progress. In this country, from here on out, we leave no one behind.

"We must honor our past and First Peoples. After all, we are all Americans and can no longer sweep this under the rug of history. Columbus Day will be replaced with Indigenous People's Day and will be a national holiday for all."

Chip Wegney stands off to the side applauding. It's been a few months since his album "Reservation Home" went platinum in the first week. It was still party music but with more depth and power.

As one critic said, "He grew up." There are some traditional American Indian beats mixed with modern rhythm and sound. "His lyrics are more personal."

This event changed his career trajectory. He's become one of the most vocal advocates for Native American rights. No longer just an entertainer, he's used his platform to keep the conversation going long after the media spotlight faded.

"You can't go back to singing empty party songs after what we witnessed," he says to reporters gathered at the event. "That day changed everything, not just for Native Americans, but for all of us who saw what's possible when people choose understanding over fear."

His fundraising efforts have expanded beyond celebrity phone banks to year-round initiatives supporting reservation development, educational programs, and cultural preservation projects.

Crystal teaches advanced self-defense at the new rec center. Her classes are always full, but she saves special sessions for young girls, teaching them more than just how to fight. She shows them how to stand tall and how to trust. Tom Sr.'s plumbing business has expanded into a full construction company, though he still manages to find time to attend every one of her classes. They're planning a spring wedding, with TJ as best man.

Estranged from her parents, Crystal asked Samuel to give her away, who nodded and cried when she asked him.

He's softer these days, more prone to smiling, especially when Crystal brings her students out to learn about the horses. He's even convinced Bull Nose Pete to help, the mime's silent gestures somehow perfect for spooking kids into paying attention.

Ben Blackfeather still rides the Maine coast but now leads wilderness retreats combining Apache wisdom with veteran healing. He rides his motorcycle along the coast at dawn, but he often has the company of other warriors seeking to find peace.

Denni moved to the reservation permanently, her green hair now streaked with traditional colors. She and TJ run the youth archery program together, teaching precision and patience to a new generation.

Mack and the boys are still playing warriors in their own ways, helping the less fortunate.

Alex is starring in an off-Broadway play he wrote about the Ghost Dance, though he claims any similarity to recent events as "purely coincidental."

Back at the reservation, Black Cloud and White Feather watch the President's speech together. The children lean forward on the couch, wearing their now-faded Yankees and Mets caps.

"Look at that big crowd," Lilyanna points at the screen.

"One parade changed everything," White Feather says, giving her brother a sideways glance.

"No," Black Cloud responds softly. "People changed everything. They just needed to see each other. Really see."

"Isn't that what all of us want, to be seen?" She rests her head on his shoulder.

Little Wonder tugs at his uncle's sleeve. "Tell us again about New York, Unca Cwoud."

"Oh no," White Feather laughs. "Not that story again. It seems to grow and get more embellished each time."

But she settles back on the couch anyway, watching her brother light up with pride.

Black Cloud's phone buzzes. It's a text from Samantha Blue, *Save me a spot on the couch. I'll be home for Christmas.*

He looks at his sister and smiles.

After the speech ends, Black Cloud says, "It takes just one

good man to make a difference."

White Feather corrects him clearing her throat, "Or one good woman."

Black Cloud nods, and they high five.

"Come on White Feather! We've got more cooking to do. This turkey is huge!" Morning Sparrow shouts after preparing the green bean casserole and wanting to baste the turkey.

Turkeys had arrived earlier in the week on reservations across the country with a note from the president saying, "In the spirit of Thanksgiving, we now break bread as a national family."

Black Cloud steps outside into the crisp November air. Bull Nose Pete, Tall Tim, and Samuel are already setting up the horseshoe stakes.

"You boys looking to lose today?" he calls out to them stepping down.

"Only thing lost around here is your aim," Samuel shoots back, but there's warmth in his voice that wasn't there a year ago.

Black Cloud holds a horseshoe in his hand, feeling its weight, remembering all the games they played while planning their mission. They're deep into their third match, when Little Wonder comes to the screen door.

"Come on Unca Cloudy, the parade's a startin'."

Black Cloud holds the last horseshoe in his hand and chants to the wind while quoting Chief Joseph, the famous Nez Perce leader who said, "We will fight no more forever." Then he adds, "For there are no more enemies left to fight."

He throws the horseshoe and nails it. The clink of metal hitting metal.

The End

Notes From the Author

I've always felt a deep and unshakable connection to the earth. Over time, that connection drew me toward Native cultures, whose reverence for land, spirit, and community echoed something I'd long carried in my own heart.

Over the years, I have visited several reservations. I vividly remember the first time I stepped onto one. I was shocked by the experience of stepping back in time—the cars were from another era, rusting away in the dust. The streets were uneven and crumbling. A part of me couldn't resolve the differences where a few miles away was a completely different story with shining streets, well-groomed neighborhoods and high-end stores.

So much about Native American history and reservation life is overlooked in our culture and schools. The broader society rarely acknowledges their part in this history. Before the reservation system, they didn't know poverty, isolation, or alcoholism. They didn't know high infant mortality rates or shortened lifespans, sometimes by twenty years. They didn't know what it was like to have their children ripped from their homes. Rarely do we confront the full picture. Rarely do we reckon with what happened—and what is still happening.

Yes, they were defeated, but how long must this defeat continue? How long must the establishment perpetuate this pain? How long will we allow outdated policies, bureaucratic indifference, and corporate greed to prolong the suffering?

Most of us think of this nation as aspiring to be honorable, with honorable intent. But we cannot move forward with this injustice hanging over us. We're defying the very ideals we claim to uphold. It's easier to marginalize, to brush aside, but doing so does a great disservice to them, to us, and to our shared history. We are an American family, yet within our borders exists a third world, not only allowed but perpetuated by policies, greed, land and money grabs.

When history is ignored or whitewashed—like so many are attempting to do now—it inevitably repeats itself. The past festers like an unchecked wound, seeping into the present. Ignorance will never lead us to a better future. We cannot move forward without acknowledging and redressing the wrongs of the past.

We must do our best to heal in order to move into the future.

The war is over. After the Civil War, the South was rebuilt. Can we not do the same? Isn't that what a higher-functioning society does? What a compassionate people do?

In writing this story, I've only scratched the surface of the injustices faced by Native peoples—then and now. I hope I've honored the spirit and resilience of the communities I sought to represent. There is so much more history I couldn't fit into these pages. The atrocities span centuries. The stories of courage, loss, and survival go far deeper.

To learn more, I've added a short reference section below.

As stated in the story, we are all part of human history—and therefore, part of its present and future. What we do matters.

If you feel moved to help, please consider supporting these vital organizations:

Healing from Boarding Schools - https://boardingschoolhealing.org/
Native American Rights Fund - https://narf.org/support-us/
Native American Enterprise Development - https://ncaied.org/

There are many other Indigenous-led causes doing extraordinary work. Find one that speaks to you—and stand with them.

Additional Quotes, Leaders, Facts, and Stats

Quotes from Native American Leaders

1. "Treat all men alike. Give them the same law. Give them an even chance to live and grow." –Chief Joseph, Nez Perce (1879)
2. "I am tired of talk that comes to nothing. It makes my heart sick when I remember all the good words and all the broken promises." –Chief Joseph, Nez Perce (1879)
3. "If the white man wants to live in peace with the Indian, they can live in peace." –Chief Joseph, Nez Perce (1877)
4. "I was born upon the prairie, where the wind blew free, and there was nothing to break the light of the sun." –Chief Parra-wa-samen (Ten Bears), Numunuu (Tampraika Comanche) (1871)
5. "So live your life that the fear of death can never enter your heart." –Chief Tecumseh, Shawnee (early 1800s)
6. "So we must be one as they are…Otherwise we shall be all gone shortly": Narragansett Chief Miantonomi who tried forming alliances against settlers in Long Island and New England in the 1640s.
7. "If the Great Spirit had desired me to be a white man he would have made me so in the first place." –Chief Sitting Bull, Hunkpapa Lakota Sioux (1877)

8. "A warrior I have been. Now it is all over. A hard time I have." –Crazy Horse, Oglala Lakota (1877)

9. "Let me be a free man, free to travel, free to stop, free to work, free to trade where I choose, free to choose my own teachers, free to follow the religion of my fathers, free to talk, think and act for myself." –Chief Joseph, Nez Perce (1879)

11. "One does not sell the earth upon which the people walk." –Crazy Horse, Oglala Lakota (1877)

12. "They made us many promises, more than I can remember, but they never kept but one; they promised to take our land, and they took it." –Red Cloud, Oglala Lakota (1870)

13. "What treaty have the Sioux made with the white man that we have broken? Not one. What treaty have the white man ever made with us that they have kept? Not one. When I was a boy the Sioux owned the world; the sun rose and set on their land; they sent ten thousand men to battle. Where are the warriors today? Who slew them? Where are our lands? Who owns them?... What law have I broken? Is it wrong for me to love my own? Is it wicked for me to cherish the things that give me life?" –Sitting Bull, Hunkpapa Lakota (1876)

Fallen Leaders

1. Crazy Horse (1840-1877) earned a reputation as a skilled and fearless fighter as well as a brilliant military strategist. He led war parties and raids on federal troops and frontier settlements, but also showed himself to be compassionate at times. In 1877, Crazy Horse surrendered to U.S. forces under promises of a reservation for his people. However, he was taken into custody and later killed when he resisted being jailed [2]. His death at Fort Robinson, Nebraska, sparked controversy and outrage among the Lakota.

Today, Crazy Horse is remembered as one of the most iconic Native American leaders of the 19th century. He became a symbol of Native American resistance in the face of U.S. expansionism. His life and legacy remain influential in Native American culture and history to the present day [3].

[1] Ambrose, Stephen E. *Crazy Horse and Custer: The Parallel Lives of Two American Warriors*. Anchor, 1996.

[2] Marshall, Joseph M. *The Journey of Crazy Horse: A Lakota History*. Penguin, 2004.

[3] Powers, Thomas. *The Killing of Crazy Horse*. Knopf, 2010.

2. Sitting Bull (1831-1890), a Hunkpapa Lakota leader, led during years of resistance against the United States government. He is most famous for his victory at the Battle of the Little Bighorn in 1876, where his forces defeated Lt. Col. George Custer and the 7th Cavalry [1]. Sitting Bull refused to be confined to a reservation and led his followers into Canada after Little Bighorn. He later surrendered in 1881 but joined Buffalo Bill's Wild West show for a time before returning to the Standing Rock Agency [2].

Sitting Bull was a spiritual and political leader who inspired his people to uphold Lakota traditions. He performed the Sun Dance and was known for his visions; his prophecy of defeating the 7th Cavalry is credited with inspiring the Lakota and Cheyenne victory at Little Bighorn [3]. Sitting Bull's leadership maintained unity among the Lakota bands during times of violence and hardship. Though he fought the U.S. government, he also wanted peace and the survival of his people.

After years of struggle, Sitting Bull was killed by Indian agency police in 1890, just before the Wounded Knee Massacre. His death marked the end of the Plains Indian Wars and traditional Lakota freedom. Sitting Bull remains one of the most famous Native American leaders and symbols of resistance in the face of U.S. westward expansion [4].

[1] Utley, Robert M. *Sitting Bull: The Life and Times of an American Patriot.* Holt Paperbacks, 2008.

[2] Utley, Robert M. Sitting Bull: The Life and Times of an American Patriot. Holt Paperbacks, 2008.

[3] Marshall, Joseph M. *The Journey of Crazy Horse: A Lakota History.* Penguin, 2004.

[4] Ambrose, Stephen E. *Crazy Horse and Custer: The Parallel Lives of Two American Warriors.* Anchor, 1996.

3. Chief Joseph (1840-1904) was a leader of the Wallowa band of the Nez Perce tribe. When the U.S. government tried to force his people to move onto a reservation in Idaho, Chief Joseph led a small band on a 1,170-mile retreat towards Canada while evading capture [1]. This epic journey, known as the Nez Perce War of 1877, saw Chief Joseph outmaneuver and battle U.S. forces led by General Oliver Howard through four states before finally surrendering just

40 miles from the Canadian border [2].

Chief Joseph possessed great military skill and strategically led a band of fewer than 200 people against a pursuing force that grew to over 2,000 troops. His speeches advocating for peace and criticism of broken treaties made him famous internationally. Though unsuccessful in reaching Canada, Chief Joseph's retreat is considered one of the most brilliant tactical achievements in American Indian history [3].

After surrendering, Chief Joseph continued advocating for the rights of his people. He later met with President Rutherford B. Hayes after being imprisoned and toured the U.S. speaking on behalf of Native Americans. Chief Joseph remains one of the most respected and well-known Native American leaders of the 19th century [4]. His defense of his ancestral lands and his people's liberty made him an icon of indigenous resistance.

[1] Josephy, Alvin M. *The Nez Perce Indians and the Opening of the Northwest.* Mariner Books, 1997.

[2] McWhorter, Lucullus V. *Yellow Wolf: His Own Story.* Caxton Press, 1940.

[3] Hampton, Bruce. *Children of Grace: The Nez Perce War of 1877.* Henry Holt and Co., 1994.

[4] Nerburn, Kent. *Chief Joseph & the Flight of the Nez Perce.* HarperOne, 2005.

4. Geronimo (1829-1909) was a prominent leader of the Bedonkohe band of the Chiricahua Apache tribe. He led raids against Mexican and American settlers and soldiers in the Southwest during the Apache Wars, resisting forced relocation onto reservations [1]. Geronimo escaped from confinement multiple times before finally surrendering for the last time in 1886. He became a celebrity pris-

oner of war and lived the rest of his life as a farmer in Oklahoma [2].

Known for his daring and strategic skills, Geronimo was feared by settlers across the Southwest. He retaliated against encroachment into Apache lands with raids on ranches, wagon trains, and military outposts across Arizona, New Mexico, and Northern Mexico. Geronimo's small band evaded thousands of Mexican and American troops for over a decade, using the rugged terrain to their advantage [3]. His surrender in 1886 marked the end of the Indian Wars era and the beginning of Apache tribes being confined to reservations.

In his later years, Geronimo capitalized on his fame to earn money. He was a featured attraction at fairs, rodeos, and exhibitions, including the 1904 St. Louis World's Fair. Geronimo also sold souvenirs and told his life story. He remains one of the most legendary Native American figures of the 19th century due to his resistance against American expansion [4].

[1] Debo, Angie. *Geronimo: The Man, His Time, His Place.* University of Oklahoma Press, 1976.

[2] Roberts, David. *Once They Moved Like the Wind: Cochise, Geronimo, and the Apache Wars.* Simon & Schuster, 1994.

[3] Utley, Robert M. *Geronimo.* Yale University Press, 2012.

[4] Barrett, S.M. *Geronimo: His Own Story.* University of Nebraska Press, 1970.

5. Black Kettle (1803-1868) was a leader of the Southern Cheyenne tribe who advocated for peace and compromise with the U.S. government during the Plains Indian Wars era [1]. He accepted resettlement on reservations in Colorado and Oklahoma to avoid further conflict. However, he was unable to control hostile factions of young Cheyenne who still waged war against American settlers [2].

Black Kettle gained fame when he and his people were victims of the Sand Creek Massacre of 1864. A cavalry regiment led by Colonel John Chivington attacked Black Kettle's camp, killing around 200 Cheyenne despite promises of safety there [3]. Black Kettle continued to seek peace agreements after this atrocity, including signing the Treaty of Medicine Lodge in 1867 that relocated Cheyenne to Oklahoma.

Tragically, Black Kettle was killed in the Washita River Massacre of 1868, when Lt. Col. George Custer attacked his camp before dawn [4]. The death of Black Kettle marked the end of hopes for peaceful relations between Southern Cheyenne and the U.S. government. He is remembered as a peacemaker who tried to avoid war through negotiation and compromise with the United States.

[1] Greene, Jerome A. *Washita: The Southern Cheyenne and the U.S. Army*. University of Oklahoma Press, 2014.

[2] Hoig, Stan. *The Peace Chiefs of the Cheyennes*. University Press of Colorado, 1980.

[3] Kelman, Ari. *A Misplaced Massacre: Struggling Over the Memory of Sand Creek*. Harvard University Press, 2013.

[4] Brown, Dee. *Bury My Heart at Wounded Knee: An Indian History of the American West*. Macmillan, 1970.

6. Cochise (1815-1874) was a prominent leader of the Chokonen band of the Chiricahua Apache. He led Apache resistance against settler encroachment and the U.S. Army in the Southwest during the early 1860s until his death [1]. Cochise is famous for his daring raids and escapes as he evaded capture in the rugged Dragoon Mountains of Arizona for over a decade.

Cochise initially maintained peaceful relations with Americans, but this changed after he was falsely accused of kidnapping a white child in 1861 [2]. His people were attacked by the U.S. Army, setting off years of war. Cochise respected treaties when made, such as the peace agreement of 1871 that settled Apaches on a reservation. But he fought fiercely when betrayed or attacked [3].

The Chiricahua Apaches held out longer than other tribes against subjugation due to Cochise's leadership. However, after his death, the tribe was forced to move to reservations in Arizona and New Mexico. Cochise remains an iconic figure of Native American independence and resistance during the Indian Wars era. His military skills allowed his small band of Apaches to evade defeat for over a decade [4].

[1] Sweeney, Edwin R. *Cochise: Chiricahua Apache Chief.* University of Oklahoma Press, 1991.

[2] Roberts, David. *Once They Moved Like the Wind: Cochise, Geronimo, and the Apache Wars.* Simon & Schuster, 1994.

[3] Ball, Eve & Kaywaykla, James. *In the Days of Victorio: Recollections of a Warm Springs Apache.* University of Arizona Press, 1970.

[4] Thrapp, Dan L. *The Conquest of Apacheria.* University of Oklahoma Press, 1967.

7. Osceola (1804-1838), whose birth name was Billy Powell, was a leader of the Seminole tribe in Florida who resisted relocation to Indian Territory. In 1835, he led Seminole warriors in the Second Seminole War against U.S. forces attempting to forcibly remove the tribe from their lands [1]. Osceola employed guerrilla warfare tactics to defeat American troops in several battles, inflicting heavy casualties. He came to symbolize Seminole courage and independence [2].

Osceola refused to sign a treaty in 1832 that relinquished Seminole lands, arguing it was invalid because not all tribal leaders agreed to it. After Wiley Thompson, the Indian agent, put him in chains, Osceola led raids on army outposts and maintained Seminole resistance despite being vastly outnumbered [3]. In October 1837, Osceola was captured under a flag of truce when attending peace talks. He died in captivity a year later, never having surrendered [4].

Chief Osceola left a legacy as the most famous Seminole leader who resisted forced relocation and retained freedom for his people in Florida. Though the Second Seminole War continued, Osceola's guerrilla campaign showed the ability of smaller Native American groups to effectively battle U.S. forces for years and retain autonomy.

[1] Covington, James W. *The Seminoles of Florida*. University Press of Florida, 1993.

[2] McReynolds, Edwin C. *The Seminoles*. University of Oklahoma Press, 1957.

[3] Missall, John & Missall, Mary Lou. *The Seminole Wars: America's Longest Indian Conflict*. University Press of Florida, 2004.

[4] Mahon, John K. *History of the Second Seminole War 1835-1842*. University Press of Florida, 1967.

8. Wovoka (1856-1932), also known as Jack Wilson, was a Northern Paiute religious leader who founded the Ghost Dance movement in the late 1800s. The Ghost Dance was a spiritual practice that envisioned a peaceful end to white expansion and restoration of lands and way of life for Native Americans [1]. Wovoka preached this message of deliverance, unity, and pacifism among tribes of the Great Plains during a time of violence and displacement [2].

In 1889, Wovoka had a prophetic vision during a solar eclipse where he was taken into heaven and told Christ would return to restore Native American lands [3]. This vision inspired the Ghost Dance rituals, which spread rapidly among tribes between 1889-1890. Government agents saw the ghost shirts worn during the ritual as symbols of war, leading to the Wounded Knee Massacre of Lakota in 1890 [4].

Wovoka outlived this tragedy and continued to promote unity, preaching into the 20th century. He succeeded in bridging Pine Ridge Lakota and his own Paiute people. Wovoka remains a significant figure for fostering a sense of common purpose among far-flung Native American groups through his mystical teachings and the Ghost Dance movement.

[1] Kehoe, Alice Beck. *The Ghost Dance: Ethnohistory and Revitalization.* Waveland Press, 2006.

[2] DeMallie, Raymond J. *The Sixth Grandfather: Black Elk's Teachings Given to John G. Neihardt.* U of Nebraska Press, 1984.

[3] Mooney, James. *The Ghost Dance Religion and Wounded Knee.* Dover, 1973.

[4] Brown, Dee. *Bury My Heart at Wounded Knee: An Indian History of the American West.* Holt, Rinehart & Winston, 1970.

9. Tecumseh (1768-1813) was a Shawnee leader who worked to unify Native American tribes east of the Mississippi against the encroachment of American settlers [1]. He led a confederation of tribes against the United States during Tecumseh's War and the War of 1812, when he allied with the British. Tecumseh envisioned a pan-Indian alliance that could resist American expansion through united armed struggle [2].

Along with his brother Tenskwatawa, Tecumseh established a religious and political community at Prophetstown in Indiana that drew followers from many tribes [3]. Tecumseh argued that no single tribe could sell communal native lands to the U.S. government without consensus. He emerged as a prominent resistance leader, demanding the repeal of land cession treaties [4].

Tecumseh died fighting alongside British forces during the Battle of Thames in Canada in 1813. His death marked the end of native unity east of the Mississippi. However, Tecumseh became a folk hero for advocating Indian independence and armed resistance to protect tribal lands against encroachment. His vision of pan-Indian solidarity remained influential.

[1] Edmunds, R. David. *Tecumseh and the Quest for Indian Leadership*. Little, Brown, 1984.

[2] Sugden, John. *Tecumseh: A Life*. Holt Paperbacks, 1998.

[3] Cave, Alfred A. *Prophets of the Great Spirit: Native American Revitalization Movements in Eastern North America*. U of Nebraska Press, 2006.

[4] Allen, Robert S. *His Majesty's Indian Allies: British Indian Policy in the Defence of Canada, 1774-1815*. Dundurn Press, 1992.

10. Chief Seattle (1786-1866) was a leader of the Duwamish and Suquamish tribes around the Seattle area. He is best known for a speech in 1854 that advocated peaceful coexistence with white settlers at a time of rapid encroachment [1]. The speech highlighted Chief Seattle's wish that his people be able to live undisturbed while also accepting the reality of sharing the land with American settlers [2].

Chief Seattle reluctantly signed the Treaty of Point Elliott in 1855, ceding Suquamish and Duwamish lands but securing a reservation for his people. Despite great cultural losses from settlement pressure, Seattle's nonviolent resistance enabled his tribes to persist when many Northwest tribes were wiped out fighting removal [3].

The actual words of Chief Seattle's most famous speech in 1854 were not recorded at the time. However, it was later reconstructed from memory by Dr. Henry A. Smith who attended the speech [4]. Scholars debate the accuracy of this reconstruction, but the ideas expressed align with Chief Seattle's efforts to coexist with settlers while protecting his people's land and cultural rights as much as conditions allowed [5].

[1] Kaiser, Rudolf. "Chief Seattle's Speech(es): American Origins and European Reception." *Recovering the Word: Essays on Native American Literature.* Ed. Swann. U of California Press, 1987.

[2] Kluger, Richard. "Chief Seattle: A Man Alone." *Chief Seattle and His Times.* Ed. Ballard. University of Washington Press, 2000.

[3] Ruby, Robert H. & Brown, John A. *The Chinook Indians: Traders of the Lower Columbia River.* University of Oklahoma Press, 1976.

[4] Marr, Carolyn J. "'The Day Chief Seattle Spoke'." *Journal of Northwest Anthropology* 50.1 (2016): 79-99.

[5] Bierwert, Crisca. *Brushed by Cedar, Living by the River: Coast Salish Figures of Power.* University of Arizona Press, 1999.

Sterilization Program

The law that led to the mass sterilization of Native American women in the 1970s was the Family Planning Services and Population Research Act of 1970 (Public Law 91-572). This law expanded federal funding for family planning programs and gave the Indian Health Service (IHS) authority to perform sterilizations. However, due to a lack of proper consent protocols and coercive practices, thousands of Native American women were sterilized without fully informed consent. Investigations in the mid-1970s, particularly by the U.S. General Accounting Office (GAO), revealed that between 1973 and 1976, around 3,406 Native American women were sterilized, many without their knowledge or under pressure.

1. Lawrence, Jane. "The Indian Health Service and the Sterilization of Native American Women." American Indian Quarterly, vol. 24, no. 3, 2000, pp. 400-419.

• This article explores the history of coerced sterilizations, examining policies, legal loopholes, and the impact on Native American communities.

2. Torpy, Sally J. "Native American Women and Coerced Sterilization: On the Trail of Tears in the 1970s." American Indian Culture and Research Journal, vol. 24, no. 2, 2000, pp. 1-22.

• Torpy details the systemic sterilization abuse and how it violated Indigenous sovereignty and reproductive rights.

3. U.S. General Accounting Office. "Investigation of Allegations Concerning Indian Health Service: Report to Senator James Abourezk." 1976.

• This government report documents findings on non-consensual sterilizations performed by the IHS.

Indian Relocation Act of 1956

The Indian Relocation Act of 1956, also known as Public Law 959, was a U.S. federal law aimed at encouraging Native Americans to leave their reservations and assimilate into urban areas. The Act was part of the broader Termination Policy, which sought to dissolve tribal sovereignty and integrate Indigenous people into mainstream American society. Under the program, the Bureau of Indian Affairs (BIA) offered financial assistance for job training, relocation expenses, and initial housing costs. However, many Native Americans faced significant challenges, including discrimination, unemployment, and lack of community support in cities. The Act ultimately contributed to the rise of urban Native American communities but also led to economic hardship and cultural dislocation for many individuals.

1. Fixico, Donald L. Termination and Relocation: Federal Indian Policy, 1945-1960. University of New Mexico Press, 1986.

• This book provides a detailed examination of U.S. policies affecting Native Americans during the mid-20th century, including the Indian Relocation Act. Fixico explores the social and economic consequences of relocation on Native communities.

2. Rosier, Paul C. Serving Their Country: American Indian Politics and Patriotism in the Twentieth Century. Harvard University Press, 2009.

• This source discusses how the relocation program affected Native American identity, politics, and economic conditions, highlighting both struggles and resilience.

3. Smith, Paul Chaat. Like a Hurricane: The Indian Movement from Alcatraz to Wounded Knee. The New Press, 1996.

• This book connects the Relocation Act to the rise of Native activism in the late 20th century, showing how urbanization played a role in political movements.

4. Bureau of Indian Affairs. "Indian Relocation Program." U.S. Department of the Interior, 1956.

• A government document outlining the official intent, policies, and support structures of the relocation program.

5. Lobo, Susan, and Kurt Peters. American Indians and the Urban Experience. Altamira Press, 2001.

• This book provides an analysis of urban Native American experiences, discussing how the Relocation Act shaped modern Indigenous communities.

Native American Boarding School System

The Native American boarding school system, primarily implemented in the late 19th and early 20th centuries, was a U.S. government and religious institution-led effort to assimilate Indigenous children into Euro-American culture. The schools operated under the principle of "Kill the Indian, save the man," as articulated by Richard Henry Pratt, founder of the Carlisle Indian Industrial School in 1879. These institutions forcibly removed Native children from their families, suppressing their languages, traditions, and spiritual practices while subjecting them to harsh discipline, forced labor, and abuse (Adams, 1995).

The long-term effects of these schools have been profound. Many students experienced psychological, physical, and sexual abuse, leading to intergenerational trauma in Indigenous communities (Child, 1998). The loss of language and cultural knowledge contributed to the erosion of tribal identities and community cohesion. Additionally, the schools often provided substandard education, leaving many students unprepared for life outside the institutions or within their tribal nations (Lomawaima, 1994). The legacy of the boarding schools continues to affect Indigenous populations today, contributing to disparities in education, mental health, and cultural preservation efforts.

• Adams, D. W. (1995). Education for Extinction: American Indians and the Boarding School Experience, 1875-1928. University Press of Kansas.

• Child, B. J. (1998). Boarding School Seasons: American Indian Families, 1900-1940. University of Nebraska Press.

• Lomawaima, K. T. (1994). They Called It Prairie Light: The Story of Chilocco Indian School. University of Nebraska Press.

Smallpox and Disease

It's difficult to give an exact number for how many Native Americans died from smallpox, but we can look at some estimates and sources:

• In 1492, before Europeans arrived in the Americas, there were an estimated 10-15 million indigenous people living north of Mexico. By 1650, after years of disease epidemics, conflict, and loss of territory, that number had declined to about 1 million. Smallpox was a major cause of this population decline. [1]

• Historian Alfred W. Crosby estimates that smallpox killed more than 50% of the indigenous populations between Canada, the United States, and Mexico between 1520 and 1580. [2]

• Another study found that Native American populations declined 88-99% from smallpox epidemics between the 1770s and 1870s in the western United States. [3]

• Yet another historian, David S. Jones, estimates that from 1520 to 1920, 56 million Native Americans died from imported diseases like smallpox, influenza, and measles. [4]

So while an exact number is unknown, historians agree smallpox killed millions of Native Americans after contact with Europeans starting in the 1500s. The high mortality was due to Native Americans having no prior exposure or immunity to the diseases brought by Europeans.

[1] Thornton, Russell. *American Indian Holocaust and Survival: A Population History Since 1492*. University of Oklahoma Press, 1987.

[2] Crosby, Alfred W. "Virgin Soil Epidemics as a Factor in the Aboriginal Depopulation in America." *The William and Mary Quarterly*, vol. 33, no. 2, 1976, pp. 289–299.

[3] Thornton, Sherburne F. "American Indian Holocaust and Survival: A Population History since 1492." *American Indian Quarterly*, vol. 15, no. 2, 1991, pp. 209–210.

[4] Jones, David S. "Virgin Soils Revisited." *The William and Mary Quarterly*, vol. 60, no. 4, 2003, p. 703.

Massacres

The U.S. government engaged in many violent massacres of Native American peoples throughout the 18th and 19th centuries as part of a larger process of settler colonialism and westward expansion. One of the most notorious was the Sand Creek Massacre in 1864, when a 675-man Colorado militia led by Colonel John Chivington attacked a village of Cheyenne and Arapaho in southeastern Colorado Territory, despite the Native tribes' demonstrated peaceful intent and the fact the tribes were flying an American flag (1). The militia killed and mutilated approximately 200 Native Americans, mostly elderly men, women, and children. This act of violence from the US cavalry against innocent people shocked the nation (2). Another infamous massacre was the massacre at Wounded Knee in 1890, when the 7th Cavalry surrounded a Lakota encampment in South Dakota and massacred at least 150 men, women, and children. Some were killed while fleeing, and survivors were left to freeze to death in a blizzard (3). These massacres represent some of the darker acts of violence and cruelty on the part of the U.S. government towards Native peoples.

1. Brown, Dee. *Bury My Heart at Wounded Knee: An Indian History of the American West.* Holt McDougal, 2001.

2. Madley, Benjamin. "Reexamining the American Genocide Debate: Meaning, Historiography, and New Methods." *The American Historical Review*, vol. 120, no. 1, 2015, pp. 98–139.

3. Ostler, Jeffrey. *The Plains Sioux and U.S. Colonialism from Lewis and Clark to Wounded Knee.* Cambridge University Press, 2004.

Trail of Tears

The Trail of Tears refers to the forced relocation of Native American nations from southeastern parts of the United States to lands west of the Mississippi River in the 1830s [1]. The Cherokee, Chickasaw, Choctaw, Muscogee, and Seminole tribes were removed under the Indian Removal Act of 1830, opening 25 million acres of land for white settlers [2].

The Cherokee people suffered most heavily. Between 1836-1839, around 15,000 Cherokee were forced to march 1,200 miles to present-day Oklahoma on foot, by wagon, and by steamboat. Harsh conditions led to the deaths of 4,000 Cherokees on this "Trail of Tears" [3]. The Creek, Choctaw, Seminole and Chickasaw people also faced devastating removals in which hunger, disease and poor travel conditions contributed to thousands of deaths [4].

The Trail of Tears was the result of President Andrew Jackson's policy of Indian removal, leading to the expropriation of traditional tribal homelands to make way for white settlement. It became symbolic of the suffering experienced by Native Americans facing colonization and expansionism in North America during the 19th century [5].

[1] Ehle, John. *Trail of Tears: The Rise and Fall of the Cherokee Nation*. Doubleday, 1988.

[2] Anderson, William. *Cherokee Removal: Before and After*. University of Georgia Press, 1991.

[3] Perdue, Theda and Green, Michael. *The Cherokee Nation and the Trail of Tears*. Viking, 2007.

[4] Wallace, Anthony. *The Long Bitter Trail: Andrew Jackson and the Indians*. Hill and Wang, 1993.

[5] Moulton, Gary. *John Ross, Cherokee Chief*. University of Georgia Press, 1978.

Broken Treaties

The United States government signed over 500 treaties with Native American tribes between 1778 and 1871, when treaty-making with tribes ended [1]. Many of these treaties were broken or violated by the U.S. government and settlers soon after they were signed [2]. Exact numbers are difficult to determine, but estimates indicate dozens of treaties were outright violated or quickly undermined through illegal encroachment on tribal lands.

One of the most systematic violations stemmed from the Indian Removal Act of 1830, which aimed to forcibly relocate tribes east of the Mississippi to lands west of the river [3]. This broke the terms of multiple treaties guaranteeing possession of ancestral homelands to the Five Civilized Tribes—Cherokee, Chickasaw, Choctaw, Creek, and Seminole. Their horrific removal on the Trail of Tears violated at least nine treaties [4].

In total, historians have estimated that the U.S. government violated or nullified over 370 Indian treaties in the years between the Revolutionary War and 1871 [5]. A few egregious examples include illegal prospecting during the Gold Rush, which violated at least 18 treaties with tribes in California, and the Fort Laramie Treaty of 1868, which was broken within two years as miners flooded the sacred Black Hills [6].

[1] Wilkinson, Charles. *Messages from Frank's Landing: A Story of Salmon, Treaties, and the Indian Way*. University of Washington Press, 2000.

[2] Deloria, Vine and DeMallie, Raymond. *Documents of American Indian Diplomacy: Treaties, Agreements, and Conventions, 1775-1979*. University of Oklahoma Press, 1999.

[3] Ehle, John. *Trail of Tears: The Rise and Fall of the Cherokee Nation*. Doubleday, 1988.

[4] Anderson, William. *Cherokee Removal: Before and After*. University of Georgia Press, 1991.

[5] Lieder, Michael and Page, Jake. *Wild Justice: The People vs. The Treaties and the United States*. Harbour Publishing, 1997.

[6] Lazarus, Edward. *Black Hills White Justice: The Sioux Nation Versus the United States, 1775 to the Present*. University of Nebraska Press, 1991.

Current Statistics

Unemployment Among Native Americans

• The unemployment rate for American Indians and Alaska Natives was 12% in 2015, compared to just 5% unemployment nationwide (1).

• Among Native American groups, the unemployment rate varies. In 2013, unemployment was highest among Sioux tribes at 16%, versus only 9% unemployment for Cherokee tribal members (2).

• Native American unemployment is higher in rural areas and reservations—unemployment averaged 22% across reservations in 2016 compared to 15% in urban areas with large Native populations (3).

• Factors contributing to high Native American unemployment include rural isolation, lack of infrastructure, education gaps, discrimination, and cultural barriers (4).

• The COVID-19 pandemic caused severe job losses among Native populations, with unemployment peaking at 26% in May 2020 versus 13% nationwide (5).

(1) Stebbins, S. (2016). American Indian and Alaska Native Heritage Month: November 2016. United States Census Bureau.

(2) Austin, A. (2013). Native Americans and Jobs: The Challenge and the Promise. EPI Briefing Paper #370. Economic Policy Institute.

(3) Donovan, B. (2017). Crisis in Indian Country: An Analysis of the Unemployment Disaster in Reservation Counties. Nationwide.

(4) Sarche, M. & Spicer, P. (2008). Poverty and Health Disparities for American Indian and Alaska Native Children. Annals of the New York Academy of Sciences, 1136(1).

(5) Rho, H.J., Brown, H. & Fremstad, S. (2020). A Basic Demographic Profile of Workers in Frontline Industries. Center for Economic and Policy Research.

Healthcare Issues

• American Indians/Alaska Natives die at higher rates than other Americans from tuberculosis (600% higher), alcoholism (510% higher), diabetes (177% higher), unintentional injuries (140% higher), and suicide (74% higher) (1).

• The life expectancy of Native Americans is approximately 5.5 years less than the U.S. all races population—73 years compared to 78.5 years (2).

• Native American infants die at a rate of 8.3 per 1,000 live births, compared to 5.7 per 1,000 for white infants (3).

• Native youth suicide rates are 2.5 times higher than the national average and the highest of any racial/ethnic group (4).

• Native Americans have a higher mortality rate from diabetes (38.2 per 100,000) compared to the general population (21.8 per 100,000) (5).

• American Indians/Alaska Natives have a lower rate of health insurance coverage (25%) compared to whites (11%) and overall U.S. population (11%) (6).

• There is a lower physician-to-patient ratio for Native Americans

(1 physician per 2,848 patients) compared to the U.S. average (1 per 385 patients) (7).

(1) Indian Health Service. Disparities. https://www.ihs.gov/newsroom/factsheets/disparities/

(2) CDC. Health of American Indian or Alaska Native Population. https://www.cdc.gov/nchs/fastats/american-indian-health.html

(3) IHS. Indian Health Disparities. https://www.ihs.gov/newsroom/factsheets/disparities/

(4) CDC. Leading Causes of Death in Native American Populations. https://www.cdc.gov/minorityhealth/lcod/aian.html

(5) IHS. Diabetes in American Indians and Alaska Natives. https://www.ihs.gov/newsroom/factsheets/diabetes/

(6) Kaiser Family Foundation. Health Coverage by Race and Ethnicity. https://www.kff.org/racial-equity-and-health-policy/state-indicator/health-insurance-coverage-by-raceethnicity/?currentTimeframe=0&sortModel=%7B%22colId%22:%22Location%22,%22sort%22:%22asc%22%7D

(7) AMA. Physician Distribution and Health Access in Rural Areas. https://www.ama-assn.org/about/research/physician-distribution-health-access-rural-areas

Poverty

• In 2017, the poverty rate for American Indians and Alaska Natives was 25.4%, compared to 14% for the nation as a whole (1).

• Among Native American groups, poverty rates vary significantly. In 2017, the poverty rate was 31.5% for American Indians living on reservations, versus 18.3% for American Indians living off reservations (2).

• Approximately 28.4% of Native American children under age 18 lived in poverty in 2017, versus 17.5% of children nationwide (3).

• The highest poverty rates by Native American group in 2017 were: 40% for those identifying as American Indian and Alaskan Native; 38% for Chippewa; 35% for Navajo; and 33% for Sioux (4).

• Factors linked to higher poverty among Native populations include lower educational attainment, lack of infrastructure in tribal areas, higher rates of disability and single parenthood, prejudice in hiring, and loss of traditional land bases (5).

• From 2007 to 2017, the Native American poverty rate fell 8 percentage points, from 33.5% to 25.4%. But it still remains almost double the national poverty rate (6).

(1) Kaiser Family Foundation analysis of 2017 Census data

(2) recalculation by Families USA of 2017 Census data

(3) NICWA analysis of 2017 Census data

(4) 2017 Census American Community Survey

(5) Norris, T. et al. (2012). The American Indian and Alaska Native Population: 2010. U.S. Census.

(6) Macartney, S., Bishaw, A., & Fontenot, K. (2013). Poverty Rates for Selected Detailed Race and Hispanic Groups by State and Place: 2007–2011. U.S. Census.

Acknowledgements

This book has been a labor of love for many years. During that time, it has slowly taken shape, with characters and tone gradually coming together. I hope I have done it justice and honored the people, ideas, and intentions that chose to come forward.

I want to thank my wife, Jennifer Dawn. She has been my guiding light and wrestling partner, whether it's refining ideas or even debating the placement of a comma, she has always been there. Thank you, honey. I love you.

I also want to thank my good friend, Chris Schneider, who has been a sounding board along the way—and still takes my calls.

My cousin and friend Luke Zaientz was kind enough to read a draft (when I thought it was finished, and it wasn't) and provide some much-needed suggestions.

Sometimes in writing, or any large project, you can no longer see the forest for the trees…We don't accomplish anything great alone.

I'd also like to thank my friend, Kate Rosenberg. Though she was on vacation in Turkey she was kind enough to read it and provide much valuable feedback, and just under the wire too. So, thank you Kate.

Lastly, my gratitude goes to the brave men and women who have written books and articles on these painful subjects, illuminating them as the only way forward.

About the Author

Douglas Robbins writes about what truly matters—often the stories and struggles that are overlooked or pushed aside. His work shines a light on human nature, with all its flaws, beauty, and potential for redemption.

He is the author of several books, each one exploring a different facet of the human condition. He is also the host of The Douglas Robbins Show, a podcast where he dives into the deeper layers of life, creativity, and consciousness.

Douglas lives in the Catskill Mountains of New York with his family, where the trees, sky, and stillness inspire his work.

To learn more, visit: **www.DouglasRobbinsAuthor.com.**

A Favor to Ask

This story came from a place of deep passion and years of research and reflection. If it moved you, made you think, or helped you see the world differently—even just a little—I'd be truly grateful if you'd leave a review. Your words can help others discover this book and the message behind it.

Thank you for taking this journey with me. And remember:

Be kind to yourself and others.

We are all part of the human family.

—Doug

www.ingramcontent.com/pod-product-compliance
Lightning Source LLC
Chambersburg PA
CBHW030537310726
48979CB00010B/1938/J
* 9 7 8 1 7 3 3 3 9 7 8 3 4 *